"He's the one, Officer."

Lisa gestured toward Gabe as she spoke. "He kidnapped my sister."

"Kidnapped?" Gabe's voice boomed out his astonishment. "No one mentioned anything about kidnapping."

"My sister has disappeared and she was last seen with you—the day she interviewed you about a job."

"Lady, I told you. I don't know your sister. And I don't need a job, because I already have one." His clipped voice revealed his growing irritation.

Lisa shivered. She looked up at him. His eyes were the color of a cloudy, Arctic sky—cold and relentless. Her instinct was to back off, simply turn around and leave.

Then she thought of Dixie and she knew she couldn't walk away.

Dear Reader,

February is the month for hearts and flowers, and this month's Superromance selections definitely call for a few hearts to be lost—and found.

In Patricia Chandler's *Mooncaller,* Dr. Whitney Baldridge-Barrows knows she should hate Gabriel Blade. He's planning to turn the Havasuapai village where she works into a tourist resort. Instead, she finds she's losing her heart at the bottom of the Grand Canyon....

Texas journalist Lacy Kilpatrick comes home to a family feud. Though her family calls sexy Austin Fraser "the enemy," and forbids her to see him, Lacy discovers she has other ideas. Lynda Trent weaves lighthearted romantic magic in *If I Must Choose.*

And sparks really fly between Tatum McGillus and Jonathan Wright. In Tara Taylor Quinn's *McGillus V. Wright,* hero and heroine stand on opposite sides of the law. Besides that, the timing is wrong, and the two agree on absolutely nothing. This is one relationship that will need a miracle in order to survive.

Louisiana author Anne Logan sets *Dial "D" for Destiny* in her home state, where Lisa Le Blanc is hot on the trail of her missing sister, Dixie. And the trail leads straight to Gabriel Jordan. But the man denies ever speaking to Dixie. Still, she's sure he knows more than he's telling, and sticking close to him is the only way to discover the truth. Strangely, her heart seems to be in danger, too....

And speaking of hearts and flowers, this year's edition of Harlequin's popular Valentine anthology, *My Valentine,* features short stories by four favorite Superromance authors—Margot Dalton, Karen Young, Marisa Carroll and Muriel Jensen. Be sure to look for it wherever Harlequin books are sold!

Happy Valentine's Day!

Marsha Zinberg,
Senior Editor, Superromance

Anne Logan

DIAL "D" for DESTINY

Harlequin Books

TORONTO • NEW YORK • LONDON
AMSTERDAM • PARIS • SYDNEY • HAMBURG
STOCKHOLM • ATHENS • TOKYO • MILAN
MADRID • WARSAW • BUDAPEST • AUCKLAND

ISBN 0-373-70585-9

DIAL "D" FOR DESTINY

ABOUT THE AUTHOR

When a friend of Anne Logan's called the author to say that she was about to meet a man she'd been communicating with by phone for several weeks, an idea for a book took hold. "I remember worrying about her meeting this stranger," says Anne. "What if she were to disappear? What would I do? Of course, she didn't disappear—her meeting was everything she dreamed of. But I carried the 'what if' game much further."

This is Anne Logan's third Superromance novel. Her first, *Gulf Breezes*, won the 1992 National Readers' Choice Award. She lives with her husband in Luling, Louisiana. The couple have three grown children and a one-year-old grandson.

Books by Anne Logan

HARLEQUIN SUPERROMANCE
507—GULF BREEZES
550—TWIN OAKS

Don't miss any of our special offers. Write to us at the following address for information on our newest releases.

Harlequin Reader Service
P.O. Box 1397, Buffalo, NY 14240
Canadian address: P.O. Box 603,
Fort Erie, Ont. L2A 5X3

To my parents, Doris and Charles Logan,
and in memory of my grandmother, Norma Wilson

Special thanks to Valorie Boyles,
for her help, friendship and inspiration,
and to Blake Selman, musician extraordinaire,
who graciously allowed me to borrow his name
and his lyrics to "Destiny Calling."

PROLOGUE

DIXIE MILLER GLARED at the ringing phone, then eyed the mountain of file folders that had been dumped on her desk earlier that morning. With all of the recent hirings and firings, it was all she could do to keep up with her work. She was sorely tempted to let the damn thing just keep ringing. Even without interruptions, at the rate she was going, she was never going to get caught up.

Finally, with a sigh of resignation, she snatched up the receiver. "Southern Phone, personnel department."

"It's me." The deep masculine voice vibrated through the telephone line. "Are you busy?"

A delicious shivery feeling washed over her as she instantly recognized the caller, and her heart skipped a beat. Once again, she eyed the stack of file folders. "No, not at all," she lied. Then a flirtatious imp from somewhere inside prompted her to add, "But we've got to stop meeting like this."

His answering chuckle was exactly what she had hoped for. The fact that they had never met face-to-face had added a certain mystique to the unusual long-distance relationship they shared.

"I *am* glad you called," she said. "I finally have some good news."

"There's an opening?" The excitement in his voice was unmistakable.

"Maybe, maybe not," she teased.

"Ah, come on. You wouldn't torture a guy, would you?"

"Maybe, maybe not," she repeated in a singsong voice.

"Dixie!"

"Oh, all right. Yes, there is finally an opening. A new guy we hired was late one too many times, and they fired him."

He gave a war whoop that made her smile. "Finally! Oh, thank the powers that be."

Dixie laughed along with him for a moment, but then she sobered. "You understand I can't promise anything, but if you can be here for an interview on Thursday, I think you've got a good shot."

"Oh, I'll be there, all right. You can bet on it. What time?"

"One o'clock." She paused and laughed again. "And for Pete's sake, don't be late."

He chuckled. "No chance, lady. No chance."

For agonizing seconds silence hummed over the lines and Dixie held her breath. Would he want to keep talking this time as he had the other times?

In each of their previous conversations, once the job question had been dealt with, they had gone on to discuss more personal things. By the third time he'd called, she had finally coaxed him into describing himself, and that's when she had realized that despite the way he flirted with her, he was really kind of shy. From what he'd told her, she knew that he was tall, almost six foot four, had dark brown hair and blue eyes. Since she was a petite five foot three, they would probably look like Mutt and Jeff, but Dixie didn't really care, since she liked tall men.

The next time he'd called, they had discussed favorite books and movies. Not only did they have similar tastes in both, but she could tell just from the way he spoke that he was way above average intelligence.

Dixie sighed. If he was half as attracted to her as he had led her to believe, he'd ask her out, wouldn't he? Had she misjudged all the calls he'd made to her? Had she read more into their lengthy personal conversations than she should have? There was always the possibility that he had only flirted with her in the hope that she would help him get a job.

"By the way," he finally drawled, "what are you doing Thursday night? I'm going to need *someone* to help me celebrate."

Dixie smiled and all of her doubts disappeared like a puff of smoke. "I think I have a date with this guy I've been talking on the phone with for the past month."

CHAPTER ONE

GATHERING HER COURAGE, Lisa LeBlanc walked up
to the steps leading to the front porch that ran the
length of the old home. At the door she quickly
knocked before she had time to change her mind.

A man appeared, shoved the wooden screen door
aside and stepped out of the shadows, giving Lisa an
unobstructed view.

Lord, he was tall, she thought, as her gaze traveled
upward: scruffy boots, well-worn jeans, a plaid shirt
that outlined broad shoulders and a deeply tanned
face. It was the kind of face that was neither handsome nor ugly, but totally, uncompromisingly masculine. And his eyes. She shivered. His eyes were the
color of a cloudy arctic sky, cold and relentless.

No, she thought. He wasn't exactly what she had
anticipated—not her sister's type of man at all. He was
older than she had expected too. Mid-thirties. A lot
closer to her age than to her sister's.

When the door softly thudded closed behind him,
she willed her shaky legs to back up a couple of steps
toward the edge of the porch so she wouldn't have to
crane her neck.

"Are you Gabriel Jordan?"

He reached up and removed the toothpick that was clamped between his even white teeth. "If you're selling something, I'm not interested," he said.

"I'm not selling anything," she answered, hoping her voice sounded braver than she felt. She raised her chin. "I'm looking for my sister."

"Your sister?" His rough voice was polite enough, but she also detected a hint of aggravation.

Lisa swallowed hard. "Dixie—Dixie Miller—is my sister," she stammered. "Is she here?"

His brow furrowed. "Lady, there's no one here but me, and I don't know any Dixie Miller." He paused, looking confused. "Who are you? And why would you think your sister would be here?"

Lisa ignored his question and glanced down at the piece of paper in her hand. She mentally compared the house numbers to the numbers above the door behind him. The address was the same. In a town as small as Ponchatoula, Louisiana, there couldn't be more than one St. Arthur Street.

"Your name *is* Gabriel Jordan?"

He nodded. "Yeah, just like my father and just like my son. So what?" His voice grew impatient. "I still don't know anyone named Dixie Miller, so if you'll excuse me?" He stuck the toothpick back into his mouth and reached for the screen door handle.

"No!" Lisa grabbed his shirtsleeve and the man went stone still. He looked first at her hand, then he stared into her eyes.

In that split second, caught up in his gaze, Lisa experienced a subtle awareness that she hadn't been conscious of at first, an awareness that was simmering with sexual overtones and totally at odds with the circumstances. Then, as suddenly as the sensation had manifested itself, it was gone, leaving her feeling even more nervous than before.

She quickly released her hold. "Sorry." She motioned toward his arm. "It's just that—" Her fingers fluttered uselessly, and she clasped them tightly in front of her with her other hand. She took a deep breath. "If your name is Gabriel Jordan and this is your address, then you *have* to know my sister. Dixie's been talking to you for weeks. She interviewed you for a job with Southern Phone in Shreveport last Thursday."

Lisa paused, hoping for a sign, a slip in his puzzled expression that would confirm that he was the man she was looking for. Except for a slight tightening of his jaw, nothing about his face changed. "My sister's been missing since then—the day she interviewed you—and she was seen leaving the office with you, too."

The man's eyes widened in astonishment. He turned his head to the side, spit out the toothpick, then faced her. "Lady, I told you I don't know your sister. In the first place, I don't need a job because I already have one." His clipped words revealed his growing irritation. "In the second place, I don't have time to argue about someone I've never heard of or spoken to."

Lisa's heart thudded painfully in her chest, and her first instinct was to back off, give up, to simply turn around, walk to her Jeep and drive away. Then she thought about Dixie, thought about the last conversation they'd had, and she knew she couldn't just walk away. This man was her only lead to finding her sister.

Lisa opened her mouth to argue, then snapped it shut when she saw him narrow his eyes and focus his attention on something behind her. She glanced over her shoulder. A sheriff's squad car pulled up alongside the curb in front of the house, and she almost groaned out loud with relief. Now maybe they could get to the truth. The two deputies would know what to do.

The minute the deputies stepped onto the porch, Lisa moved back, aligning herself with the burly men. "He's the one that was last seen with my sister, but he won't even admit he knows her." She directed her remark to the officer on her left. He looked to be the older of the two, so she figured he might be more sympathetic. "Make him tell *you* where she is."

The older officer raised a bushy eyebrow but ignored her for the moment. "Mr. Gabriel Jordan?"

For the first time since she'd confronted the man, she was gratified to see that he looked a bit nonplussed. He took a moment to glare at Lisa then nodded curtly. "I'm Gabriel Jordan."

"Sir, we've been asked to follow up on a possible missing-person report concerning a Miss Dixie Miller, ah, unofficially, that is." He turned his head and stared at Lisa for a moment. "I take it that you're the lady who filed the complaint."

Lisa nodded vigorously. "I'm Dixie Miller's sister."

"Don't you live in Des Allemands?"

"Yes, but—"

"Weren't you told the sheriff's department would check things out and get back to you?"

Feeling more uncomfortable as each minute passed, Lisa nodded a bit more slowly this time.

"So what are you doing here?"

Lisa bit her lower lip. It was the same question she'd asked herself several times before she'd worked up the courage to drive to Ponchatoula and knock on Gabriel Jordan's front door.

"I—I waited, but no one called me, and when they did, they said Mr. Jordan wasn't home. They told me they would get back to me later, but—"

The officer shook his head. "Do you have any idea what kind of trouble you could get into?"

"Me!" Lisa stiffened. "What about him?" She gestured toward Gabriel Jordan. "He's the one who probably kidnapped—"

"Kidnapped!" Gabriel Jordan's voice boomed out his astonishment. "Now just a minute here." He jerked his thumb at the officer. "He said *missing*. No one mentioned anything about a kidnapping."

"My sister has disappeared, and she was last seen with you—"

"Whoa, just hold on there, both of you," the officer said, stepping between them. "If you don't mind," he drawled, giving Lisa a stern look, "I'll handle this."

Lisa ground her teeth to keep from voicing her thoughts. As far as she could tell, no one had handled anything since she'd talked with the authorities in Shreveport early that morning.

The officer pulled out a small notepad and a pen. He directed his attention to Gabriel Jordan. "Do you know a woman named Dixie Miller?"

The man glared at Lisa. "No, I don't." He turned back to the officer. "Never heard of her."

"Can you tell us where you've been the last few days?"

"Working," he answered. "I'm a petroleum engineer for GMO—Gulf of Mexico Oil." He gave Lisa a pointed look. "Have been for fifteen years." He shook his head. "Look, Officer, I've been hopscotching from rig to rig the past two weeks, and I just got home an hour ago."

The officer nodded and spent a couple of minutes jotting down notes. "That accounts for why you weren't home when we came by earlier. Can you prove it?"

For several seconds Gabriel Jordan hesitated as if making up his mind about something. Then with a resigned sigh, he reached into his back pocket, pulled out a well-worn leather billfold and extracted a card. He handed it to the officer.

In a voice that sounded weary even to Lisa's ears, he said, "If you'd like to call those numbers, I'm sure they'll verify what I've just told you." He gestured toward the front door. "Please... feel free to use my phone."

Again the officer nodded and wrote on his notepad. After a brief meaningful glance at his partner, he said, "After you, Mr. Jordan. I'll make a couple of calls and maybe we can clear up this misunderstanding."

"Now just a minute." Lisa reached out and grabbed the officer's arm. "What do you mean, misunderstanding? There's no misunderstanding. My sister was last seen with this man and now she's missing. Why, he could have—"

"Ma'am, I told you once to let me handle this." The officer pulled his arm free. "You shouldn't be here in the first place, and if you can't restrain yourself, I'll have to ask you to wait in your car... or leave."

Wondering how she ever could have thought the sheriff's office would be on her side, Lisa glared at the officer for several seconds. She could feel hot anger burning her cheeks, and she could taste even hotter words on the tip of her tongue. Finally she pivoted around and stomped to the edge of the porch to wait.

As she gazed out over the quiet neighborhood, she was well aware of the other officer staring at her, and she was tempted to stare right back. After all, *she* wasn't the suspect. Instead she strained to hear the mumbled voices from within the house. With a sigh of disappointment, she crossed her arms tightly below her breasts and tried to concentrate on anything but the fury and frustration knotting up her stomach.

Squinting against the late-afternoon sun, her photographer's eye noted that most of the homes on the street were of a similar architecture that hinted at Victorian. They were old houses but well maintained with carefully manicured lawns, shaded by oaks, pines and the occasional magnolia tree. With the array of colorful flower beds and the number of azalea bushes already in bloom, the whole setting would have been perfect for a Norman Rockwell painting, she thought.

After several minutes that seemed like hours, she heard footsteps. She turned around.

The older officer, followed closely by Gabriel Jordan, emerged from inside the house. "Sorry to have bothered you, Mr. Jordan," he said, "but we have to check out all complaints. Do you have any idea who could be using your name?"

"What do you mean, using his name?" Lisa marched across the porch.

"Look, Ms...." The officer glanced down at his notepad.

"LeBlanc." She filled in the gap and felt her stomach tighten even more. "My name is Lisa LeBlanc, and I—"

He held up his hand to interrupt her. "Ms. LeBlanc, there are no fewer than twenty men who can attest to the fact that Mr. Jordan was working on a rig in the Gulf of Mexico at the time your sister turned up missing. Now, ma'am, I know how you feel but—"

"You have no idea how I feel!" The arrogance of the man was too much. Dixie was more than just her younger sister. Panic invaded her senses, threatening to shatter what little semblance of calm she had left.

Her mind raced as she glanced from one officer to the other, then to Gabriel Jordan. *"Do you have any idea who could be using your name?"* The officer's words reverberated in her head. If this man wasn't the Gabriel Jordan she was looking for, then— *"Yeah, just like my father and just like my son."* There *was* more than one Gabriel Jordan. Was it possible she'd picked the wrong man? she wondered.

She whirled around to face the older officer. "What about his father...or his son? He said their names were Gabriel Jordan, too." She knew she sounded desperate, but she was beyond caring. The name was all she had to go on. Her heart beat wildly in her chest as she waited for someone to answer her.

The older officer hesitated several seconds as if thinking about what she'd said. Finally with a resigned sigh, he turned to Gabriel Jordan. "Well?" he asked.

Lisa could see every muscle in Gabriel Jordan's jaw tighten. "My father has been dead for over twenty years," he answered. "My son is only seventeen. He's still in school, so he'd have no reason to apply for a job with the telephone company, and he has absolutely no reason to kidnap anyone."

His words left Lisa feeling as if she'd just been punched in the stomach. Her cheeks grew warm with embarrassment, and her eyes suddenly burned with threatening tears. She ducked her head and concentrated on the toes of her tennis shoes.

The officer had been right. She shouldn't have come. She should have let the sheriff's office handle things. All she had accomplished was to make a fool of herself. The only thing left to do was apologize and leave while she still had some measure of dignity.

She drew in a deep, steadying breath and faced Gabriel Jordan. "Look. I—I'm sorry. I'm not usually like this." For a second she thought she detected a slight thaw in the arctic coolness of his gaze. "I—I apologize for any inconvenience I've caused," she added, the carefully spoken words almost choking her. "It's just that I've been so worried, I've—" Her voice cracked.

What's the use, she thought. With a defeated shrug, she quickly turned away and hurried down the porch steps.

Wrenching open the Jeep's door, she climbed inside.

Without looking she knew that none of the men on the porch had moved. She could feel all three pairs of eyes watching her.

"Come on, Lover," she whispered, using Barry's pet name for the Jeep. "Please don't fail me now." She prayed that for once the stubborn machine would start without having to be coaxed.

Lisa depressed the clutch, held the accelerator to the floor and switched on the ignition. The engine turned over once, with a groan of protest, and she pumped the accelerator. The engine caught, rumbled to life and she shoved the grinding gearshift stick into reverse.

A few minutes later when she braked at a red light on the main street of Ponchatoula, she tried to think of anything but the past humiliating hour.

All around her, the streets were full of crews of workmen, cleaning and repainting most of the main street buildings. Since April was only a couple of weeks away, she figured they were probably sprucing up the town for the annual Strawberry Festival.

As she remembered the one time she'd attended the festival, Lisa's throat ached even more, and a lone tear escaped to slide down her cheek.

She swiped at the tear. "You're just feeling sorry for yourself," she whispered. "So stop it right now."

But there was no way she could stop the bittersweet memory of her husband or of their last day together before he'd had to report for duty to his National Guard unit.

Sipping strawberry daiquiris, she and Barry had leisurely roamed the streets with the rest of the crowds. They had explored each one of the many craft booths set up near the railroad tracks, and they had checked out every antique shop that lined the main street, enjoying their last few hours together.

The light turned green. Lisa depressed the clutch and shifted into first.

Barry's Guard unit had been assigned to the Persian Gulf. When he *had* finally come home, he'd been forever sealed away from her in a casket, one of the few casualties of Desert Storm.

First her parents' death, she thought. Then her husband's death, and now... "No," she whispered, her grip tightening on the steering wheel. "Dixie is not dead. She's just missing."

Lisa took a deep breath. She'd find her sister. She had to.

Once Lisa turned the Jeep onto Interstate 55, she thought back to the last conversation she'd had with Dixie. In the five years since Lisa had married Barry and moved to south Louisiana, neither sister had ever missed those Saturday-morning calls, no matter where they were—not until three days ago when Dixie hadn't answered.

Lisa swallowed hard, remembering the argument they'd had. If only she had been more understanding. Even now, she could recall every word of that conversation....

"Oh, Lisa, I can't believe I'm finally going to meet him. I just know he's got to be gorgeous. Every time he calls, and I hear that deep sexy voice, I get goose bumps."

"Come on, Dixie, give me a break. You don't know anything about the man except what he's told you over the phone. Did it ever occur to you that he's been feeding you a crock of bull for the past month?"

"I know all I need to know, and if you're going to give me another Lisa lecture, then I'm hanging up."

"Okay, okay, but will you do me one favor?"

"Depends," Dixie retorted.

"Will you at least make sure that you meet him where there will be lots of people around? And call me afterward."

A groan from Dixie hummed over the phone line. "Talk about a one-track mind. Geez, I swear. Haven't you heard anything I've told you? He's applied for a job. He's being interviewed in my office first, then we're going out to dinner. Give me a little credit, will you? I'm not completely stupid."

Lisa sighed. "Of course you're not stupid, but I still don't like this—not any of it. Call it intuition or whatever, but—"

"Oh, good grief, Lisa. Look, I know you mean well, but back off, will you? I'm not a kid, and you don't have to play mother anymore."

Play mother? The hurtful words ripped through Lisa with the precision of a surgeon's scalpel. "Is that what you think?" she said, trying to keep her voice even. "You think that for the past twelve years, all I've been doing is *playing?*"

"I didn't say anything that hasn't needed to be said for a long time," Dixie snapped, her tone defensive. "Lisa, you know I love you, but for Pete's sake, will you please cut the apron strings? I'm twenty-three years old, I pay my own bills and you still treat me like I was a child. Maybe if you'd get a life—"

"Get a life! I have a life, thank you very much. And my life is not the issue here anyway—"

"Ha! You have a *career,* not a life. All you do is stay holed up in that studio of yours down in Des Allemands, hiding behind your cameras."

"That's not true."

"Oh, yeah? So when's the last time you had an honest-to-God date with a man? Huh? Just when?"

"I've dated."

"Yeah, I can count the number of times on one hand. Barry is dead, Lisa, but you're not. Maybe if you would—"

"That's enough."

"Enough...enough..." The word still echoed in Lisa's mind.

"Oh, Dixie, I'm sorry," she whispered. As she crossed the bridge over Pass Manchac, the wind whipped through her hair and she breathed in the humid air of nearby Lake Maurepas.

There was no mistaking that the man in question called himself Gabriel Jordan.

Immediately, a picture of the man flashed in Lisa's mind. A long-forgotten but familiar feeling stirred deep in her stomach, a feeling she hadn't experienced since Barry.

Lisa shivered, gripped the steering wheel tighter, and willed Gabriel Jordan's image and her improper reaction to him to disappear. It was easier to think of him as a liar.

Had he been lying? she wondered.

What about his alibi?

His cronies at the rigs could have lied for him, she argued silently, couldn't they?

Lisa groaned. But why would they? And why would Gabriel Jordan have applied for a job as a lineman with the phone company when it was evident that he already had a perfectly good job?

He wouldn't have, came the silent, accusing answer. She had been wrong about him...embarrassingly wrong.

An hour later, when she pulled into her driveway, she eyed the late-model Ford parked next to her usual spot. The last person she felt like dealing with was Clarice LeBlanc. She loved Barry's mother and she would always be grateful for the support she'd received from Clarice after Barry's death, but sometimes the tiny woman got on her nerves. Clarice had raised six children and still thought she had the right to run their lives.

With a resigned sigh, Lisa shoved the gearshift into reverse, set the brakes and switched off the ignition.

When Lisa rounded the corner of her home, she pasted a smile on her lips. Clarice was sitting on the porch swing, reading a book. From the looks of the cover, Lisa figured it was the latest in the batch of romance novels she received each month. Clarice was a devout reader and had several bookcases of novels she'd saved over the years.

Clarice looked up and raised one curious eyebrow. "Where have you been, *chere?*" Clarice called out in her thick Cajun accent. "I've been waiting for almost an hour." She carefully marked her place in the book and closed it.

Lisa dug out her keys, buying time to avoid answering. "Let's go inside," she said. "I could use a cup of coffee." She stuck the key in the lock, twisted it and shoved open the door.

"Sounds good, but I can't stay long. I just came over to tell you we're having a crawfish boil this Saturday. They're not really big enough yet, but *Pépère* wants some, so..." She shrugged as if to say, what can I do? "Everyone is supposed to come," she added.

Lisa almost smiled. And whatever *Pépère* wants, *Pépère* gets, she thought. Clarice's father, known to everyone as *Pépère*, was in his late eighties, but still called the shots in the LeBlanc family. Lisa had fallen in love with the old man the first time she had met him, and though he had blustered and fussed about the fact that she was Protestant instead of Catholic, she had known by the twinkle in his faded eyes that he had approved of her.

Knowing Clarice would follow her, Lisa walked briskly through the living room and headed for the kitchen. She figured that Clarice could have called instead of coming to her home, but she suspected her mother-in-law paid her these unexpected visits just to check up on her.

"I'm not sure I can make it Saturday," she called over her shoulder. "I may go to Shreveport."

"I guess you still haven't heard from that sister of yours yet, eh?"

Lisa deposited her purse on the counter and began preparing the coffeemaker to brew a fresh pot. "No, I haven't." She didn't dare tell Clarice about her trip to Ponchatoula just as she hadn't told her that she had filed a missing person's report. Telling Clarice was tantamount to broadcasting the news to the whole LeBlanc family.

"She'll turn up. You shouldn't worry so. What that girl needs is a husband to keep up with her."

Lisa sighed but kept silent, deciding that arguing with Clarice was useless. A husband was Clarice's solution to every woman's problems...except where she was concerned. To Clarice's way of thinking, Lisa was still and always would be married to Barry.

Thinking back, Lisa supposed that some of her reluctance to date more stemmed from the fact that she would have to face her mother-in-law's disapproval.

Many times since Barry had died, she had considered moving back to Shreveport, but she truly loved south Louisiana, and her successful photography studio afforded her the kind of financial security she wouldn't be able to attract in the more depressed Shreveport area.

"So, *chere,* we will see you Saturday, then."

Lisa faced Clarice. "If I am in town, you know I'll come."

Half an hour later, Lisa strolled down to the bayou that ran alongside her home and studio. Clarice had quickly finished her coffee and left.

For several moments, Lisa stood, trying to absorb the peaceful sights and sounds around her. She sighed and breathed in the humid bayou smells, hoping that she could somehow relax, somehow find a moment of solace.

But it was no use. Her mind wouldn't be soothed and she couldn't let go of all the questions and horrible scenarios that swirled through her head.

Lisa closed her eyes against the tears that threatened. *Oh, Barry. What do I do now? I can't lose Dixie, too.*

CHAPTER TWO

IN PONCHATOULA, Gabriel Jordan heard the protesting groan of the front screen door being opened.

"Gabriel? It's just me."

Recognizing his aunt's voice, he looked up from the letter he'd been reading and sighed, a small indulgent smile pulling at his lips. For ten years, his aunt Bessie had lived next door and had helped him raise his son. She never bothered to knock, but he didn't mind...at least, most of the time he didn't.

As the tiny, birdlike woman rushed into the room from the foyer, he refolded the letter and tucked it into his shirt pocket.

"Oh, Gabriel, I'm so glad you're finally home."

Her usually sparkling blue eyes were clouded and the few aging lines on her normally smooth face were deeply etched. From worrying, Gabe concluded. He gently hugged the frail woman and bent to brush her cheek with a kiss.

"Have you heard anything?" she asked, a hopeful note in her voice. "Has he called yet?"

Gabe shook his head. For a moment he debated whether he should mention his strange visit from Lisa LeBlanc and the sheriff's deputies, but only for a moment. His aunt was worried enough, and he was too weary to try to explain.

"Oh, dear." She fumbled with the opening of her handbag, pulled out a crisply starched lacy handkerchief and blotted her eyes. "Where could that boy be?"

Using every bit of willpower that he could muster, Gabe fought down his own panicky feelings for his aunt's sake. "Stop worrying," he admonished softly and squeezed her thin shoulder. "You know Danny. If he dropped out of school, he had a good reason. At least we know he's okay."

Gabe couldn't really imagine any reason why his usually levelheaded son would drop out of college and simply disappear, but there was no use upsetting his aunt more than she already was. He was upset enough for the both of them.

When her frantic message had finally caught up with him early that morning, he'd commandeered the next available helicopter back to shore, gone straight to Tulane University in New Orleans and questioned the dean and Danny's roommate. Neither could tell him anything useful to help him locate his son.

Gabe tried to summon an encouraging smile for his aunt. "He'll show up eventually. But right now I'm starving. I haven't had anything since breakfast this morning." Food was the last thing on his mind, but feigning hunger was all he could think of at the moment to distract his aunt.

The older lady sniffed and stuffed the handkerchief back into her handbag. "Oh, you poor thing. Of course you're hungry." She backed away toward the foyer. "You wait right here. I still have some chicken and dumplings left over from last night that I'll bring over. Just give me a minute to heat it up. There should be just enough."

She hesitated in the doorway, then turned to look at him. "Gabriel, about the letter he sent . . . You know he didn't mean those things he said. Danny loves you and you've been a good father."

Gabe's fingers tightened into fists. "I know, sweetheart. He was probably upset about a grade or a test or something."

For several long seconds she continued staring at him, and Gabe tried his best to give her another reassuring smile. Then, as if finally satisfied with what she saw, she nodded, turned, and he watched her disappear through the doorway. Seconds later, he heard the front screen groan and thump closed as Bessie left.

Hooking his thumbs into his pockets, he turned back to stare at a two-year-old graduation picture of his son sitting on the mantel above the fireplace.

Even at fifteen Danny had been tall and broadshouldered for his age. He'd also been the youngest student to ever graduate from Ponchatoula High School and one of the youngest who had ever entered Tulane University as a full-time student. His son's genius IQ was still a source of amazement to Gabe.

And dropping all of his classes and taking off was completely out of character.

Gabe shook his head and paced the length of the living room, halting in front of the window that faced his aunt's house. He reached up and touched the letter still in his pocket, his son's angry words still burning in his brain.

He shook his head as if the action would scatter the words and make them disappear. And as another thought crossed his mind, a shiver of unease ran down Gabe's spine. Was it mere coincidence that Danny and Lisa LeBlanc's sister had turned up missing at the same time? If it was, then why had the LeBlanc woman come looking for Gabriel Jordan?

Just because Danny's full name was Gabriel Daniel Jordan, too, didn't necessarily mean he was mixed up with Lisa LeBlanc's sister... did it?

He frowned. And it certainly didn't mean he had kidnapped her. Christ, Danny was just seventeen. Realistically Gabe knew that there were kids even younger than Danny who got into trouble, what with the influx of drugs, gangs and random shootings. But not Danny, he thought. Danny was as straight an arrow as they came, the quintessential all-American boy.

Through the window Gabe saw his aunt emerge from the side entrance of her home, her arms loaded with dishes. He shoved his fingers through his hair and took a deep breath. Only Danny could give him the answers he needed. But he'd have to find him first.

Gabe glanced over his shoulder to once again stare at the picture of his son. "Where are you, Danny boy?" he whispered.

THREE HUNDRED MILES northwest of Ponchatoula, in a dilapidated log cabin, Danny Jordan stared across the room at the bed where a woman lay, trussed up like a calf waiting to be branded. One of her eyes was swollen shut. Dark purple-and-yellow bruises radiated down her cheekbone and across her nose. The other eye was closed.

Was she unconscious or simply asleep? He couldn't tell. At least she's still alive, no thanks to him, he thought, noting the slight rise and fall of her chest.

"Dixie? Are you awake?"

As he waited, hoping for some kind of response, nothing but the eerie twilight sounds of chirping crickets and hooting owls filtered in from outside of the cabin.

The floor where he lay was hard and unyielding. If only he could loosen the ropes around his wrists.

He turned and strained, but a sudden sharp pain ripped through his chest. Danny groaned.

Bruised or cracked ribs, he decided, concentrating on the feel of the coarse rope burning his skin and fighting the overwhelming desire to simply give up and sleep.

As he waited for the pain to subside, he rested his head on the cold floor.

"Are you okay?"

The sound of Dixie's voice roused him. Had he fallen asleep? He couldn't tell.

"Danny?"

"Yeah, I'm okay," he finally answered. "How's your head?"

She made a noise, but it was a pitiful excuse for laughter. "Probably about the same as your ribs."

"They're not too bad," he lied. "Any luck with your ropes?"

"Just as tight as ever."

Even from where he was lying he could see tears forming and spilling from her good eye. He winced. "Aw, come on Dixie, don't cry." It was the first time she had done so, and the sight twisted his gut. "We'll get out of this somehow...." His voice trailed into a whisper. "I'm sorry...so damned sorry. I should have fought harder."

She sniffed and rubbed her face against the mattress. "Oh, God," she groaned. "Don't start that again. For Pete's sake, and for the last time, none of this is your fault."

"Yeah, but I'm bigger than him...and younger. I should have been able to beat that guy to a pulp."

"Oh, right. And just how many fights have you ever been in?" she taunted.

Danny felt his face grow warm. "Enough," he grumbled.

"Listen!"

"What is it?" But even as the words left his mouth, he heard the sound of a car engine and crunching gravel.

"Maybe it's someone else this time. Maybe it's not him. Think we should yell out or something?"

Danny shook his head. "Not yet."

A car door slammed and the sound of footsteps on the porch reached their ears. Within seconds the door opened.

The smell of food was the first thing that registered in Danny's mind as the man, carrying a white sack, entered the room.

"So, how is everyone today?" he said, setting the sack on the crude wooden table. "Enjoying your vacation?"

"Go to hell, you bastard."

He glared at Dixie. "Shut up or you can forget about anything to eat or drink."

"You're a real tough guy, aren't you? Especially when it comes to women and boys, huh?" she continued.

"Dixie, don't." But Danny knew his words fell on deaf ears and his heart began to race.

"Just one more word," the man threatened as he pulled a gun from his coat pocket and walked toward her.

"Leave her alone!" Danny shouted, straining against his ropes and ignoring the pain in his chest.

MIDNIGHT.

It had taken him awhile, but Gabe had finally

calmed his aunt's fears enough to persuade her to go home and get some sleep. He'd immediately called all of Danny's old friends, but the results had been the same. Nothing. It was as if his son had dropped off the face of the earth without a trace or a clue.

Sitting at his desk, Gabe stared at the small, cylindrical glass tube lying near the pages of Danny's letter. Encased in the tube was a cigarette. Danny had given it to him as a joke on New Year's Day. He had laughed and said it was Gabe's trophy, a testament to the day that he'd finally quit smoking.

Gabe picked up the tube and turned it to read the writing on the label wrapped around it. "Break only in case of emergency," it read. And for the first time in months, he was tempted. He could almost taste the acrid smoke, feel the soothing results as the nicotine raced through his bloodstream.

"Damn!" Gabe tossed the tube into a nearby trash basket. Reaching inside his breast pocket, he pulled out a toothpick and stuck it between his teeth.

Glaring at the letter, he snatched up the pages and began reading. He'd already read the letter so many times that he'd almost memorized it, but each time he had hoped he would find something that would give him a clue where Danny might be.

Dear Dad,

I'm sorry for taking what you will probably think is the coward's way out by writing a letter instead of talking to you face-to-face. But I've tried talking and that didn't work. You never listen. You only hear what you want to hear, so I figured you might pay more attention to a letter.

"You never listen. You only hear what you want to hear."

Each word was a dagger, inflicting a mortal wound. Gabe shoved his fingers through his hair. *That's ridiculous,* he thought. Of course he listened. Just because he didn't give the boy everything he wanted didn't mean he never listened, dammit.

Dismissing the words, he continued reading.

There's no other way to say this but straight out. I'm quitting school.

I know Aunt Bessie will worry, but please assure her that I'll be okay. Please tell her that I've got great prospects and I won't starve.

"Great prospects. Won't starve."

Gabe closed his eyes and cursed. What the hell did that mean—a job of some kind? But what kind of job could a seventeen-year-old get except working the counter in a fast-food restaurant?

Gabe wondered if Danny actually thought he could support himself on minimum wage? If he did, Gabe decided his genius son wasn't as intelligent as everyone had declared he was all these years.

Gabe opened his eyes and glared at the page.

Dad, I know you've done the best you knew how, but I also know that you would never agree to let me quit school. What you don't understand is that I never wanted to graduate early, to go straight to college, to be so different. All I've ever wanted was to be like everyone else. Instead, everyone—you, Aunt Bessie, all my teachers—pushed and pushed and pushed. Well, I'm tired of doing what's expected. I'm tired of being the "wonder boy." I'm seventeen and it's time I had some say-so about my own life.

I'm sorry if this hurts you, but it seemed to be the only way.

Love,
Danny

Gabe reread the last sentence again, then dropped the letter. He closed his eyes and pinched the bridge of his nose. "Damn fool boy!" he muttered.

Abruptly he stood, then headed for the kitchen. As he peered into the almost-empty refrigerator, he wondered what the hell he was going to do. Selecting a canned soft drink, he removed the toothpick he'd been chewing, popped the top and took a swallow. The cool liquid slid down his throat. He rubbed the sweating can against his forehead and thought about turning on the air-conditioning. For the end of March, it was unseasonably hot and muggy.

Gabe walked to the back door, opened it and breathed in the humid air. Other than an occasional car passing or a dog barking, only the night sounds of frogs and chirping crickets could be heard.

Sleep.

If only he could get some rest, maybe he could think more clearly in the morning. But every time he tried, his mind raced, weighing and discarding the places his son might have gone to.

And hovering just above his thoughts was the one thing he didn't want to admit. That somehow, some way, Danny's disappearance *was* linked to Dixie Miller's disappearance. None of it made sense.

A vision of Lisa LeBlanc's shining auburn hair and her dark intense eyes floated across his mind. Those brown eyes had snapped with determination and almost glowed with passionate loyalty for her sister.

Gabe blinked several times and the vision vanished. She had spunk. He'd give her that. And it was crystal clear she was fiercely devoted to her sister, but everything else that had happened during her visit seemed like a blur or a bad dream.

Gabe frowned, trying to remember what else he knew about her. She'd said that she lived in Des Allemands, but that was about all he could recall. He'd been too upset about Danny to think clearly.

Was she married? And if she was, why hadn't her husband come with her? And why did he care one way or the other?

Was it possible? he wondered. Was Danny somehow mixed up with Lisa LeBlanc's sister? He'd never heard Danny mention anyone by that name. The vision of Lisa LeBlanc floated across his mind again. If the sister looked anything like Lisa LeBlanc, he could hardly blame Danny. At seventeen, raging hormones had a tendency to overrule good sense. And genius IQ or not, his son was one hundred percent male.

"You never listen."

Gabe squeezed his eyes shut against the haunting refrain of Danny's words. There had to be some other explanation for the bizarre coincidence. He didn't want to believe that Danny was mixed up in a kidnapping...and he didn't want to face Lisa LeBlanc again, but Danny's full name was Gabriel Daniel Jordan, and at the moment, the only clue he had was Lisa LeBlanc's sister. As much as he hated to admit it, especially given the way he'd rudely reacted to the woman, the only answer he could come up with was to find the sister.

But how?

EARLY TUESDAY MORNING, Gabe pulled his truck into Lisa LeBlanc's driveway alongside the same battered old Jeep that she'd been driving the day before. He figured the Jeep had to be at least ten years old.

He switched off the ignition. Finding where she lived had been easier than he had expected. He'd stopped at a gas station and asked to see a local phone directory. The attendant had asked if he could help, and when Gabe told him who he was looking for, the attendant had laughed. It turned out that the attendant was a cousin-in-law of sorts.

Stepping out of his truck, Gabe stared at a huge sign that informed him that Lisa was a professional photographer and owned the studio located in the main house. The idea intrigued him, and his admiration of her climbed another notch.

He was a total disaster when it came to cameras, and because of his lack of skills in that one area, he'd spent a fortune over the years just so he could have photos of Danny growing up.

As he walked toward the studio entrance, he glanced around the surrounding property. The lot was at least half an acre, he figured, and it bordered a small bayou. The yard was landscaped with azalea bushes, a few ornamental trees and was well maintained. The house was an old double, built to accommodate two families. The exterior was white with dark blue shutters and trim, and it seemed in excellent condition.

Once at the front door, Gabe raised his hand to knock, then lowered it. He still didn't know just exactly what he was going to say to her. And there was always the possibility that she might refuse to even talk to him. After the way he'd treated her the day before, he couldn't much blame her if she did. Still, he had to try. Finding Danny was too important not to.

Drawing himself up to his full height, he took a deep breath for courage and knocked on the door.

WHEN LISA PEEKED through the curtain of her studio door, the last person she'd expected to see was Gabriel Jordan. A tremor of unease rippled through her.

What reason would he have for showing up on her doorstep? she wondered. She could think of none except the possibility that he knew more about Dixie's disappearance than he'd admitted the day before.

That he had taken the trouble to look her up and find her address was a little unnerving, especially when he could have simply phoned her instead. After all, she thought, the man was a perfect stranger, a stranger she'd accused of kidnapping. For all she knew, he could want some kind of revenge for all the trouble she'd caused him.

Wary of his reason for being there, she decided to leave the security chain firmly in place. Gathering her courage, she cautiously opened the door.

"Ms. LeBlanc, may I come in? I think we need to talk."

Lisa swallowed. "Talk about what?"

"About your sister."

Maybe he did know something, after all. But still Lisa hesitated.

As if sensing her reluctance, he added, "I promise I won't take up much of your time."

Lisa glanced at her watch. Her receptionist, Carla, would be in soon, she rationalized. She should be safe enough for the next ten or fifteen minutes until Carla showed up.

Finally, with a curt nod, Lisa gave in and allowed her curiosity to overrule her caution. She closed the door long enough to unfasten the security chain, reopened it and gestured for him to enter.

"Nice place," he said.

"Thanks."

"I love these old doubles. Do you use both sides for your studio?"

Lisa shook her head. With Gabe standing just an arm's length away, the entry foyer suddenly felt too small, too intimate. She backed up a step. "My husband and I remodeled the other side to live in and this side for the studio."

"Is your husband a photographer, too?"

She shook her head. "No. My husband was a fisherman."

"Was?"

"He died in Desert Storm—" Thinking of Barry in the past tense was still hard . . . and painful. "Look, Mr. Jordan. I thought you wanted to talk about my sister." She made a show of checking the time on her watch. "I've got a busy day ahead and I can only give you a few minutes. My receptionist is due any minute, and I've got a ten o'clock appointment scheduled this morning." She motioned for him to precede her down the hallway. "We can talk in the reception room."

"Of course . . . sorry."

Lisa followed him, careful to give him a wide berth. For such a large man, he was perfectly proportioned. He was wearing the same scruffy boots she'd noticed the day before, but today his jeans didn't look quite so faded.

With each step he took, the muscles in his shoulders and back strained against the fabric of his knit shirt. Her fingers itched for her camera, and she wondered if he looked as good with his shirt off as he did with it on. She could just picture him bare chested, barefoot, dressed in nothing but a pair of faded jeans.

When Lisa realized the directions her thoughts were taking, her face grew warm. Now was not the time to indulge in ridiculous, useless fantasies. *Get a grip,* a silent voice warned. *"Hiding behind your cameras."* Dixie's accusation from their last conversation taunted her.

As soon as they entered the reception room, Lisa took refuge behind the receptionist's desk.

Gabe stopped in the middle of the room and slowly turned in a circle, his gaze taking in each of the framed photographs of people, animals and still lifes that filled the walls.

Lisa drew in a deep breath and tapped her fingers impatiently against the desktop.

After a moment, he walked over to the back wall and stared at a particular portrait of a dark-haired young boy dressed all in white. The boy, just one of Barry's many nephews, was lounging on a white wicker daybed and surrounded by sheer white billowy curtains. Lisa had titled the shot *Provocative Innocence.* To her, the picture embodied the innocence and purity of childhood but at the same time hinted of the virile man the boy would become. The portrait had won her numerous awards and had gained her a healthy measure of national attention.

"You do nice work," he said, a definite reverence and respect evident in his tone.

"Mr. Jordan—"

"Call me Gabe." He smiled and seated himself in a nearby chair.

"About my sister?" she prompted.

His smile faded. He leaned forward, and with his hands clasped loosely together, he rested his elbows on his knees. "Have you heard anything else from the police?"

Lisa shook her head.

"Have you checked with her friends?"

Lisa nodded. "I called Nicole early Monday morning—Nicole is one of Dixie's closest friends. She drove by Dixie's apartment several times during the day, but Dixie wasn't home and her car was gone."

"I'd like to help you find your sister."

Stunned, Lisa simply stared at him. Gabe stared back. "Why would you want to help me?" she finally asked when she found her voice.

"If you'd discovered that someone had used your name, had involved you with the police, wouldn't you want to know who and why?"

Lisa thought about his reasoning for a moment. If their situations were reversed, she would be pretty damn angry, too. Yes, she decided, she would want to know who and why; still, there was something—a certain wariness—in his expression that didn't ring true, something that made her suspect that there might be another motive behind his offer. But what?

"I do see your point," she reluctantly conceded. "So what do you propose?"

"What had you planned to do next?"

Lisa bit her lower lip. She'd been up half the night going over what few facts she had, and she'd finally concluded that if she wanted to know what had happened to her sister, she'd have to find out for herself.

"I've decided to go to Shreveport," she said, opting to tell him the truth. "It will take most of today to clear my calendar of appointments, so I'm leaving early in the morning. I want to check out Dixie's apartment and talk to her boss. I figured I could get more information in person than over the phone."

Gabe nodded in agreement. "You're right." He paused. "What about...I mean—" He took a deep breath and seemed to hesitate. When he lowered his gaze and stared at the floor again, she got the feeling that he was hiding his *real* reason for offering to help. "I'd like to go with you," he finally said.

"Go with me..." Caught off guard, Lisa let her voice trail away. For long seconds all she could do was stare at him. The man was a complete stranger, she didn't trust him and she still couldn't shake the feeling that he knew more about Dixie than he had said. As she was blessed or cursed—Lisa could never decide which—with an active imagination, a myriad of thoughts swirled through her head. What if he had done away with Dixie? What if his offer was just a ruse to get rid of her, as well?

No. Stop thinking like that. Dixie is okay. She's alive.

Lisa firmly shook her head. "No. Sorry, but I don't think that's such a good idea."

"Look, I know we kind of got off on the wrong foot yesterday, and I apologize for that. I had just gotten home ... and then you showed up, accusing me of kidnapping, then the police—well, you can imagine how I felt. I think you owe me a chance to make up for it and to clear my name."

Being reminded of her humiliating mistake made Lisa want to squirm in her chair. No one liked to admit being wrong, and Lisa thought it was kind of tacky of him to remind her of her mistake.

"You'd be safer traveling with a man than by yourself," he added.

Safer with a man? Suddenly the guilt she'd felt fled, and all of Lisa's defenses went on alert. As a woman, especially a widowed woman in business for herself, she'd had to fight tooth and nail to gain the respect that most men took for granted, and it really irritated her that this man—this stranger—would be so condescending.

She narrowed her eyes. "That's a matter of opinion," she retorted evenly. "I'll have you to know that I've gotten along just fine for quite a while without a man's so-called protection."

Gabe held up his hand. "Whoa. Hold on. No offense intended. All I meant was that *if* someone else is involved with your sister's disappearance, he'd think twice before he tackled both of us."

Lisa had to think about that one. What he'd said made sense; so if it made sense, why did she get the feeling she was being manipulated by an expert, an expert with a silver tongue?

"I suppose you're right, but—"

Gabe stood. "Good. Then it's settled. I'll be back in the morning."

Yep, she thought. *An expert.* And she'd played right into his hands. The realization that she'd been had was a bit unnerving, and as far as Lisa was concerned, nothing was settled, but before she could think of a suitable argument, she heard the rattle of the front door opening.

"Lisa, it's just me. Sorry I'm late."

"Your receptionist?"

Lisa nodded and stood. Seconds later, Barry's cousin, Carla, entered the room. As Lisa watched Gabe and Carla exchange greetings, she wondered what she'd let herself in for. Not only did she distrust Gabriel Jordan, but each time she thought of being confined with him in the Jeep for the six-hour trip to Shreveport, her heart picked up a beat and a flash of heat shot through her. Something about the man, something in the way those cool eyes looked at her, made her much too aware that she was still a woman with a woman's needs.

Gabe turned to face her. "See you tomorrow, say about eight?"

Lisa leveled a no-nonsense look at him. "You can come along, but you might as well know up front that I don't trust you. And just in case you get any funny ideas—" she motioned toward Carla "—my husband's relatives will know that I left with you."

Gabe nodded. "I understand, and believe me, I won't give you any reason to worry. All I want is to clear my name."

The minute the front door closed, Carla rounded on Lisa. "What's going on here?"

Lisa sighed. "I'm leaving in the morning for Shreveport."

"I gathered as much, but that's not what I'm talking about. Why is that man going with you?"

"Oh, Carla, it's a long story, but the bottom line is that he might be able to help me locate Dixie."

Carla stared at her as if she had lost her mind. "*Pépère* and *Tante* Clarice will have a fit."

"Only if they know," Lisa said matter-of-factly. "What they don't know won't hurt them."

The look on Carla's face was comical. It would never occur to the young woman to do anything that her family wouldn't approve of.

Lisa reached out and patted Carla's arm. "Just trust me, and please don't tell them until I've left. After that—" she shrugged "—there won't be much they can do about it."

Carla's eyes widened. "Nothing except give me hell for not telling them in the first place."

"Please, Carla, promise me."

The young woman hesitated then finally nodded her head. "Okay, *chere,* but I hope you know what you're doing."

"Me too, Carla. Me too."

CHAPTER THREE

ON WEDNESDAY MORNING, Gabe turned into Lisa's driveway and pulled up beside her Jeep. The hood was raised and all that was visible beneath it was a shapely behind and a pair of legs outlined by skintight jeans.

Lisa no doubt, he thought as he stepped out of his truck. Just as he'd suspected, the auburn-haired woman emerged from beneath the hood, holding up an oil dipstick.

Gabe narrowed his eyes and fished out a toothpick from inside his pocket. Surely she didn't intend to drive that rattletrap all the way to Shreveport, he thought, slipping the toothpick into his mouth and clamping down on it with his teeth.

He walked to the front of his truck. Leaning against the bumper, he crossed his arms and watched her wipe the dipstick clean, shove it back into the crankcase, then pull it out again.

"I'm just about ready," she called over her shoulder. "As soon as I check—"

"I kind of figured we'd take my truck."

Without missing a beat, she shoved the dipstick back into place and slammed the hood. "She doesn't look like much," she said, wiping her hands on the greasy rag she'd used, "but Lover will get us there and back just fine."

Gabe removed the toothpick. "I'd still rather drive my truck... Lover?"

A sudden tinge of pink appeared on her pale cheeks, and if he hadn't known better, he would have suspected she was blushing. But he did know better. She might have looked like the epitome of the helpless female, but looks—as he was fast finding out with Lisa LeBlanc—were deceiving.

She raised her chin a degree. "Sorry, we go in my Jeep or we don't go, at least not together anyway. And Lover is the Jeep's name," she added, her tone a bit defensive, then she quickly turned away.

Gabe watched as she walked around to the back left side of the Jeep. She squatted down by the tire and unscrewed the cap of the inflation valve. The woman was an amazing and complete contradiction, he thought. The term "steel magnolia" came to mind, and Gabe almost smiled as she pulled a tire gage out of her shirt pocket and tested the tire.

"It's a little low, so we'll have to stop and air it up."

Gabe walked up behind her. "My tires are new." Just as she stood, he caught her by the arm. "And so is my truck." He felt her muscles stiffen beneath his fingers and knew instantly that he'd made a grave error in judgment. The lady didn't like to be touched. When she jerked her arm loose, he let go, even though he knew he could have easily held on to her.

She backed up a step and placed her hands on her hips. "Look, Mr. Jordan—Gabe," she corrected herself, when he raised an eyebrow in obvious objection to the formality. "Either you go with me in my Jeep or you stay here. One way or the other, it doesn't matter to me. As I said yesterday, I don't trust you, and if you try any funny stuff between here and Shreveport, I'll leave you standing on the side of the road." Deliberately preempting any further conversation, she said, "End of discussion," and marched off toward the house. Just as she reached the door, she pivoted. "And another thing. I'm driving."

Gabe stuck his toothpick back into his mouth and watched her disappear into the house. For a moment he was tempted to just get in his truck and leave without saying a word to her. It would serve the little hellcat right, he thought.

Reaching up, he shoved his fingers through his hair, switched the toothpick to the other side of his mouth and sighed. It might serve her right, but letting his temper get the best of him wouldn't find Danny. And right now, Lisa LeBlanc and her missing sister were the only clues he had to go on.

Shaking his head, he strolled to the back of his truck and grabbed his duffel bag.

Inside the house, Lisa stood over her suitcase and tried to control the tremors racing through her. She took several deep breaths and silently cursed her wretched temper. Usually she could control it, but the past three days of worrying about Dixie, then trying

to rearrange her schedule, had stretched her nerves to
the limit.

She was sure Gabe had only meant to be helpful
when he'd offered to use his truck and equally sure he
hadn't meant anything sinister when he'd grabbed her
arm. And if she was honest, she would have to admit
that all in all, the man seemed like a pretty decent sort
of guy.

Lisa sighed. If she was going to be honest, she
would also have to admit that fear hadn't been the
only emotion to have contributed to her tremors. The
man—in Dixie's vernacular—was a hunk. She'd have
to be blind, deaf and dumb not to notice.

With a shaky hand, Lisa closed the suitcase and
zipped it up. At the moment, she was just too tired and
uptight to deal with being honest, she decided.

A few minutes later, dragging her suitcase behind
her, Lisa emerged from the house. Out of the corner
of her eye, she could see Gabe standing by the passenger door of Lover, waiting for her.

From the morose look on his face, she figured he
wasn't too happy about their traveling arrangements.
Too bad, she thought as she locked the front door and
grabbed the handle of the suitcase. Besides, she had
already thought things through. If she drove, she'd
have more control. And if he did try anything funny,
there was always Barry's old handgun that she kept
beneath the driver's seat for protection.

Before she had dragged the suitcase very far, Gabe
met her and grabbed the handle. When he lifted it, he

grunted and a look of surprise widened his eyes. "What have you got in this thing? Bricks?"

"I don't recall asking for any help."

He stared at her for several seconds, then shook his head. "No, I guess you didn't. My mistake." Before she could object further, he turned, suitcase still in hand, walked to the Jeep and heaved it into the back seat.

Lisa felt heat creep up her neck. She couldn't remember the last time she'd behaved so ungraciously. She slid inside the Jeep and fastened her safety belt.

When Gabe climbed inside, she felt obligated to apologize. It wasn't his fault that she was a nervous wreck. "Sorry," she muttered as she waited for him to fasten his seat belt. "I'm not usually so...so..."

The withering look he gave her cut off the rest of her explanation. So much for graciousness, she thought. Tight-lipped, she directed her attention to starting Lover. She pumped the accelerator several times.

"You'll flood it doing that."

Lisa closed her eyes and counted to ten. Ignoring his warning, she pumped the accelerator again just for good measure, then she switched on the ignition. When Lover started, Lisa threw him a smug look, ground the gears into reverse and started backing out of the driveway.

"There's a car coming."

"I see it," she said evenly.

Looking as if he'd just bitten into a sour apple, Gabe shrugged and slumped down in the seat.

A few minutes later Lisa pulled out onto Highway 90 and accelerated up to the fifty-five speed limit. Well, one thing for sure, she thought, the trip wouldn't be boring. Sparring with Gabriel Jordan would certainly keep her on her toes.

As the miles sped by, Lisa tried to concentrate on anything but the quiet man seated beside her. On either side of the four-lane highway, there were stands of lush green trees interspersed with open fields, some solely cleared for the natural-gas lines and others for livestock.

Lisa let up on the accelerator and slowed the Jeep as they passed through the small town of Paradise. Several minutes later, Gabe sat up, his gaze following the 310 exit sign. "You passed the exit to the bridge."

Lisa took a deep breath and prayed for patience. "I need air in the tire. Remember? And there's a station in the next town."

Gabe raised an eyebrow. "We passed up two stations in Des Allemands."

Lisa shrugged. "I like the station in Bouttc," she fibbed, unwilling to explain why she hadn't stopped at the other stations. They both belonged to Barry's relatives. If she had stopped at either station, she would have been expected to explain who Gabe was and where they were going. Except for their argument over who was going to put air in the tires, Lisa was feeling a little less apprehensive about her passenger by the time they approached the on-ramp to Interstate 10. For miles, the raised highway was surrounded by wetlands and swamps that, so far, seemed relatively untouched by modern man.

As she approached the end of the merge lane, the car in front of her suddenly stopped. Lisa slammed her foot on the brake. Behind them, tires squealed.

"Good Lord, woman. We almost hit that car."

Lisa's insides began to shake, more from fear of almost hitting the car than from Gabe's comment. She gripped the steering wheel. The traffic thinned out and the car in front of them sped up and merged into the traffic. Sparing Gabe a brief, furious glance, Lisa watched for an opening, then stomped on the accelerator.

"That car had no business stopping," she said through gritted teeth, "so I would appreciate you keeping your comments to yourself."

"Oh, hell," Gabe said, rubbing his neck. "I didn't mean anything by it." He glanced at her but only got her thin-lipped profile for his effort. "Okay, okay. I'm sorry," he finally offered. "And from now on, I'll keep my mouth shut...about your driving," he added grudgingly. "There, does that make you feel better?"

Lisa sighed. "No, I don't feel better because I'm the one who should apologize...again. I tend to overreact when I get nervous—I mean scared. I've never had an accident," she rushed on to explain, hoping he didn't catch her slip. She certainly didn't want him thinking that he made her nervous, even if he did, since she still had her suspicions about his so-called motive for wanting to help her find Dixie. Figuring that her explanation was sufficient, she reached down and flipped on the radio.

The oldies-but-goodies station filled the Jeep with a rock and roll song that Gabe remembered listening to as a teenager. Personally he preferred country-western, but he decided to keep those thoughts to himself.

He settled farther down in the seat. He'd suspected all along that part of the reason she was so uptight was that he made her nervous. And that was the last thing he wanted to do, but something about her made him touchy, too.

Maybe it was that damn perfume she wore, he thought. He'd read somewhere that certain smells could have adverse effects on behavior.

Still, he didn't relish the thought of being put out on the side of the road, which was exactly what she would do if he didn't learn to keep his mouth shut.

Hoping to block out all thoughts of her, he rolled his window down halfway, leaned back his head and closed his eyes. It didn't work. Her scent still filled his nostrils, teasing him and making him just as ill-tempered as before.

They were on the interstate approaching Baton Rouge before Lisa noticed that he'd opened his eyes again. While he'd slept or pretended to sleep—she wasn't sure which—she had tried to think of some way to call a truce. Butting heads with him wouldn't give her the answers she needed. If her initial suspicions were right, the only way she was going to find out if he did know more about Dixie than he'd claimed was to get him to talk.

Gabe yawned and stretched, then patted his shirt pocket.

"Did you lose something?"

Gabe frowned and shook his head. "Just a bad habit," he answered, producing a toothpick from inside his pocket.

Lisa threw him a curious glance. "Pardon?"

"I used to smoke," he explained, a sheepish expression on his face. "Quit a few months ago." He held out the toothpick. "These aren't quite the same but they help."

"Oh, I see. Guess the antismoking stuff finally got to you, huh?"

"That and being nagged day and night."

"Your wife?"

Gabe shook his head. "I'm not married, but my son, Danny, stayed on my case."

It wasn't so much what he had said but the way he'd said it that made Lisa even more curious than before. Was his wife dead or was he divorced?

What difference does it make?

Makes no difference at all, she told herself. *Just keep him talking.* "I smoked when I was younger but when I got custody of Dixie, I didn't think it was a good example to set for a young girl."

Gabe turned in his seat toward her, a frown on his face. "Custody?"

Lisa bit her bottom lip. Talking about that time in her life always brought back sad memories. Even now, she still missed her mom and dad. "Our parents were killed in a pile-up on the interstate." She cleared her throat to ease the tightness. "With no other close relatives," she shrugged, "the court awarded me custody."

"How old were you...and how old is your sister?"

Lisa sighed, remembering those first awkward months. "I was twenty-two, eleven years older than Dixie, and fresh out of college. She's twenty-three now."

Just five years older than Danny, he thought. "That makes you about thirty-four," he said absently, but his mind was on her sister's age. Five years wasn't much of an age gap between Dixie and Danny. With Danny's good looks, his broad shoulders and his height, it stood to reason that a woman could easily mistake him for being older than he was. And any boy Danny's age would feel flattered by the attentions of what he would perceive as an older woman.

"Must have been tough on you. And your sister," he added.

She nodded. "We had our share of ups and downs, and it took me a few months to make the transition from being the older sister to becoming the surrogate parent. I'm afraid that at first I spoiled her rotten— you know, feeling sorry for her and all. And believe me, she took full advantage of the situation. But like most kids, she finally grew up."

Once a spoiled brat, always a spoiled brat. The phrase popped into his head. So far Lisa had said nothing to persuade him any differently.

"When she enrolled in college," Lisa continued. "I was so proud. I thought I had it made, that I'd finally succeeded in raising her to be a responsible adult."

Suddenly she laughed, a husky sound that did funny things to Gabe's insides. "After the first year, she dropped out. Said college just wasn't her bag."

In spite of himself, Gabe's interest was piqued. "So what did you do... I mean, how did you handle it?"

"At first I was furious—"

"I can sympathize with that," he mumbled, thinking about his initial reaction to Danny's letter.

"Pardon?"

Gabe shrugged. "Nothing."

Lisa threw him a quick puzzled look, then returned her attention to the road. "Anyway, after I'd calmed down, we had a long heart-to-heart talk. And you know what?" She glanced over at him and smiled. "I learned that sometimes people have to find their own way, and that what I wanted for Dixie wasn't necessarily what was best for her. In the past four years, she's worked her way up at Southern Phone and even got herself elected as the treasurer for their labor union."

It took a moment for Gabe to recover from seeing her smile. She had a nice smile, the kind that made a person feel all warm inside, and it occurred to him that it was the first time she had done so since he'd met her.

Listening to her talk, he was surprised at how much he had in common with Lisa LeBlanc. And he recognized the parental pride in her voice. How many times had he felt the same way about Danny? But there was one difference.

"You don't listen. You only hear what you want to hear."

Regret and guilt coursed through Gabe. Had he ever just sat down and talked to Danny? Had he ever really listened to his son? *If you had, Danny wouldn't have felt the need to write that damn letter.*

"Anyway," Lisa continued. "As the old saying goes, all's well that ends well...." Her voice trailed off into a whisper. "Except that all isn't well," she added.

The anguish in her voice made Gabe feel peculiar, and for a moment he had the most absurd longing to reach out to her, to try to physically shield her from the pain and anxiety she was feeling. The moment passed, but he still felt a certain kinship with her problem.

"For what it's worth," he said. "I understand how you feel...having a son myself," he quickly added. "Try not to worry until we know more," he finally offered. It was inane advice, but since he was in the same position, it was the best he could come up with under the circumstances.

Lisa sniffed and raised her chin. "I keep telling myself that she's okay, that I would know if...if she wasn't."

Gabe had told himself the same thing, over and over, about Danny. But he couldn't tell that to Lisa. If she suspected his son might be involved with her sister, she would probably stop at the nearest pay phone and call the police. And he'd probably end up walking to Shreveport.

"There's a fast-food restaurant up ahead. Why don't you pull over for a few minutes? I could use a cup of coffee." *And a break,* he added silently. The smell of her perfume was getting to him again. At least that's what he tried to tell himself.

Lisa nodded.

Once in the restaurant, Gabe sat nursing a cup of coffee while Lisa made a trip to the rest room. *God, what a mess,* he thought, looking out the window at the passing traffic on the highway.

Being around Lisa was like being on an emotional roller coaster. One minute she was the epitome of independence and stubbornness and the next minute he found himself wanting to comfort her and protect her. He tried rationalizing his topsy-turvy feelings by telling himself that at least she wasn't boring.

"Aw, hell," he muttered, reaching up to rub the ache in his neck.

Face it, Jordan.

Gabe took a deep breath. Whether he wanted to admit it or not, he was truly beginning to like the woman, more than any woman he'd met in a long time, and the fact that he was damn attracted to her, too, could really become a problem.

Dangerous thoughts, buddy boy.

Too dangerous, he realized. At the moment, he didn't need any additional complications, and if he wasn't careful, if he didn't keep a tight lid on his libido, he might end up having to deal with more than he'd bargained for.

NOTHING BUT LONELY, remote interstate and acres of uninhabited land stretched out before them. It was Lisa's least favorite leg of the journey to Shreveport, since there wasn't an exit or any sign of civilization for miles. She had made the trip many times over the past few years, but this particular stretch of highway had always made her nervous.

Leaning forward, she twisted the radio dial, but the only stations she could find without static were hard rock and country-western. "I give up," she grumbled, finally settling on a country-western station. Any noise was better than nothing, she decided, glancing over at Gabe.

Since they had left Baton Rouge, he'd been sleeping, or pretending to sleep—again, she wasn't sure which. She figured he was probably pretending so he wouldn't have to make conversation.

Suddenly there was a loud bang like a muffled shotgun blast.

Lisa yelped and the steering wheel almost jumped out of her hands.

Gabe jerked to attention. "Don't hit the brakes!" he shouted.

The Jeep lurched to the left, and Lisa's right foot hovered just over the brake pedal as she held on to the steering wheel for dear life.

"Hold it steady."

Her heart pounding, she tightened her grip and tried to hold the Jeep between the white lines of the highway. "A blowout?" Her voice quavered.

"Probably. Atta girl. Just take it easy. Turn on the blinker, and let it slow itself down."

Gabe's voice was confident and reassuring, and Lisa concentrated on doing exactly what he said.

"Now ease it over to the shoulder."

When the Jeep finally thumped to a stop, it was several seconds before Lisa could pry her fingers loose from the steering wheel. Offering up a prayer of thanks, she took a deep breath and ventured a look at Gabe.

To her surprise, he grinned. "Hey, lighten up," he teased. "You did real good, and it could have been worse."

Lisa didn't want to think about worse. She was trying to remember the last time she'd had her spare tire aired up, and she was dreading the moment Gabe was going to say, I told you we should have taken my truck.

Instead, he unbuckled his seat belt and shoved open his door. "It won't take more than a few minutes to change the tire, and we can get it fixed in Alexandria."

Lisa unbuckled her own belt, opened her door and crossed her fingers, hoping against hope that the spare would be in good enough shape to get them that far.

As Gabe dismounted the spare from the back of the Jeep, Lisa shifted from one foot to the other. "Is it okay? Enough air?"

He bounced it on the ground a couple of times, then shrugged. "It's a little bald on the edges, but it'll get us there okay." He rolled it around and propped it against the front fender.

Lisa dug out the jack and the lug wrench from beneath the seat and handed them to Gabe.

Once the jack was firmly in place, he picked up the wrench and began loosening the lug nuts.

Cars whizzed past and an eighteen-wheeler roared by, leaving them in a cloud of dust. Lisa hovered near the back of the Jeep, still waiting for Gabe to say I told you so.

When minutes went by and he still hadn't said anything, she began to wonder if maybe she had been wrong about him. Maybe he really was just a nice man with no other motive for wanting to come along than to clear his name.

CHAPTER FOUR

WHEN LISA TURNED DOWN the narrow street that led
to Dixie's apartment complex, she glanced at her
watch: 3:00 p.m. Even with the blowout, stopping to
get the tire fixed and eating a quick lunch in Alexandria, they had still made good time.

Gabe never did make any comment, derisive or
otherwise, and with each mile that had passed, she'd
found herself becoming more comfortable around
him.

Maybe too comfortable, she thought with concern,
especially since the whole purpose of letting him tag
along was to find out if he knew more about Dixie's
disappearance than he had admitted.

It was his quiet, confident manner, she decided, that
had made it easy to forget she didn't trust him—that,
and the flat tire incident. She should have been
pumping him for information, but instead she'd rattled on and on about Dixie's accomplishments at
Southern Phone and her contributions to the union.

Except for mentioning bits and pieces about his job
and a few tidbits about his genius son, she still didn't
know much more about him than when they had

started off. From now on she'd have to remember to be more inquisitive and less talkative.

When Lisa pulled into an empty parking space in front of Dixie's apartment, she glanced around. A sudden tingle of hope bubbled inside her.

"Her car is still gone," she said, unable to disguise her excitement. She turned to Gabe. "She could be just off somewhere, couldn't she?" But even before the words were out of her mouth, she knew Dixie wouldn't have just taken off without letting her know where she was going.

With a frown, Gabe turned to face her. "I hate to bring this up, but is it possible she's had an accident . . . I mean, have you checked?"

Lisa nodded. "The first thing I did when I realized she was missing was to call all the hospitals in the area."

"What about the police? Did they check out accidents elsewhere?"

She shrugged. "They said they had, but I don't trust the police. In my opinion they haven't been a whole lot of help." She shoved open her door.

"Unless you have *proof* of something, there's not much they can really do. Have you got a key?"

Lisa shook her head. "No, but I know where Dixie keeps a spare one."

With Gabe following close behind, she walked over to one of the potted plants on either side of the front door. The police might need proof, she thought, but

she didn't. Dixie *never* missed their Saturday morning calls.

Lisa stooped down and dug her fingers into the dirt
surrounding the plant. Only a couple of seconds
passed before she pulled out a key. She blew the dirt
off it, inserted the spare key into the keyhole and
opened the door.

When he stepped inside, Gabe glanced around.
"Interesting decor."

Lisa winced at the slightly veiled sarcasm in his tone
as she took in her surroundings. The walls and carpet
were stark white. The sofa and matching chair were
black leather, accented with a red lacquered coffee table and two end tables. Red and black throw pillows
of all shapes and sizes were haphazardly strewn about.

"She just recently redecorated, and she's been after me for weeks to come visit." The whole room
vaguely reminded her of a crazy checkerboard. "She
always has been, ah, creative," Lisa offered, for lack
of a better term to describe her sister's unusual taste in
furnishings. Then Lisa's eyes widened. "Oh, no, look
at that."

Gabe followed as Lisa walked over to the edge of the
sofa. One of the end tables was lying on its side. A
couple of magazines and several tiny black-and-white
china animals were scattered nearby on the carpet.

"Maybe we should call the police—I mean *something* happened here. Wouldn't this be proof?"

Gabe shook his head. "Not enough." A frisson of uneasiness made his spine tingle. Had there been a struggle of some kind? he wondered.

He bent down and reached for the table.

"No, don't touch anything!"

Gabe hesitated, turned his head toward Lisa and raised his eyebrows in question.

"It's just that... well, maybe there could be fingerprints.... The police might want to investigate."

Although he could tell she was trying to remain composed, she had paled and her voice was thin.

Gabe straightened without touching the table. "I would like to think you're right," he said. "And I might even agree with you except that I don't think just one upturned table by itself warrants calling the police... yet."

His indulgent tone rankled, making her feel like a child accused of still believing in Santa Claus. Facing the truth of what he'd said hurt... because, deep down, she knew he was right. The police would probably laugh at her, she thought, remembering the call she had placed to them before Gabe had arrived that morning. It had taken them a full thirty minutes to locate the file they had started on Dixie after Lisa's call on Monday.

Lisa lifted her chin and spared him a brief, cool look. He might have been right but that didn't mean she had to like it. "I still think we should be careful about touching stuff." Without waiting for his answer or any more comments he might have to offer, she headed toward the hallway. "It's a two-bedroom apartment," she called over her shoulder. "I'll check out Dixie's room while you check out the other one."

Gabe stared at her retreating back. Now, what had he done, except point out the obvious? But however well-meaning he'd meant to be, she invariably took exception to whatever he said.

On his way to the bedroom, he stopped to take a look at the bathroom first. As he stood in the doorway of the totally feminine room, he noted a bunched-up towel thrown across the shower rod. He walked over and touched it. *Dry as a bone,* he thought. He turned and eyed the small vanity cabinet.

Except for the usual paraphernalia women used—makeup, perfume and hairbrushes—nothing seemed out of the ordinary. There were even a couple of toothbrushes still in the holder, he noted.

When he stepped through the doorway into the spare bedroom, he thought the small room with its rose colored drapes and matching bedspread seemed almost bland when compared to the living room. And unless he missed his guess, it had been used recently, he decided, noticing the unmade bed.

He glanced around. Other than an indented pillow, the wrinkled sheets and the comforter that lay half on the bed and half on the floor, nothing seemed out of place. Except...

Gabe's gaze zeroed in on the comforter on the floor, and a suspicious-looking bulk underneath the right-hand corner. When he bent down and pushed aside the satiny bedcover, his breath caught in his throat and his heart skipped a beat.

Telling himself that there were thousands of green camouflage knapsacks in the world, Gabe lifted the top pocket flap, with a not-so-steady hand. The knapsack was stuffed with what looked like clothes. He shoved his hand inside and pulled out a wad of familiar-looking shirts, yet still he didn't want to believe what his mind was telling him.

It was the last item he pulled out that finally convinced him. Gabe closed his eyes and slowly shook his head. There was no doubt that the black T-shirt belonged to his son. Gabe remembered arguing with Danny over which color to buy and what design to have air-brushed onto the shirt. He had favored the famous Tulane insignia, since Danny was a student there. But Danny had preferred a caricature of Blake Selman, the lead singer of a trendy new rock group.

Gabe crushed the T-shirt in his fist. He'd suspected his son might be somehow involved with Lisa's sister, but he hadn't wanted to believe it, had hoped that the whole name thing was just a coincidence.

He let out a muffled curse, and as he stuffed the shirt back into the knapsack, his mind raced. One thing he *was* sure of—Danny was no kidnapper. But how did Danny come to know someone like Dixie? Why would Danny have applied for the job at Southern Phone? Was that his idea of "great prospects"? And if they left together, where were they? Questions, he thought. Nothing but damn questions and not even a clue that could lead them to an answer.

He tilted his head and listened. He could still hear Lisa moving around in the next bedroom. What was he going to tell her? What could he tell her?

Sorry, Lisa, but I believe my seventeen-year-old son is involved with your sister.

No.

In a split second, he made up his mind and shoved the knapsack back beneath the comforter. He'd tell her nothing...yet, he decided as he stood, his back to the door. If he told her what he suspected, he'd have to explain why he'd lied about Danny. She might then go to the police and actually accuse Danny of kidnapping her sister. Until he knew more, there was no use making her more suspicious than she already was.

"Gabe."

Gabe whirled around. Lisa was standing just inside the room. He took a deep breath to calm his racing pulse. *Take it easy, man, or she'll wonder why you're so spooked.* From the worried look on her face and the way she was wringing her hands, he could tell she'd found something. Determinedly he walked toward her.

"What is it?" he asked. As he'd expected, she backed out of the room, stopping just outside the doorway.

"There's a suitcase laid out on the bed and Dixie's clothes are scattered everywhere, as if she was packing in a hurry. Now I'm sure something has happened to her."

"She could have been unpacking," Gabe suggested. "There are a lot of cosmetics in the bathroom."

Lisa frowned. "I hadn't thought of that."

"Anything else?"

She slowly shook her head. "What about you? Did you find anything?"

He hesitated only a moment then shook his head. "Nothing in here, except it's obvious she had a guest at some point." He figured he could at least tell her that much of the truth.

With a puzzled frown, Lisa peered past him and eyed the rumpled bed.

"Does she have an answering machine?" Gabe asked, hoping to distract her.

Lisa shook her head. "Nope. She hates talking on them—mine especially—and swore she'd never get one."

"Kind of strange for someone who works for a phone company, don't you think?" But after everything Lisa had told him about Dixie and after seeing her living room, he was beginning to think that Lisa's sister, besides being spoiled, was a bit strange. And definitely not the type of person Danny should be mixed up with. After all, he thought, what kind of twenty-two year old woman would take up with a seventeen year old kid?

Gabe stepped past Lisa, into the hallway, and gambling that she would follow, he headed toward the living room.

"What now?" he asked over his shoulder.

"Her office."

IT WAS ALMOST FOUR-THIRTY when they finally located Southern Phone Incorporated. Lisa wasted no time in explaining the situation to the trim well-dressed receptionist. According to the nameplate on her desk, the woman was Nora Walker. And to Gabe, for some reason he couldn't pinpoint, Nora seemed a bit nervous.

"Ma'am, did you make an appointment with Mr. Snelling?"

Lisa glared at the woman. Gabe could have sworn that the red highlights in her hair had begun to glow.

"No, I did not make an appointment," she replied slowly, sparks shooting out from her dark eyes as she carefully enunciated each word. "I told you, I just arrived in town." She leveled the woman a no-nonsense look. "You get Mr. Snelling on that phone and tell him I demand to see him right now."

As if she'd been jolted by a bolt of electricity, the receptionist snatched up the phone and punched three digits.

After several unintelligible murmurs, she replaced the receiver. "If you'll please be seated, Mr. Snelling will see you in a few minutes."

After cooling their heels for at least fifteen minutes, they were finally directed through a set of double doors and down a long hallway to an office.

Gabe didn't like Dixie's boss from the moment he laid eyes on the slight, balding man. Something about Snelling reminded him of a fidgety little kid who needed to go to the bathroom and was afraid that any minute, he might have an accident.

"How can I help you, Ms. LeBlanc, Mr.—?"

Lisa turned to Gabe. "This is Mr.—"

Gabe cut her off. "You can tell us where Dixie Miller is."

Gabe ignored Lisa's pointed, suspicious look. It made sense that if Snelling didn't know his name and didn't recognize him, Lisa would finally believe that he had nothing to do with her sister's disappearance. Of course there was always the possibility that even if Snelling had conducted the interview, he might not remember Danny's name.

"Dixie?" Snelling's eyes widened.

"Dixie Miller, your assistant, who happens to be my sister," Lisa retorted impatiently.

Snelling glanced first at Lisa then at Gabe. "Oh, Dixie. Yes, yes, of course." He took a step backward. "Won't you please be seated?" He gestured at the chairs in front of his desk and let out a nervous laugh.

Gabe sat. Lisa remained standing.

"Do you know where she is?" Lisa asked.

"Why, Ms. Miller is on vacation. Let's see." He scurried around to the back of his desk and made a show of riffling through some papers stacked on the corner. "Yes, here it is." He held up a piece of paper.

"Last Thursday she requested emergency leave for a few days."

Lisa frowned. "I thought you said vacation."

Gabe narrowed his eyes when he saw Snelling tug at the knot in his tie. Yep, he thought. The man was definitely nervous. Even more nervous than Nora Walker had been. But why?

Snelling shook his head. "They're one in the same, the only difference being that vacation is scheduled well in advance and emergency leave is—"

Lisa held up her hand. "Okay, okay. I understand, but did she say why she needed the emergency leave?"

"No—no, she didn't give a reason. I just assumed it was a family difficulty of some kind. It was all very sudden. She had just finished interviewing a job applicant when she asked me for a few days off."

"You wouldn't happen to remember who the applicant was, would you?" she asked.

"Oh, my, I'm not sure I should give out that kind of information."

Gabe stood up to emphasize his full six-foot-four frame. "We won't tell anyone if you won't."

To Gabe's satisfaction, Snelling's eyes grew round with fear. "I-I believe the applicant's name was Gabriel Jordan, but I was so busy that I didn't sit in on that particular interview."

"So you didn't see him." Lisa's voice sounded just as disappointed as Gabe felt, and she looked as if someone had knocked the air out of her.

Snelling shook his head. "No, I'm afraid I didn't."

So much for the physical identification theory that would have let him off the hook, Gabe thought.

He sighed in frustration. Instead of answers, all they had done was add more pieces to the puzzle.

Stepping over to Lisa, he placed his hand against the small of her back. "Have you got a business card with you?" To his surprise she didn't shrink from his touch. As if in a trance, she looked up at him and nodded.

"Why don't you leave one with Mr. Snelling just in case he needs to reach us."

While Lisa dug in her handbag, Gabe directed his attention toward Snelling. "If you happen to hear from Dixie, we'd appreciate you giving us a call. We'll be staying at the—" Gabe thought a second and remembered the name of a motel they had passed. "We'll be at the Sunrise Inn."

Snelling's eyes darted back and forth between Lisa and Gabe. "Of course, of course," he readily agreed, and Gabe couldn't help thinking the skinny little man looked more relieved than he should have.

When Lisa finally produced a card, she handed it to Snelling. "If we're not there," she said, "then you can leave a message at the number on this card."

With his hand still firmly at her back, Gabe nudged her toward the door.

As they stepped out into the hallway, Gabe was surprised by the strength of the empathy he felt for Lisa. Up until now, she'd been so strong and sure of herself. And she'd been so convinced that when they went to Dixie's office that someone would have known where she was or what had happened to her. He wished there was something he could say or do that would make her feel better, that would make things easier for her.

Halfway down the hall, Gabe knew that she was well on the way to recovering her spirit when she stiffened and pulled away from his touch. "That little twerp was hiding something," she said in a low voice. "I'm sure he knows more than he told us."

"Yeah," Gabe agreed. "I think you're right, but there's nothing we can do about it...at least not now."

"Lisa?"

The woman's whispered voice came from behind them. Both Gabe and Lisa stopped and turned.

"Do I know you?" Lisa asked the short, slightly plump young woman.

Her eyes grew round with fear. She quickly pressed a finger to her lips and shook her head. "Shh. Not so loud." She glanced over her shoulder, then back at Lisa. "We've never met, but we've talked. This will explain." She shoved an envelope into Lisa's hand, then scurried down the hallway and slipped into one of the offices.

With a puzzled frown on her face, Lisa glanced up at Gabe. Equally puzzled, he shrugged and they both looked down the empty hall where the woman had disappeared.

When Lisa started to open the envelope, Gabe grabbed her arm. "Not here," he cautioned. "Wait till we're back in the Jeep."

The minute they closed Lover's doors, Lisa tore into the envelope. She pulled out a folded piece of paper and Gabe leaned over to get a better look.

"Now I remember," she said. "That was Nicole, one of Dixie's friends. I talked with her Monday morning." Suddenly she looked up at Gabe and frowned. "Funny she didn't seem to recognize you. She's the one who told me that Dixie left with Gabriel Jordan."

Gabe took a deep breath and sighed. "Maybe she didn't recognize me because I'm not the man your sister left with."

When he saw that she still wasn't completely convinced, he took the note from her and read it aloud.

"It says that she has some information she thinks you need to know, and she wants you to meet her at a restaurant called Pedro's on Airline Highway tonight at seven." Gabe glanced at his watch. "It's five-thirty now. We've got time to check in to the motel and get cleaned up first."

Lisa stared straight ahead. Her fingers absently tapped a staccato rhythm on the steering wheel. "I wonder what kind of information she has. And why does she need to be so secretive about it?"

Gabe wondered, too. He had a gut feeling that the answer had something to do with the reason the receptionist and Snelling had been so nervous.

Lisa suddenly cleared her throat and sighed. "I guess we'll just have to wait until later to find out." She pulled her keys from her handbag and jammed one into the ignition. "We don't have to stay at a motel, though," she said as she pumped the accelerator. "We can stay at Dixie's apartment."

Gabe thought a minute, then shook his head. "I'd feel better staying at a motel. Besides, that's where I told Snelling he could reach us. It's the one we passed not far from your sister's apartment." He didn't want to alarm Lisa, but there were several things that had bothered him about Dixie's apartment.

One nagging piece of the puzzle was the upturned end table and tiny animal figurines strewn on the carpet. He was pretty sure there *had* been a struggle of some kind. Then there was the half-packed suitcase as well as Danny's knapsack to consider. He didn't want to chance Lisa finding that knapsack . . . not yet.

Within reason, he knew everything could be explained, but he still had an uneasy feeling about it all.

SIXTY MILES AWAY, Danny felt one of the ropes around his wrists give. Straining against his bindings, he glanced at the sleeping woman. Was she asleep or had she passed out? He wasn't sure. The past two days, she had refused to eat, and he could tell she was growing weaker.

Danny glanced toward the only window in the cabin. Twilight was fast fading into darkness. Time was running out, he thought.

Any minute, the bastard could show up. And it seemed that the longer he kept them, the nastier he got. Danny twisted his mouth, but the tape across it wouldn't budge. They were lucky he'd only taped their mouths instead of shooting them after the last stunt Dixie had pulled. And if they didn't escape, Danny wasn't sure what the bastard would do if he came back and found his ropes loose.

Danny strained even harder. Suddenly the remaining ropes gave way. He was free. As he struggled upright, he only took a moment to flex his fingers and inspect his bruised and rope-burned wrists. His hands tingled with a thousand pinpricks as circulation returned. He reached up and ripped the tape off his mouth, skinning his lips in the process. When he bent forward, he groaned. He'd already decided his ribs weren't cracked, but they were still sore as hell. After several clumsy attempts, he loosened the ropes that bound his feet.

He stumbled across the room toward Dixie. When he shook her, she roused to consciousness, opening one eye. The other was still swollen shut. He eased the tape from her mouth, then began working on the ropes at her wrists.

"We've got to hurry," he said, tugging at the knots. They finally gave way, and she pulled her hands free. While he concentrated on her bound feet, she rubbed her wrists.

"I feel so dizzy," she said.

Danny pulled the loosened ropes away. "Try to stand . . . easy now."

"Oh, Danny, I'm not sure I can."

He steadied her with his arm around her waist. "You should have thought about that when you threw the food at him. It's a wonder he didn't punch you again."

"Just shut up, will you?"

"Well—"

They heard the sound at the same time and froze. It was faint at first—a car engine and crunching gravel—but it steadily grew louder.

"Oh, God," she whispered. "It's too late. He's back. We're not going to make it."

Danny glanced around the room, searching for something—anything—he could use as a weapon. "Oh, yes we are," he retorted sharply. "He still thinks we're tied up." Danny pulled her toward the door. "Flatten yourself against the wall on this side." Satisfied that by leaning against the wall she could stand alone without passing out, he hurried to the lone table and chair in the room and grabbed the chair.

"What are you doing?" Dixie whispered urgently.

Approaching footsteps sounded outside on the wooden porch. "Shh," he hissed, as he positioned himself against the opposite side of the door and raised the chair above his head.

There was the scrape of a key being inserted in the lock. When Danny saw the doorknob twist, he took a deep breath and prayed for strength.

The door opened. "What the hell?"

The man's eyes widened with surprise, but Danny surprised him even more. He slammed the chair down over the man's head. With a groan of pain, the man crumpled to the floor. Danny bent to check the man's pockets.

"What are you doing?" Dixie cried.

Danny glanced up then resumed his search. "Looking for the car keys." Finding none, he grabbed Dixie's hand. "Come on. He must have left them in the ignition."

Dixie stumbled after him. "Is . . . is he dead?"

"I don't know and I don't care," Danny snapped.

The keys were in the car, as he'd suspected. As soon as Dixie got in, Danny yanked the gearshift into reverse and backed around until the car was facing the gravel path that served as a road.

"Oh, God!" Dixie screamed. "Look, he's coming."

Danny only took a second to glance over his shoulder. The man was stumbling out the doorway, waving a gun in his hand.

Danny cursed and stomped down on the accelerator. The engine roared and gravel sprayed from beneath the tires. "Duck," he yelled as gunfire exploded.

Dixie screamed again.

"Are you hit?" he shouted, flooring the accelerator and gripping the steering wheel. The car bucked and bounced and fishtailed over the potholes. It was all Danny could do to keep it from careening off into the woods, and he didn't dare take his eyes off the road.

"Dixie!" he shouted again.

CHAPTER FIVE

LISA AND GABE waited for Nicole in the reception area of the crowded Mexican restaurant. Outside a steady rain shower obscured the streetlights and turned passing car lights into a distorted blur.

Gazing out a nearby window at the dark, dismal scene, Lisa took a deep breath and tried to relax.

After they had checked into separate rooms at the Sunrise Inn, she had finally had some much-needed time alone to think. Not only had Nicole's message seemed ominous, but Nicole was the one person who had actually seen the man Dixie had left with on Thursday afternoon.

"Maybe she didn't recognize me because I'm not the man your sister left with."

Each time Lisa thought about Gabe's words, she couldn't help but wonder if she had been wrong about him from the very beginning. Either she was wrong and he had nothing to do with her sister's disappearance, or she was right, and he was damn good at pulling the wool over her eyes.

But if Gabe was the same man Dixie had left with, surely Nicole would have recognized him back at the office. And if he wasn't the same man, Lisa was still sure he knew more than he had admitted, but what? Other than her nagging woman's intuition, she couldn't put her finger on just why she still didn't trust his reasons for coming along in the first place.

And if she was wrong? Lisa felt embarrassing heat creep up her neck. If she was wrong, she owed Gabriel Jordan one huge apology.

Lisa sneaked a quick peek at Gabe and thought that he didn't appear very nervous about coming face-to-face with Nicole. In fact, dressed in a pair of casual gray slacks and a blue-and-gray pullover, he could have been any ordinary man out for an evening of casual dining.

Well, not just any man, she silently amended, and not quite ordinary. Gabe would always stand out in a crowd. His size alone made sure of that. And his virile good looks could never be classified as ordinary. In fact, she was finding that the more time she spent with him, the more her thoughts strayed toward things she had no business thinking, things that had nothing to do with their reason for being together in the first place, and had everything to do with her topsy-turvy libido.

"All you do is stay holed up in that studio of yours, hiding behind your cameras." Dixie's accusations popped into her head and she winced. Was her sister right? Was she having such a hard time dealing with Gabe because she had hid behind her career, hid from the pain a relationship with a man could cause?

Lisa sighed. Now was not the time for self-analysis. There were other more important issues to deal with.

Willing Nicole to show up soon, Lisa glanced at her watch. "She's late," she said out loud. "Do you think she's coming?"

Gabe looked at his own watch before he answered. "It's only ten after. Let's wait a few more minutes, then I suggest we go ahead and eat. I don't know about you, but I'm starved."

A waiter hurried past, and Lisa marveled at how he expertly balanced and maneuvered a huge serving tray loaded with steaming platters. In spite of her nervous stomach, her mouth watered at the wonderful spicy aromas that lingered even after he had disappeared around the corner.

At that moment the front door opened, letting in a blast of cool damp air that made Lisa shiver.

She turned in time to see Nicole step inside. "Sorry I'm late," she offered, shaking off the dripping umbrella in her hands. "I got hung up in traffic."

Lisa had thought about this moment back at the motel, and she had decided then exactly how she would handle it. She stepped aside, giving Nicole a full view of Gabe. The grim expression on his face told her that he knew what she was up to, but to his credit, his only response this time was a tight-lipped look of resignation.

"Nicole, I want to introduce you to Gabriel Jordan."

Gabe stuck out his hand.

Frowning, Nicole automatically shook his hand, all the time peering at Gabe with a puzzled look on her face. Then with a firm, negative shake of her head, she turned to Lisa. "The name may be the same, but he's not the man I saw your sister leave with."

Until that moment, Lisa hadn't realized she'd been holding her breath. What confused her even further was the overwhelming feeling of relief that flooded through her.

"The other man was much younger," Nicole continued. "Too young, in my opinion, to be applying for a job as a lineman." She shot Gabe an apologetic look. "Not that you're old," she hastened to add, her cheeks turning pink.

"No offense taken," he assured her.

Tilting her head, Nicole continued to stare at him several seconds longer. "You do favor him, though," she finally said thoughtfully. "Same eyes, same hair color and same build. Humph, guess we all favor someone." She turned to Lisa and motioned at Gabe. "What's going on here?"

Before Lisa could answer, Gabe spoke up. "It's a long story but the bottom line is that someone used my name and I intend to find out who."

To Lisa, Gabe's tone lacked the intended conviction of his words. As Gabe and Nicole continued talking, Lisa thought about the short exchange she had just witnessed. She'd watched Gabe carefully, and when Nicole had begun making physical comparisons, he had paled and seemed downright uncomfortable . . . and worried.

The initial relief Lisa had felt earlier began to dissipate quickly. She could think of only one reason for him to react that way. He had to know or at least suspect who the other man was. Fathers and sons often shared physical similarities, didn't they? But Gabe's son was only seventeen . . .

". . . can't believe they're accusing Dixie of such a thing. And now with her missing—I've been so worried."

Nicole's words jolted Lisa back to reality. "What did you say?"

"Why don't we get a table first?" Gabe suggested.

Lisa gave a curt nod.

Gabe signaled to the maître d', and they were led to a small table and given menus. Gabe stared at his, but his thoughts were on Nicole's description of the man she had seen with Dixie. And from the furtive looks Lisa kept giving him, he figured his lies were about to catch up with him.

Lisa was no fool. It wouldn't take her long to add two and two and come up with Danny.

A waitress appeared and took their orders. When she left, Nicole turned her attention to Lisa. "I'm sorry for all the cloak-and-dagger stuff back at the office, but I couldn't say anything then. The place was crawling with FBI agents, and I was afraid you'd leave town before I had a chance to talk to you."

With her hand clutching her napkin, Lisa stiffened as a frisson of alarm raced through her. "FBI?"

Nicole's eyes held a well of sympathy. "They think Dixie stole money from the union retirement fund."

"What?" Lisa felt as if every drop of blood had drained from her face. "That's ridiculous!" she cried, her raised voice attracting the attention of a couple seated at a nearby table. She glared at them then lowered her voice. "Dixie is not a thief," she hissed.

Nicole reached over and patted Lisa's hand. "I know that and you know that, but..." She withdrew her hand, and unable to look Lisa in the eyes, she lowered her gaze to the tabletop. "So far, all the evidence they've gathered points to her," she whispered.

Lisa threw the napkin back onto the table. "I don't give a damn what kind of evidence they have. My sister would never steal anything."

At that moment, their waitress appeared with the food they had ordered. Lisa snatched back her napkin and stared at the steaming plate that was set in front of her. Her stomach knotted, and she took several deep breaths to stem the sudden nausea Nicole's words had caused.

As soon as the waitress left, Gabe turned to Nicole. "You said evidence. What kind?"

His outward calm along with his steady tone of voice was an unexpected, soothing balm to Lisa's outraged emotions. And she wondered yet again how and why he had the power to make her feel so at ease, so safe, in spite of all of her suspicions about him.

Nicole swallowed the bite of food she had taken, then drank a sip of water before she answered. "Once a year an annual audit is performed on the union's accounts," she said. "The accountants came in on Monday and went over the books. On Tuesday night, the union held its monthly meeting, and when the auditors gave their preliminary report, all hell broke loose. They had discovered that over two hundred thousand dollars is missing from the retirement fund account."

"That still doesn't explain why they would suspect Dixie," Lisa retorted.

Nicole gave her a sad little smile. "I'm getting to that."

Lisa closed her eyes for a moment. "Sorry. It's just that all of this on top of Dixie disappearing is upsetting."

"Of course it is," Nicole agreed.

Before he thought, Gabe reached out and squeezed Lisa's hand. "We'll find her." *And Danny,* he added silently. "But first we have to know what we're dealing with."

Lisa nodded. "You're right," she whispered, making no attempt to pull away from his touch.

Gabe gave her hand one last squeeze then he turned to Nicole. "Okay, let's have the rest."

"The president of the union immediately notified the National Labor Relations Board, who, in turn, notified the FBI. Early this morning, agents from both organizations showed up and started digging. Within a few hours they had determined that the money was transferred systematically over the past six months to a local bank account."

Nicole paused to give Lisa a sympathetic look. "I'm sorry, Lisa, but a woman employee at the bank confirmed that the account was in Dixie's name. The bank's records also showed that the account was closed out last Friday...the day after Dixie had requested emergency leave. And since she is the treasurer and no one can locate her..."

Lisa groaned. "I can't believe this." Suddenly she straightened in her chair. "No!" She adamantly shook her head. "I won't believe it. There's been some mistake. I know my sister would never do anything like that. Signatures can be forged or copied."

"For what it's worth," Nicole offered quietly, "I've only known Dixie for a few months, but I agree with you. I don't believe she did it, either."

Lisa nodded. "Thanks, I appreciate your support...and your help."

"No thanks required," Nicole replied. "Dixie has been a good friend to me. The reason I couldn't say anything at the office earlier was because there were too many eyes and ears."

"I guess that's why Snelling was so jumpy."

Nicole snickered. "If you think he was jumpy this afternoon, you should have seen him this morning when they cross-examined him about your sister. Anyway," she said, waving her fork in the air, "just before you showed up, we were given strict instructions not to discuss anything with anybody. They don't want the news leaking out to the media before they recover the money."

"At least that's something in our favor," Gabe interjected. "We won't have to worry about her name and picture being plastered on TV or in the newspapers."

Nicole cleared her throat. "There's just one other thing. Do you remember Kevin Striker?" she asked Lisa.

"Oh, I remember him, all right," she answered, unable to disguise the disgust in her voice. "I never did like that man, and in my opinion, Dixie was lucky to be rid of— Oh, no! Don't tell me she started seeing him again?"

"No—at least I don't think so. Anyway, yesterday I overheard him telling one of the other secretaries that Dixie was in hock up to her eyebrows. I thought that was kind of strange since Dixie hasn't said anything to me about it. He claimed she owed a ton of money and was getting desperate."

Lisa frowned. "That *is* odd. As far as I know, she pays cash for everything. Doesn't believe in charge cards or loans." Lisa shook her head. "Nope. Not true. Besides, she would have told me if she was having financial problems. She knows I would help her if she needed it."

Gabe marveled at Lisa's loyalty to her sister, a loyalty that he sorely feared was misplaced.

Gabe reached up and rubbed his neck. Even if it turned out that Dixie hadn't masterminded the theft, he had the distinct feeling that she was knee deep involved in some way, and he was afraid that Lisa was in for a nasty surprise.

Just thinking about Lisa's being hurt and disillusioned did funny things to his insides, and he decided those strange feelings would be better left unexplored for now. Besides, he thought, he had enough on his plate without adding a complication like Lisa Le-Blanc.

He scowled at the remaining food on his plate. Just how in the devil had Danny gotten mixed up with Dixie Miller in the first place? he wondered. But even as the thought formed in his mind, Gabe knew the answer. Danny had said in his letter that he had great prospects, and given his son's size, Gabe could well imagine Danny trying to pass himself off as much older in order to apply for the lineman position.

And if Danny was, as he'd indicated in his letter, dissatisfied with his life, it stood to reason that he would be prime pickings for an unscrupulous woman like Dixie Miller. Gabe could well picture his otherwise, highly intelligent son being bowled over by the attentions of a woman like that. Danny might have a genius I.Q., but Gabe knew that no seventeen-year-old male, regardless of his intellect, was immune to the sexual urges that tended to plague their young, changing bodies.

Gabe's insides knotted. With the FBI involved, Danny could be in real trouble, and it wouldn't matter whether he had intentionally aided Dixie or whether he had unknowingly aided her.

Without looking up, Gabe suddenly felt Lisa staring at him. *Danny's not the only one in trouble,* he thought, and when he did look up, he saw what he'd been dreading all along. She had finally put two and two together.

AN HOUR LATER, Gabe and Lisa made a mad dash from the Jeep to their motel rooms. The ride back to the motel had been tense, but Gabe knew that the weather wasn't the only cause. The steady shower had turned into a driving rain, and he figured that the only reason Lisa had held her tongue so far was that her full concentration had been required to keep Lover on the road during the storm.

Dripping wet and shivering, Lisa shook as she unlocked the door to her room. When she turned to face him, she wore an expression that brooked no argument. "You've got some explaining to do." She stepped aside and motioned for him to enter.

Inside, Lisa stopped long enough to adjust the heat controls, then headed straight for the bathroom. Seconds later she emerged with two towels and tossed one of them to Gabe. After she'd blotted her face, she leaned forward, wrapped the towel around her damp hair, then twisted it into a turban on top of her head. When she straightened, she placed her hands on her hips, pulling her damp blouse tightly across her breasts.

Gabe turned away and buried his face in the towel to block out the alluring sight. As if punishing himself for inviting such thoughts, he dried his hair a bit more vigorously than necessary.

Only when he had slung the towel around his neck did she finally speak. "I saw the look on your face when Nicole was describing the man who left with Dixie—the other so-called Gabriel Jordan. Either you tell me what you know or you can walk back to Ponchatoula starting now."

Still holding on to the ends of the towel and knowing he could no longer put off what he had to tell her, Gabe finally faced her. "You're right," he said, drawing in a deep breath. "I think that the man Nicole saw with your sister is my son. In the beginning I wasn't certain, but now I am."

"Your son?" Lisa's eyes narrowed. "And what makes you so sure now?"

There was an edge to her voice, an edge that warned of building anger, and Gabe felt his gut tighten. "Nicole's description, for one thing," he answered. "Danny is almost my height and size." He glanced at the floor; then, taking another deep breath, he looked her straight in the eyes. "I also found Danny's knapsack."

"Knapsack?"

Gabe nodded slowly. "Yeah, I found it in your sister's spare bedroom."

"Why, you—" Lisa stalked toward him. "Why didn't you say so earlier?" she demanded. "Why lie?"

Gabe had to remind himself that the only way out of this was to stay calm and explain things rationally. If he could only appeal to her parental instincts, he might have a chance to convince her he was simply trying to protect his son, just as she was trying to protect her sister.

"I wasn't sure how you would react," he said evenly. "After all, you were making some pretty wild accusations and I thought if I could find Danny first, there was bound to be a reasonable explanation for all of this."

It was as if she didn't hear him. "I knew it." She shook her head in disgust. "I knew from the start that something was fishy, especially when you volunteered to *help* me find Dixie. What a dope I was. And to think, I had considered your son at first, but when you said he was only seventeen—" She shook her head again then glared at him. "No. There's no way my sister would get involved with a high school kid. And besides, a schoolboy would never get hired on at Southern Phone."

"Danny is not your average seventeen-year-old."

"Just what does that mean?"

"Danny has the IQ of a genius and he's in his second year at Tulane University, majoring in pre-med."

For several seconds, Lisa stared at him with a mixture of surprise and bewilderment. Then she backed up and sat down on the bed. "But that makes even less

sense," she finally said. "Why would someone...
someone with his obvious academic potential be applying for a job as a lineman?"

For a second Gabe was sorely tempted to tell her just
exactly why he thought Danny was involved, but he
figured that accusing Dixie of seducing and duping his
son into helping her commit theft wouldn't go over too
well at the moment.

Instead he gave a negligent shrug and made an attempt to hide his contempt for Dixie Miller. "Danny
quit school. The day you showed up, I had just finished reading a letter he sent, telling me that he was
dropping out."

Gabe shifted uneasily. It was hard to admit that he
had problems with Danny, but he figured that if he
expected Lisa's cooperation from now on, he ought to
tell her as much of the truth as possible. "He said it
was because he was tired of everyone else running his
life. It seems that Danny thinks we have a communi-
cation problem, and I guess he was afraid I would try
to talk him out of leaving school if he told me face-to-
face. No one has seen or heard from him since last
Friday. It seemed like too much of a coincidence that
Dixie was last seen with someone calling himself Gabriel Jordan. Finding your sister was the only lead I
had in finding Danny."

Gabe braced himself for more of Lisa's anger, but
he still wasn't sure how to handle it if she tried somehow to blame Danny for Dixie's dilemma. He didn't

want to hurt her, but Danny was his son, *his* flesh and blood.

Lisa stood and slowly walked toward the window. For several seconds she stared thoughtfully out at the pouring rain. "It's all so confusing," she finally whispered. Turning, she faced him. "Instead of answers, all we're coming up with are more questions," she continued softly. "My sister missing and accused of theft... your son missing without a clue."

Gabe didn't know what to say. He'd expected more accusations. What he hadn't expected was the compassion in her voice, and he certainly hadn't expected the sympathy he saw reflected in her dark eyes.

"You should have told me about Danny from the beginning," she continued. "In many ways, Dixie is more like a daughter to me than a sister, so I can truly understand how you feel. I've already told you that I went through something similar with her after her first year of college." She sighed. "This is all some kind of terrible mistake...."

As Lisa continued talking, each kind, encouraging word pricked at Gabe's guilty conscience. He'd sensed from the beginning that Lisa was a rare and special woman. And except for her blind loyalty to her sister, nothing she'd done so far had convinced him otherwise. On the contrary, he thought, the longer he was around her, the more he truly liked her...and the more guilt he felt for thinking so badly of her sister.

Gabe felt sorry for Lisa. In spite of all her good intentions and nurturing love while raising her sister,

Dixie had gone astray somewhere along the way. Dixie Miller was guilty. He was sure of it. There was just too much condemning evidence to think otherwise. And as far as he was concerned, she had a lot to answer for: the theft, Danny's disappearance and the disappointment and hurt she would cause Lisa when the truth came out.

Gabe stared at the floor. Lisa was the kind of woman who would be fiercely loyal and freely give of her love to those close to her. She was also the kind of woman who would be devastated if that trust was ever betrayed.

What about your betrayal?

He'd not only betrayed her once, but if he continued to play along as if he, too, believed in Dixie's innocence, he would be betraying her yet again.

"Gabe . . . is something wrong?"

Lisa's question jolted Gabe out of his reverie. "What?" He shook his head. "I mean, no, nothing's wrong." He blinked several times. "Sorry. Guess I was—" *Was what, you idiot?* Gabe rubbed a hand over his weary face. "Look, it's been a long day and I'm sure you're as tired as I am. I can't even think straight anymore."

Gabe backed up toward the door. "Maybe after a good night's sleep, we can decide what to do next." *And maybe if I put some distance between us, I can think, period,* he silently added. "We'll talk more in the morning . . . over breakfast. Why don't we meet at that small café next to the motel?"

Lisa nodded and followed him to the door. "What time?"

With his hand already on the doorknob, Gabe hesitated. "Is seven-thirty too early for you?"

She smiled. "Seven-thirty is fine."

He turned to leave.

"Gabe?"

Her gentle touch on his arm came as a total surprise. Every nerve ending seemed to center around the pressure from her fingers, and for several seconds he couldn't move.

When he willed his body to turn around to face her, she was close...too close. She smelled damp and musky, a combination of lingering wetness from the rain and perfume...that damn perfume that seemed to drive him crazy.

Then she stepped even closer and wrapped her arms around his waist. Without thinking, Gabe automatically responded, hugging her close, as if doing so was the most natural thing in the world.

"I'm sure we're going to find Danny and Dixie, so don't worry," she whispered against his chest. "And I'm sure they will both have a reasonable explanation for all of this."

Gabe didn't want to release her. He was sure that her gesture was merely meant to comfort, but no matter how sweet and unselfish it was, her closeness was having an instantaneous, lightning effect on him. Thoughts of crushing her even closer and tasting her lips exploded in his head, and his traitorous body reacted accordingly.

Lisa suddenly stiffened, pulled away and stepped back. Gabe dropped his arms to his side, but he could still feel the lingering shock of their intimate contact clear to his toes.

And from the slight flush stealing upward from her neck to her cheeks, he figured that either she'd felt his unexpected response or she'd had an unexpected response of her own.

Gabe wanted to tell her *she* had no reason to be embarrassed, that if anyone should be embarrassed, *he* should.

But yet again, as had so often happened when he'd tried to express himself with his son, words failed him. He couldn't think of anything to say that wouldn't make matters worse, and he didn't trust himself to stay a minute longer than absolutely necessary.

"See you in the morning," he finally choked out, the words more gruff than he'd intended.

LISA DIDN'T DARE breathe until the door closed firmly behind him. For long minutes, she continued standing there, staring into space. A myriad of emotions swirled inside her.

When Barry had died, she had thought she would never get over the pain. Then months had passed, and though the pain was still there, she had accepted that she had to get on with her life.

A couple of times she'd tried to form relationships. The men were handsome, nice men, and they had liked her well enough, and had tried to get close to her, but there had never been that certain something, that spark of oneness that she had experienced with Barry. And then there had been Clarice and Barry's family to consider. Even now they still talked as if she were still married to him.

Lisa sighed. Dixie had accused her of using her career as a shield. Had she? Or had she simply been waiting for the right man to come along? What had begun as an impulsive, innocent gesture of comfort on her part had quickly escalated. Even now, minutes later, she still couldn't believe what she had done, couldn't believe that she had actually wanted to stay wrapped in Gabriel Jordan's strong arms forever.

So why now? she wondered. *And why him, of all people?*

Lisa shivered, then reached up and slipped the night chain into place. Sympathy, she decided. She had simply, innocently, sympathized with his dilemma, having been a parent herself and having had the same experience with Dixie.

From what Gabe had told her, he truly loved his son, just as she loved her sister. And he was trying his best to protect Danny just as she wanted to protect Dixie.

But there was one major difference between them. It was obvious from what he'd said and how he'd acted that Gabriel Jordan didn't have the slightest idea how to really communicate with Danny, or how to cope with his son's growing independence.

Lisa turned and strode purposely toward the bathroom. A shower and a good night's sleep were what she needed. As far as her actions toward Gabriel Jordan went, she'd slipped up and let her compassion overrule her good judgement. Nothing else. Nothing more.

Liar, a tiny voice taunted. *And what about his reaction?* the voice persisted.

Lisa ignored the voice as she hastily undressed, stepped into the shower and turned on the tap labeled *C*.

"DIXIE, ANSWER ME."

Blinding rain had forced Danny to slow the car to a crawl. He took a chance and glanced over at Dixie, but all he could see was her silhouette in the darkness. She hadn't been shot, but one of the back tires had caught a bullet. He'd had to drive on it for miles until he'd felt they were far enough away from the cabin to risk stopping to change it.

He chanced another glance at Dixie. Either she was ignoring him, sleeping again or she had passed out.

"Damn," he muttered. She must have passed out, he thought. He squinted through the windshield but didn't have the vaguest idea of where they were except that the last sign he'd passed said Highway 164. Without a map, a lot of good that did him, he thought.

He swore again. He was so tired that he could barely keep his eyes open. His chest ached and he'd have given his last nickel for a hamburger and fries.

Dixie groaned.

"Dixie, wake up! Talk to me."

"Okay, okay. You don't have to shout. I'm not deaf."

Danny heard the rustle of her clothing as she shifted in her seat, and he breathed a sigh of relief. "Geez, you had me worried."

"Sorry," she mumbled. "I'm just so damn sleepy... and queasy—my stomach doesn't feel so good."

"Well, maybe if you could help me figure out where in the hell we are, we might find something open—a restaurant or a gas station."

"Danny, stop the car!"

"What?"

"I'm going to be sick. Stop the car."

"Okay, okay, just hold on a second." Danny spotted a narrow side road and quickly pulled off the highway. The minute he stopped the car, Dixie opened the door and leaned out into the pouring rain.

When she finally pulled her head back inside, she was soaked and shivering. She reached up and pushed wet tendrils out of her face. "I forgot to tell you I get carsick. Most of the time it's not so bad except on winding roads like these. I usually wear a patch if I have to travel very far."

Danny turned, giving the back seat a cursory glance, searching for something she could dry off with. There was nothing. He quickly unbuttoned his shirt.

"What are you doing?"

He shrugged out of the shirt and offered it to her. "You're wet to the bone. Dry off with this."

"Thanks," she whispered, accepting the shirt. Then she leaned over and kissed him on the cheek. "You're one of the nice guys, Daniel Jordan. It's a crying shame you couldn't be a few years older."

Yeah, he thought, *and nice guys finish last.* Danny resisted the urge to reach up and touch the place where she'd kissed him. For weeks, after each phone conversation they'd had, he'd fantasized about meeting her, kissing her. Sure, he'd stretched the truth about his age, but five years' difference wasn't such a big deal, or so he'd thought.

Danny felt his face growing warm as he remembered when they had finally met. She had taken one look at him and all hell had broken loose.

"You're just a kid," she had shouted. "My sister warned me, but no, I wouldn't listen. All these weeks, all that big talk over the phone was one big lie."

Danny turned to stare out his window, and in the dim light, his reflection seemed to mock him as the rain continued to beat against the dark glass.

"Danny?"

"Yeah," he answered.

"Maybe we should just spend the night here. This rain isn't letting up, and we're both tired."

A STORM FRONT pushed through during the night and left Thursday morning bright with sunshine but breezy and cool.

Wishing she had packed something heavier than just a jacket, Lisa shivered when she stepped inside the café where she had agreed to meet Gabe. The smell of bacon and eggs and the warmth of the small restaurant were welcome after her short chilly walk from the motel.

She hesitated just past the doorway and searched the crowded room. It didn't take her long to spot Gabe. He was seated at a corner table next to a plate-glass window. Judging by the huge yawn he made no attempt to hide and his slouched posture, she figured he hadn't slept much better than she had during the stormy, seemingly endless night.

Had their brief but potent physical contact affected him as much as it had her?

Probably not, she thought, suddenly feeling warmer as each second passed. More than likely, he'd been worrying about his son. After all, finding his son was his only reason for coming along in the first place.

And you have more important things to worry about than what some man thinks or doesn't. Best to act as if nothing out of the ordinary had happened, she decided.

Lisa strode determinedly toward the table. "Am I late?" Gabe jerked his head up and around. He scrambled out of his seat. "No, not at all," he answered, motioning to a chair opposite him. "I was early. Want me to take your jacket?"

Lisa shook her head. "No, thanks," she answered. For several seconds his penetrating gaze held hers. Then his blue eyes darkened, sending shivers of awareness down Lisa's back.

With an effort, she tore her gaze away and quickly slid into the chair, but even after Gabe had reseated himself, she could still feel him watching her. And with each passing minute, she could also feel her face growing warmer under his close scrutiny.

Hoping to divert his attention, she picked up the plastic-coated menu, which was stuck between the napkin holder and the salt and pepper shakers, and made a show of studying the food items listed.

"Coffee?"

When Lisa glanced up at the young waitress holding a steaming carafe, she smiled, grateful for the woman's prompt arrival. "Yes, please. And I'd like an order of waffles and bacon and a small glass of orange juice."

The waitress nodded, poured Lisa coffee, then she turned to Gabe, forcing his attention to switch to her. "Are you ready to order, sir?"

"I'll have the same as the lady," he answered as the waitress topped off his cup with more coffee.

All too soon, he returned his gaze to Lisa. This time, to her relief, there was nothing in his expression but frank curiosity.

"What's on the agenda today?"

Lisa shrugged. "I'm not quite sure what to do at this point. I'd like to go back to Southern Phone and talk to some of the other office personnel, but with the FBI hanging around, I don't guess that would be such a good idea."

"You could call instead."

Lisa laughed. "I wouldn't know who to ask for. I'm sure Dixie has mentioned people she works with, but other than Nicole, I don't recall anyone in particular...except..."

"Except?"

Lisa glanced up at him. "Except Kevin Striker."

At that moment, the waitress brought their food. Lisa immediately doused her waffles with syrup, and Gabe waited until the young woman had left before he continued.

"Isn't that the man Nicole mentioned last night, the one spreading the rumors?"

Lisa had just taken a bite of waffle, but she managed to convey her distaste with a scowl as she nodded.

Gabe chuckled. "From that look and the little you said last night, I take it you don't much care for the man."

Lisa finished chewing and swallowed. "That's putting it mildly," she said, picking up her glass of orange juice. "The man is a sleaze and Dixie was well rid of him when he dumped her."

THE WAITRESS had just cleared away their empty plates and was pouring Lisa and Gabe each a final cup of coffee when Gabe felt a prickle of apprehension crawl down his neck.

Years of working with sometimes unruly roughnecks in the middle of the gulf had taught him to trust his gut instincts. Gabe had learned the hard way to recognize danger signs.

Without being obvious, he casually glanced around the restaurant until he spotted two men standing just inside the entrance. Both were dressed in dark blue suits, and since most of the restaurant's patrons were wearing jeans and flannel shirts, it was more than obvious that the men didn't exactly fit in.

But what really caught his attention was the way the men kept staring at Lisa.

Gabe leaned forward to get her attention. "Don't look now, but I think we're about to have company."

Her curiosity aroused, Lisa looked, anyway. Sure enough, the two men were headed straight for their table.

CHAPTER SIX

DANNY JERKED AWAKE and squinted against the bright sunlight. It took several moments for his fuzzy brain to clear and for him to remember he was in the front seat of a car in the middle of nowhere. His neck was stiff, his mouth felt as if it were stuffed with cotton, but worse, nature called.

A sudden, loud unfamiliar noise sounded close by, and Danny went rock still. He could feel the hairs on his neck bristling. Then it finally dawned on him just what he'd heard, and with a frown of disgust, he turned and peered out of the side window.

A cow. A stupid cow. Here he was getting all flipped out because of a cow.

A soft rustling sound from the back seat diverted his attention. He glanced over his shoulder. Dixie was curled up, her head pillowed by her arm and her knees pulled up to her chest. Her long blond hair was a mass of tangles, her face was still too pale and her clothes were beyond the wrinkled, dirty stage. So how come just the sight of her still did funny things to his insides, he wondered, especially since she had made her own feelings about him crystal clear?

Stupid question, he thought, as he turned away and eased open his door. He'd fallen for her—and fallen hard—even *before* he'd ever laid eyes on her. Even now, he wished they could somehow go back to those long phone conversations. At least then he still had some hope that she cared as much for him as he did for her. Now there was no hope... But he'd get over her, he silently vowed. He had no choice.

Hoping he wouldn't disturb her, he pushed the door closed without actually shutting it, then he stood for a moment, taking in his surroundings.

In front of the car was a metal gate that led to a fenced pasture. The small open area was surrounded by dense woods. The cow he'd heard earlier was contentedly grazing on the other side of the gate several yards away. Danny headed for a nearby stand of trees, hoping they would provide him the few minutes of privacy he needed.

When he returned, the first thing he noticed was that the back door was wide open. Dixie was sitting up, staring at what appeared to be an open briefcase in her lap. She seemed preoccupied and oblivious to everything around her.

"Hey, you're awake," he called out, hoping not to startle her.

She turned her head, and he immediately sensed something was wrong when he saw the look in her eyes. "You're not going to believe this," she said, her voice quavering with fear.

Danny stopped beside the car, bent over and peered inside. "Oh, Jesus! Where did that come from?"

"It was on the floor behind the front seat," she whispered.

"Is that what I think it is?"

Dixie nodded and his stomach knotted as a sick feeling spread throughout his insides.

IN SHREVEPORT, Lisa watched as the two men approached their table.

"Ms. Lisa LeBlanc?"

Lisa narrowed her eyes at the clean-cut dark-haired man who stood within a couple of feet of where she sat. "Who wants to know?" she asked, suddenly leery of the two strangers.

The man, early forties she guessed, reached inside his suit jacket and pulled out a square leather ID holder. He flipped it open to reveal a badge. "I'm agent Johnny Monroe, and this—" he tilted his head toward the other man "—is agent Dick Tanner. We're with the FBI."

Outwardly Lisa remained calm, but inside, her stomach did a flip-flop, and her sense of uneasiness grew. How had they known that *she* was Lisa LeBlanc? How had they known that she and Gabe were at the café? Had they found Dixie and Danny? And if they had found them, were they okay?

"Ms. LeBlanc, I would like to ask you some questions about your sister. Dixie Miller is your sister, isn't she?"

Lisa nodded slowly, but was careful to keep her expression noncommittal. Since no one outside Southern Phone was supposed to know that the FBI suspected Dixie of stealing the union money, Lisa decided she needed to be careful about what she said. She didn't want to get Nicole into trouble.

"How did you know Dixie is my sister and how did you know where to find me?"

Johnny Monroe shrugged. "We were told you were looking for your sister and that you were staying at the motel."

Other than Nicole, Snelling was the only person they had talked to, so Lisa figured that the little twerp was the one who had told them where she and Gabe were staying.

"Now, about your sister."

"Why is the FBI interested in my sister?"

Monroe glanced at his partner, then back to Lisa. "We have reason to believe she might have information about a theft—"

"My sister is not a thief," she said with chilly politeness. It was all she could do to keep from shouting, but shouting at FBI agents wouldn't help Dixie. "She wouldn't—"

"Ma'am," he interrupted. "We just want to talk to her. We're not accusing her of anything."

Like hell you're not, she thought.

"We'd just like to find her and ask her some questions," he continued.

"Just what exactly was stolen?"

"I'm not at liberty to divulge that information just
yet."

The other agent stepped forward, but he looked
straight at Gabe. "The motel manager tells us that
you're registered as Gabriel Jordan. May I see some
ID, sir?"

Lisa swallowed hard, and Gabe hesitated a moment as if he were about to say something. Then, with
a shrug, he reached inside his back pocket for his billfold. "Sure. No problem." He slipped out his driver's license and handed it to the agent. "But may I ask
why?"

Monroe answered while Tanner studied Gabe's license. "A man calling himself Gabriel Jordan was the
last person Dixie Miller interviewed on Thursday.
They were seen leaving Southern Phone together."

Staring hard at Gabe, Tanner handed the license
back to him and shook his head. "Nope." He glanced
at Monroe. "He doesn't fit the description. He's too
old, for one thing."

When Gabe flinched, a smiled tugged at Lisa's lips.
First Nicole, and now an FBI agent. Poor Gabe was
going to develop a complex about his age.

"Ma'am, if we could just ask you a few questions
about your sister, we would appreciate your cooperation."

The agent's words quickly doused Lisa's amusement, and she reminded herself that this was serious
stuff. Her sister had been accused of stealing over two

hundred thousand dollars from a union retirement fund, for Pete's sake.

"What do you want to know?"

"Ah, ma'am, do you mind if we sit?"

Lisa did mind, but she figured they would do as they damn well pleased, anyway. She shook her head and motioned toward the two empty chairs. "Help yourselves," she answered.

The minute the two officers seated themselves, the same young waitress who had waited on their table earlier appeared. "Just coffee," agent Tanner told the woman.

As he emptied two packets of sugar into his cup, agent Monroe leveled his gaze at Lisa while he stirred the coffee. But it was agent Tanner who shot out the first question.

"Mr. Jordon, Ms. Miller never filed the job application she allegedly filled out during the interview, and we can find no evidence, other than your name in her appointment book, that an application was ever completed. Do you have any idea why someone would use your name to apply for a position at Southern Phone or who this person could be?"

Gabe didn't hesitate when he shook his head. "Nope, but that's a good question and that's exactly what I had hoped to find out by coming along with Ms. LeBlanc."

"How did you know someone had used your name?"

Leaving out the part about Danny, Gabe told the agent how and why he and Lisa had met. He ended his explanation by giving the agent the same reason he had given Lisa. "It was evident to me that whoever used my name must have known something about me, at least where I lived. The more I thought about it, the less I liked the idea, so I asked Ms. LeBlanc if I could tag along."

Gabe glanced at Lisa. Would she go along with his explanation or would she tell them about Danny?

"Isn't it true you have a son by the same name?"

Icy fingers of fear gripped Gabe's heart, but before he could answer Tanner's question, Lisa let out a short bark of laughter.

"Is the FBI into accusing schoolboys now?" She shook her head and laughed again. "I hope you realize that Gabe's son is only seventeen, hardly old enough to apply for a job at Southern Phone. He's also a genius and has set his sights on becoming a doctor, so why would he want to work at a job like that?"

Gabe breathed a silent sigh of relief and resisted his sudden urge to reach out and kiss Lisa LeBlanc. At that moment, his growing respect for her and his estimation of her character climbed several notches.

Monroe shook his head and sighed. "I told you we're not accusing anybody of anything. We're just trying to get to the bottom of this thing."

Liar, Lisa thought, recalling what Nicole had told them.

"Ma'am, when was the last time you spoke to your sister?"

"Saturday, a week ago."

"And you haven't seen or talked with her since?"

"No."

Monroe narrowed his eyes. "You're positive you haven't spoken to her since then?"

Lisa felt as if every nerve in her body was stretched to the breaking point. "Look, Mr. Monroe, the whole reason I'm here is to locate my sister. If you will check, you will find that I filed a missing-person report this past Monday with the Shreveport police."

"How did you know she was missing?" he snapped.

Lisa glared at the man. "I didn't know for sure, but my sister and I are very close. *Very close,*" she repeated. "Every Saturday morning we take turns phoning each other. We're two women who live alone, so we like to check on each other. When I tried to call my sister this past Saturday, and she didn't answer, I got worried. I tried all weekend to reach her, and by Monday, I knew something was wrong. Even you have to admit, with all the crime now that I had good reason to worry."

While Lisa was locked in a staring match with Monroe, Gabe could feel the other agent watching him. He was careful to keep his face expressionless, but he couldn't help but admire the way Lisa was handling the situation.

The questions seemed to go on forever as the agents took turns grilling first Lisa, then Gabe. Gabe could tell with each passing minute that Lisa was growing more and more irritated and less patient. He discreetly glanced at his watch and was surprised to find that almost an hour had passed.

Agent Monroe finally glanced over at Tanner, and it was almost as if the two were exchanging a silent message of some kind. They both stood. "I guess that's all the questions we have for now," he said. "We appreciate your cooperation." From inside his suit jacket he pulled out two cards. He handed one to Lisa and the other one to Gabe. "If either of you find out anything or hear from your sister, please contact me immediately."

Gabe and Lisa watched until the two men were barely out of hearing range. "He must think I'm an idiot," Lisa mumbled. "Please contact me immediately," she mocked. "Humph!"

When Lisa felt Gabe's hand cover hers, she turned to look at him.

"I want to thank you for not telling them about Danny."

The deep resonance of his voice did funny things to her insides and she felt the warmth of his touch spread up her arm, straight to her heart.

"I'm not sure if I did the right thing," she said softly, "but from what you've said about your son, I don't think he's the type to kidnap anyone." She pulled her hand free and lowered her gaze. "Besides, I got the feeling from just listening to those agents that once they find my sister, they aren't going to be interested in her side of the story, and I want to try to find her first."

Gabe didn't know quite what to say, so he remained silent. If their situations had been reversed, he wondered if he would have been as generous, but he didn't much like the answer he came up with.

After a moment, Lisa sighed and looked up at Gabe. "I've been thinking about what we should do next," she said. "One name keeps popping into my head. And as much as I would rather avoid any contact with the sleazy man, I think we should talk to Kevin Striker."

ACROSS TOWN, two men stood outside Kevin Striker's apartment. One man was tall and muscular and the other was short and stocky. The shorter of the two pressed his ear close to the door.

"I don't hear anything," he said. He glanced around the parking lot. "And I don't see his car."

The taller man nodded, then produced a small tool kit from his jacket pocket and proceeded to jimmy the lock. The lock gave, and both men looked up and down the apartment complex then pulled out guns from shoulder holsters.

The shorter man cautiously shoved open the door and they both slipped inside. After a careful, thorough search of the apartment, they met back in the living room.

"Think he's gone for good?" the stocky man asked.

"Maybe. Maybe not. But I think we ought to leave him a little message, a reminder, just in case he shows up."

The short man grinned. "Yeah, sounds good to me, but then what?"

"Then we hang around for a while and see if he turns up."

BACK AT THE MOTEL, Gabe alternately paced and stared out the lone window in Lisa's room, while Lisa placed a call to Southern Phone. After several long moments, she asked to speak with Kevin Striker. More moments passed with only minimum conversation, and she hung up the phone. Gabe turned from the window. "Well?"

Lisa gave him a thoughtful look. "He's not there. They said he called in sick today." She pulled out the top drawer of the table and retrieved a telephone book. Within seconds, she found Striker's home phone number, but when she placed the call, no one answered. "Now that's strange," she mumbled, hanging up the receiver.

Gabe shrugged. "Maybe he's gone to see a doctor or he could be in the shower."

"Maybe..." Lisa stared at the telephone. "I'll wait a little while and try again."

An hour later Lisa punched out Kevin Striker's phone number again, but there was still no answer. She slowly hung up the receiver. "I think we should go over there."

Gabe frowned. "Why? It's obvious he's not home."

"I just have this feeling . . ." Lisa shrugged. "Call it intuition or whatever." She stood, picked up her jacket and handbag and walked to the door. "Are you coming?"

"Might as well," Gabe grumbled. "But I still don't see the point since it's obvious he's not there. Hell, maybe the man is playing hooky."

"Maybe," she conceded, pulling on her jacket, "but there's one sure way to find out."

When Lisa and Gabe finally located Kevin Striker's address, Lisa pulled Lover into the empty parking spot in front of his apartment.

"Nice place," Gabe commented.

His sarcasm wasn't lost on Lisa. As she glanced around the run-down apartment complex, she shuddered, grateful that Gabe had come along for the ride. Even in the broad daylight, she didn't like the looks of the shabby place or the group of rough-looking teenagers who were loitering a few doors down.

"Shouldn't they be in school or something?"

Gabe eyed the group suspiciously. "Or something is more like it." He shoved open the door. "Come on. Let's get this over with and get out of here."

Lisa knocked several times on the apartment door but there was no answer. "Something's wrong. Maybe he's really ill, too ill to answer the phone or the door."

"Not likely."

The menacing tone in Gabe's voice got her attention, and the cold, hard look in his eyes sent shivers

down her spine. Lisa followed the direction of his gaze
to the noisy gang of teenagers who kept staring at
them and arguing as if trying to make a decision about
something. *Probably trying to decide if we're worth
robbing,* she thought.

"Let's get out of here."

Lisa figured that now wasn't the time to debate the
issue, so she hurried back to the Jeep.

A few minutes later, she pulled into an empty parking spot near the front of the complex.

"Why are you stopping here?"

Lisa shoved the Jeep door open. "I'm going in to
talk to the manager."

Gabe bolted after her. "Hey, hold on." He grabbed
her arm. "What the hell for?"

Gabe's grip on her arm was warm and more disturbing than Lisa wanted to think about, and despite
the turmoil that just his touch caused, she was able to
keep her voice calm. "I want to get into Kevin Striker's apartment. Like I said before, he could be too sick
to answer the phone or the door." She pulled her arm
free. "But even if he isn't there, I want to get in and
look around."

"What? That's crazy."

Lisa shook her head, and Gabe recognized the
stubborn expression on her face. "Right now, Kevin
is the only lead we have," she said, "and I intend to
find him. You can either come with me or wait here.
It makes no difference to me."

Knowing he had no choice but to go along with her, Gabe closed his eyes for a moment and sighed. He opened them just in time to see Lisa disappear through the doorway marked Office. "Damn," he muttered, stalking toward the door. He stepped inside the small, cramped room, which reeked of stale cigar smoke. By the time his vision adjusted to the dim lighting, Lisa had the overweight, grungy-looking manager cornered and was turning on the charm. Gabe pulled a toothpick out of his pocket and stuck it in his mouth, clamping it firmly between his teeth. He crossed his arms, leaned against the wall and watched.

"I'm worried about my boyfriend, Kevin Striker." Lisa smiled, but it was a tentative smile as if she was trying to be brave.

Gabe switched the toothpick to the other side of his mouth and raised an eyebrow at her blatant tactics.

"He's been ill," she continued, ignoring the smirk on Gabe's face. "But he's not answering the phone or the door."

"Look, lady—" the manager shot Gabe a wary glance "—I'm just the manager around here. I don't get involved in personal stuff."

Lisa hesitated for a second, then in a voice that Gabe would have sworn was intoned with genuine concern, she took her best shot. "I just know something awful has happened. Why, he could be dead. Maybe I should call the police instead."

For a moment Gabe thought the manager's eyes were going to pop out of his head.

"Dead? Police!"

"Well, could we please just check?" Lisa pleaded. "I thought you might have a master key of some kind."

She had barely finished the sentence before the manager was fumbling in a nearby drawer full of keys. "Striker... Striker... I think that's apartment 105," he mumbled.

When they drove up in front of Kevin's apartment, Lisa was relieved to see that the gang of teenagers had left. The manager knocked several times before he finally unlocked the door.

"Holy Jesus! Just look at this mess." The manager stepped inside and Lisa and Gabe followed.

The place looked as if it had been ransacked, and Lisa didn't have to pretend the fear she felt.

For a moment Gabe chewed thoughtfully on the toothpick, then he removed it and headed straight for the hallway. "Wait here and I'll check out the bedroom."

Neither she nor the apartment manager said a word, and for once, Lisa didn't argue. If Striker had met with an ugly end, she'd just as soon let Gabe find him first.

Glancing around the room, she could almost feel the violence still hanging in the air, and she shuddered. It was true she didn't like Kevin, but she certainly didn't wish the man dead.

When Gabe finally called out, "Nothing in here but more of the same," Lisa felt almost dizzy with relief.

A minute later Gabe walked back into the living room. "It's hard to tell," he said, "but it looks like he might have packed some things and left in a hurry. There's not much in his closet or the chest of drawers."

"Why that sorry, no-good bastard..."

Lisa tuned out the rest of the manager's tirade as he ranted about late rent payments and damages. Stepping over upended furniture and various other objects strewn across the floor, she moved to stand by the bar separating the kitchen from the living room.

First Dixie, she thought. *Then Danny. And now Kevin.* All of them had vanished, without a trace. What on earth was going on? she wondered. Maybe they should have let the FBI handle everything. Maybe she ought to call agent Monroe and tell him about this latest development.

Lisa stared at the telephone sitting on the bar, but it was the notepad next to the phone that caught her attention. She leaned closer. Scrawled onto the pad was what looked like a telephone number. Below the number, just barely discernible, almost as if the pen had run out of ink, was written one word: charter.

Lisa turned the word over in her mind, wondering what it meant. Someone's name, maybe? Possibly someone who would know where Kevin was? She glanced at Gabe, who was listening patiently while the manager continued his tirade. Neither man was paying any attention to her.

Before she had time to change her mind, she reached up, took the notepad and slid it into her jacket pocket.

She wasn't really stealing, she consoled herself. She was simply taking advantage of a possible lead.

Sure. Right! A little voice whispered.

"Lisa?"

Lisa started at the sound of her name, and when Gabe tilted his head and frowned, she knew she probably looked as guilty as she felt.

"Have you got your business cards with you? And a pen."

"Ah, yeah, sure thing." Gingerly picking her way back across the debris to where Gabe was standing, she fumbled in her handbag and produced a card and a pen.

Gabe took both and turned to the manager. "If Striker happens to show up here again, I'd appreciate you getting in touch with us," he said. "This is where we're staying. And if we're not there, you can leave a message at the number on the front." He handed the manager the card.

When the manager frowned, Gabe gave him a shrewd look and reached into his back pocket for his billfold. "Maybe this will make it worth your while." Lisa caught a flash of a twenty-dollar bill before the manager palmed it.

Gabe turned to Lisa. "It's time to go."

Past time, she thought, nodding enthusiastically. The place gave her the creeps.

They were almost to the motel before either of them spoke.

"What do you think?" she asked.

"I'm not sure what to think at this point, but from what the manager said, your sister isn't the only one who has financial problems. Striker was three months behind on his rent."

"My sister does not have financial problems," she shot back.

"Okay, okay. Sorry."

Lisa tried to ignore the nagging suspicion that Gabe didn't quite believe her, as she braked for a red light. She was just overreacting, she told herself. "So do you think Striker took off to get out of paying back rent?"

"It's possible, but that wouldn't explain why the place was trashed. The manager might not press the issue over some back rent—the initial deposit would cover some of what was owed—but it's a sure bet he'd call the police about any damage done to the place." Gabe shook his head. "Nope. I can't see Striker wanting to attract that kind of attention if he was just skipping out on rent."

"Hmm, guess not," Lisa finally replied. "So where—"

"You found something back there, didn't you?"

Lisa threw Gabe a glance as she turned into the motel parking lot. "Maybe." She shrugged. "I'm not sure." She parked Lover near their rooms and turned off the engine. Before she could open the door, Gabe reached out and clasped her arm. "What did you find?"

For several seconds, Lisa stared at his large tanned hand encircling her small pale wrist, and just as before, her stomach did a familiar flip-flop. She could feel him staring at her, waiting for an answer. But for the life of her, she couldn't remember the question.

"I saw you slip something into your jacket."

Lisa tugged on her hand and Gabe released her. "It may not be anything." For long moments, she stared at him as she absently rubbed her wrist. He hadn't hurt her, but she could still feel his touch, which was equally disturbing.

"Care to enlighten me?"

Lisa shrugged, then reached inside her pocket and produced the notepad. "All I've got is a name and a phone number. I'll know more after I make a call."

A few minutes later, she punched out the number and waited. On the fourth ring, the phone was answered.

"Destin Gulf Charter Incorporated," a woman's voice informed her.

Lisa's mind raced. Charter wasn't someone's name. "Charter? As in boats?" she asked.

"Yes, ma'am. We're the best on the gulf coast."

"Ah, yes, I'm sure you are." Lisa racked her brain for some kind of excuse to keep the woman talking. She'd said Destin Gulf Charter. That had to mean Destin, Florida.

"Well, what can I do for you? Do you want to book a fishing trip or an excursion?"

"Actually my boyfriend has already booked a trip and I promised him I would confirm it," Lisa fabricated. "His name is Striker," she said. "Kevin Striker."

"What's the date of departure?"

"I'm not sure," Lisa hedged. "That's what he wanted me to check on."

"Just a moment, please."

The woman put her on hold and Lisa took a deep breath. She glanced at Gabe and then wished she hadn't. He had a bemused look on his face and a smirk on his lips. Lisa felt as if her own face was suddenly on fire. Never in her life had she lied so much as she had today, and Gabe seemed to know it. But what was worse, he seemed to find it amusing.

"Hello, ma'am?"

Lisa turned her back to Gabe. "Yes?"

"Mr. Striker's charter for one is scheduled to leave for Cancun day after tomorrow at 7:00 a.m. Anything else?"

"Charter for one...Cancun." The words swirled in Lisa's head.

"Hello? Ma'am, are you still there?"

"Ah, yes," Lisa mumbled, trying to clear her scrambled thoughts. "You've been very helpful. Thank you." She hung up the receiver.

"Well?" Gabe asked. "What did you find out?"

After Lisa had repeated what she'd learned, Gabe gave a low whistle. "Cancun, huh? Just how does someone who is three months behind on his rent afford to book a charter to Cancun? And why a boat? Why not just fly?"

Lisa stared at Gabe, her mind sorting through the possibilities. "Maybe he scheduled a vacation."

Gabe frowned. "But Southern Phone said he'd called in sick."

"Maybe he did get sick . . . before his vacation."

"So where is he and why does his apartment look like someone trashed the place?"

Suddenly a thought struck Lisa with the force of a jackhammer. "Oh, no!" She stood abruptly and began pacing. "You don't suppose . . ." She paused in front of Gabe, then shook her head. "No." She resumed pacing, mumbling to herself, "She wouldn't, not after he—"

"Do you mind telling me what you're talking about?"

Lisa halted and whirled to face Gabe. "Don't you see? Kevin owes back rent. Dixie disappears and is accused of stealing the union money. And now Kevin—her former boyfriend who is supposed to be out sick—has disappeared and booked a charter to Cancun, Mexico . . . a charter for *one*. No one would think to check charter rentals, at least not right away, and especially if they're looking for Dixie instead.

"Kevin is the thief!" she exclaimed. "He has to be. Nicole said he was spreading rumors about Dixie needing money. So while they're looking for Dixie, he's making his getaway."

What she said made sense, Gabe thought. Sort of. But he suspected that more than likely Dixie and Kevin were both involved and had somehow dragged Danny into it. But how? he wondered. "You could be right," he finally said grudgingly, knowing he didn't dare tell her what he really thought. "Still... none of that explains Striker's trashed apartment."

Lisa frowned as she searched for some plausible explanation. "Hmm, your right," she paused. "But what if Kevin didn't trash his apartment?" she said slowly, still thinking. "What if Dixie found out he was using her and there was a fight of some kind?" Lisa remembered that Gabe had said Danny was big. Would he have tackled someone like Kevin? "What if..." Her voice trailed away as gut wrenching fear suddenly squeezed her insides. *A charter for one.* "Oh, God. What if Kevin—what if they're—"

"No," Gabe snapped, knowing exactly what she was leading up to. In two steps, he was beside her. He grabbed her shoulders. "Don't even think it. Whatever has happened, Dixie and Danny are okay. We can't afford to think otherwise."

Lisa stared up at him and wondered if he was trying to convince her or himself.

Gabe's grip tightened. "There's absolutely no reason to think any differently at this point, is there?" he demanded.

Lisa wasn't sure what to think, but she wanted to believe Gabe, wanted with all of her heart to believe Dixie and Danny were alive. She finally answered. "No, there isn't," she whispered.

Gabe released her just as abruptly as he'd grabbed her. "Now that we've got that settled, I think the next thing we need to do is find Striker."

"Go to Destin?"

Gabe nodded. "If we leave right away, we can be there waiting for him when he shows up."

While Lisa packed, Gabe gathered his own clothes. On the chance that Danny had finally called home, Gabe phoned his aunt. Danny hadn't called, and Gabe could tell by his aunt's voice that she was close to tears. He spent several minutes trying to calm her before he was able to hang up, then he headed for the Jeep to wait for Lisa.

Gabe threw his duffel bag behind the front seat. Leaning against the passenger door, he crossed his arms against his chest and waited.

The sun felt good and was quickly warming the chilly morning. As he casually glanced around the nearly empty parking lot, he thought about what he had told Lisa earlier. Even now, he wasn't exactly sure how he knew that Danny and Dixie were alive. He just did.

What puzzled him even more was his sudden desire to reassure and protect Lisa. Not that she necessarily needed protection, he thought wryly, remembering the fearless way she'd handled him when they'd first met. Still, she did evoke a feeling in him that went further than friendship, one that he had almost forgotten and hadn't experienced in a long, long time...not since his wife.

Gabe suddenly felt a chill of unease, the kind that usually spelled danger. He scanned the parking lot again. At first glance nothing seemed out of place or unusual. Several doors down a man and a woman were loading suitcases into their car. Beyond them a maintenance man was trimming a hedge. Then, out of the corner of his eye, a movement in a black Lincoln Towncar parked directly across the parking lot caught his attention.

Two men were seated inside the car, both staring directly at him. The moment that Gabe looked their way, both men suddenly tucked their heads and seemed unduly occupied with something on the seat between them—almost as if they had been caught or were guilty of something, he thought. Very peculiar, he decided, and he couldn't shake the notion that they were there for the specific purpose of watching him.

CHAPTER SEVEN

CURIOUS ABOUT THE TWO MEN, Gabe concluded he needed a closer look. Just a simple stroll past them would suffice, he decided. If they turned out to be legit, with no other reason to be parked there than to pore over a road map, he could rest easy.

He pushed away from the Jeep and took several steps toward the car.

"Gabe?"

At the sound of Lisa's voice, Gabe paused, then turned. She was dragging her suitcase toward the Jeep.

Gabe glanced back one last time at the black Lincoln. Paranoid, he thought. He was just being paranoid, looking for danger where there was none. No one but the FBI would have reason to stake out him and Lisa. And Gabe figured that supplying Towncars for agents was probably a little beyond the FBI's budget.

Chagrined at his own misplaced wariness, he gave a slight shake of his head, then strolled over to Lisa and took the suitcase.

She had changed clothes and the gray sweatsuit she was wearing fitted loosely, evidently chosen for comfort instead of style, he thought. He'd noticed that everything she wore was casual and utilitarian rather than fashionable and he liked that about her.

"Thanks," she said, with a genuine look of gratitude. "Sorry I kept you waiting, but at the last minute I decided to check my answering machine, just in case Dixie tried to call." She paused. "Other than a couple of hang-ups, the only messages were business calls. I wonder if the hang-ups were Dixie. Maybe I should have just stayed home and waited, let the police handle things instead of running all over the countryside, or maybe—"

"Lisa, stop worrying." Gabe heaved her suitcase into the Jeep. "We're doing everything we know to do to find them. Have a little faith."

"Faith? As in God?"

Her assumption caught him off guard. "Yeah, well, that too," he said. "But if the calls were from your sister, I'm sure that for once she would have broken her rule and left a message on your machine. From what you've told me, your sister is a pretty savvy lady, and I can assure you my son is no fool." *Except possibly where savvy ladies are concerned,* he added silently.

"I guess you're right . . ."

When her voice trailed off into a wistful sigh, Gabe reached out and gently captured her chin so that she would have to look at him. "Of course I'm right," he said gruffly.

But touching her was a mistake. The urge to kiss her until she forgot all of her worries, until she could think of nothing but him, ignited in him like a flash fire. Gabe had to remind himself that he was supposed to be reassuring her and not causing her more problems.

"Now—" he cleared his throat and released his hold on her chin "—the sooner we get on the road, the faster we'll get to Florida. Right?"

A tiny smile pulled at Lisa's lips. "Right," she answered.

Once they paid their motel bill, Lisa drove to the main road leading to the interstate. Out of the corner of his eye, Gabe caught sight of the black Lincoln again. The car was easing toward the edge of the parking lot.

Even when the car followed them all the way to the interstate on-ramp, Gabe kept telling himself that there was no cause for alarm. It was just coincidence that the Lincoln was headed in the same direction.

An hour later, he casually glanced over his shoulder. Sure enough, the black Lincoln was still in sight, following at a discreet distance.

Gabe tensed and silently cursed. The whole thing was beginning to get on his nerves. He turned to Lisa. Her eyes were on the highway, but he could tell from the expression on her face that her thoughts were elsewhere. He figured despite his reassurances, she was still worrying about the hang-ups on her answering machine.

He glanced at the speedometer. The red needle was hovering around fifty-five. Other cars and trucks were

-passing them, speeding ahead, so why didn't the Lincoln? he wondered.

He fished a toothpick out of his pocket and wished it were a cigarette as he placed it between his teeth. He still didn't want to believe they were being followed, but he couldn't shake the idea that they were. But why? And who were they? At that moment, he regretted that he hadn't insisted on driving. At least then, he could speed up or slow down and tell for sure if they were being tailed.

Gabe debated whether he should tell Lisa about his suspicions. He didn't want to alarm her, and as long as the Lincoln simply followed, he didn't figure that they were in any danger. He finally decided that telling her would only give her something more to worry about. But thinking about the dilemma had given him an idea. If he was careful, he could conduct a little experiment without her knowing what he was doing.

"At this rate, it's going to take us days to get to Destin," he said, careful to keep his voice even and light as if teasing her. "The speed limit *is* sixty-five."

Sparing him a distracted glance, Lisa frowned then looked at the speedometer. "You're right," she agreed. "Guess my mind wasn't on my driving."

Gabe watched the speedometer ease up to sixty-five. He waited several minutes before he ventured another glance behind him.

"Damn," he muttered, biting the toothpick in half.

Lisa shot him a puzzled look. "What was that for?"

Gabe removed the broken toothpick and deposited the remains in the ashtray. He shifted uneasily in the car seat, wondering what excuse he could come up with. "Just thought of something I forgot to do at home before I left," he finally said, for lack of an explanation other than the truth.

Lisa frowned but returned her gaze to the highway. "Well, it's a little late now, don't you think?"

"I suppose," he mumbled.

"What did you forget to do?"

"Ah, I forgot to, ah..." *Come on, think of something.* "I forgot to have the newspaper delivery stopped."

Gabe ventured a look sideways at her to see if she was buying his trumped-up excuse. She was shaking her head, and the look on her face clearly showed that she thought he was acting a bit peculiar.

During the next hour that it took them to reach the city limits of Alexandria, Gabe kept a wary eye on the car following them. The more he thought about the situation, the more puzzled he became. Except for the FBI, there was no reason for anyone to follow them.

By the time they were well within the city limits of Alexandria, he had almost convinced himself that he had been mistaken. Almost, but not quite.

"There's a gas station coming up on the right. Why don't you pull in there, and I'll top off the gas tank?"

Lisa shook her head. "I usually buy another brand. Lover is finicky about certain kinds of gasolines."

Gabe felt like groaning out loud. "Lisa...please. For once, just humor me. Okay?" He figured if the Lincoln stopped, too, then he would know for sure. Now if only Lisa would cooperate.

"Okay," she finally grumbled. "But don't say I didn't warn you when Lover starts sputtering and clattering down the road."

As inconspicuously as possible, Gabe watched the black car as Lisa pulled up to a row of gasoline pumps. Sure enough, the Lincoln pulled into a station across the highway.

The driver got out, and Gabe narrowed his eyes. The man was short and stocky, but because of the distance, Gabe couldn't see much else about him.

While Gabe continued watching for several minutes, he tried to decide what they should do. He would have to tell Lisa, but should he could call the police? And if he did, what would he say to them? He couldn't *prove* the men had followed them, and the two men had done nothing to try and harm them...yet.

No, he decided, calling the police wouldn't do any good. The only solution was to lose the Lincoln, but first he would have to persuade Lisa to let him drive.

"Well?" Lisa's voice was snappy with irritation. "I thought you wanted to get gas. Or did you want to just sit here for the rest of the day?"

Ignoring her testiness, Gabe turned in the seat to face her. "Now just stay calm and don't get nervous, but I'm almost positive we're being followed."

Lisa frowned. "Followed. That's ridiculous. Why would anyone want to follow us?"

Gabe prayed for patience. "Just take my word for it. They've been on our tail since we left Shreveport."

Her eyes grew round with alarm. "You're serious, aren't you?"

Gabe nodded. "Yes, I'm afraid so."

"Who—"

"No!" Gabe reached out and grabbed her shoulder. "Don't look around. There's a black Lincoln Towncar parked across the highway. It's been with us since we pulled out of the motel parking lot. I have no idea why we're being followed, but I don't like it, so we're going to lose them."

Gabe felt her shudder beneath his fingers. "How?" she whispered.

He squeezed her shoulder gently in an attempt to calm her, then he released her. "Just do exactly as I say."

"What are you going to do?"

"I'm going to pretend to pump gas. When I nod, you crank the Jeep, then ease over to the passenger side and buckle up."

She didn't argue, but Gabe could see by the fire dancing in her eyes that she didn't much care for the idea. *Probably doesn't want me driving her precious Lover,* he thought.

Without turning his head, Gabe could see the Lincoln, and he noticed with satisfaction that the other man had gotten out of the car. The man was taller than the driver and had the build of a weight lifter.

Gabe shoved open his door, climbed out and walked toward the pump. As he removed the nozzle, he saw that the driver was already pumping gas into the Lincoln. The other man was walking to the side of the building where the rest rooms were located.

Gabe bided his time. As soon as he saw the man disappear into the rest room, he nodded at Lisa and prayed that the old Jeep would crank. After a second of hesitation, the engine caught and rumbled to life. The minute Lisa slipped into the passenger seat, Gabe slammed the nozzle back into the gas pump.

Once he was in the Jeep, he jerked the gearshift into drive and floored the accelerator. The Jeep roared out of the gas station, burning rubber all the way to the street.

Gabe chanced a quick look in the rearview mirror, and he saw the man at the pump running toward the rest room. Almost immediately the man inside emerged, and they both sprinted for the Lincoln.

Gabe gunned the Jeep again. He sped along the service road until he came to the first turn leading to the main highway that ran through the middle of town. The stoplight was red and an eighteen-wheeler was barreling down the highway. Praying that there weren't any cops around, Gabe stomped on the accelerator. Lisa screamed, and the Jeep shot onto the highway. Behind him, he heard the blast of the truck's air horn and the squeal of brakes.

Gabe cursed and stomped on the accelerator again. He pushed the speedometer as close to seventy as he dared and deftly maneuvered between the two lanes of traffic. Coming up fast was the south traffic circle. He knew he'd never make it at the speed he was going, so he was forced to slow down.

Once he was through the circle, he ventured another quick glance in the mirror. He didn't see the Lincoln, but he decided not to take any chances. At the next service road exit, he made a sharp right, then raced through a stop sign down a side road that looked as if it led to a residential area. After two more quick turns, he finally slowed down, then pulled up beside an empty overgrown lot.

Without cutting the engine, he stared into the rearview mirror for several minutes. There was no sign of the black Towncar. "I think we lost them," he said, his heart pounding from the rush of adrenaline. Still watching for the Lincoln, he loosened his death grip on the steering wheel and flexed his cramped fingers.

"Are you okay?" he asked, turning to Lisa.

She was staring at him as if she were seeing a madman. Her brown eyes were wide with terror and looked a shade darker against her too-pale face. The few freckles across the bridge of her nose were even more pronounced than usual.

"Lisa?"

Suddenly, two dark red spots stained her pale cheeks. "You almost killed us," she whispered, her voice hoarse and unsteady.

"Lisa, I—"

"Running red lights." Her voice rose. "Driving like a bat out of hell."

"Lisa—"

"No!" She clenched her hands into fists.

Gabe grabbed both her wrists. "Calm down. We're okay." For a moment she resisted, trying to break his hold, then her face crumpled and she began to shake.

"I-I thought we were going to die," she said.

Gabe leaned over and gathered her into his arms. For once she didn't resist. "It's okay," he murmured against her hair.

Lisa wrapped her arms around Gabe's neck and clung to him. It felt good to have someone to lean on for a change, if only for a few moments. For long seconds she allowed herself the luxury of letting him comfort her. Secure in Gabe's arms, she felt safe. "I was so scared," she whispered.

"I know," he answered, tightening his hold on her.

She pressed closer and he could feel her every shuddering breath. He could feel each pounding beat of her heart. A sudden rush of desire raced through him, a desire he tried to control. He'd only meant to comfort her, somehow reassure her, but now...

"Lisa, I— Oh, Lisa, I'm sorry."

"No, I'm sorry for acting like such a—" Lisa pulled her head back just far enough to see him. "Gabe..." Her voice trailed away to a whisper when she saw the smoldering look in his eyes.

When he closed the scant inches between them, she didn't back away, didn't resist. At the first touch of his warm, firm lips, she groaned.

She'd known this moment would come, almost from the first time she'd laid eyes on him if she were truthful. Lisa had never much believed in fate or destiny, but somehow, from the beginning, even before she met him, she'd sensed that some force other than pure coincidence was conspiring to throw them together. And for once, she didn't want to think about all the reasons that she shouldn't kiss him back. She didn't want to think, period. For once she wanted to give in to the strange attraction she felt.

The moment he sensed her acquiescence, Gabe took her mouth like a man parched for water. He deepened the kiss, plunging his tongue inside to meet hers in a duel of shared passion.

Lisa reached up and burrowed her fingers into his thick hair. She pulled at him, wanting his dominance, wanting to shut out everything but the raging need she felt building deep inside. But just kissing him was like an appetizer, and she wanted the whole meal.

As if Gabe sensed her thoughts, he slipped his hands beneath her sweatshirt. Lisa held her breath in anticipation as his hands slid farther up her back, and she wondered how his bare skin would feel beneath her fingers.

With swift deftness, he unhooked the closure of her bra, then slowly he slid his hand around, cupped her breasts and began rubbing his thumb over her bare nipple. Lisa cried out against the aching maelstrom building within her. Long-forgotten sensations ripped through her, sensations that she had thought she would never feel again. She ached and throbbed, and she knew there was only one way to satisfy her escalating desire, only one inevitable conclusion.

But you barely know this man. This is wrong!

The words seeped into her thoughts like thieves. Just a few more moments, she told herself. But the words persisted, and no matter how much she wanted to ignore them, they kept whirling in her head until they finally stole her last vestige of desire.

She stiffened. "No!" She pulled away. "Please don't." She pushed against Gabe's shoulder, and for a minute she wasn't sure he was going to stop. "No," she repeated, and he went still, then finally released her.

She scooted over as close to the door as she could get. Staring straight ahead, she crossed her arms and tightly hugged her middle. "I can't. I—I'm sorry, but I just can't. I don't blame you. I blame myself. I don't even know you."

Silent seconds turned into agonizing minutes. Leftover passion still charged the air. She could hear Gabe's harsh breathing, but she couldn't bring herself to look at him. She was still too confused about how she'd responded to him. He had every right to be upset with her. She had acted like a tease, giving him the come-on then backing off.

When she finally worked up the courage to look at him, he was staring straight ahead, but there was nothing in his expression to suggest that he was angry. If anything, he looked as uncomfortable as she felt.

"Gabe?"

She could see his Adam's apple bob when he swallowed, then he turned his head. "I'm the one who should be apologizing," he said, his voice sounding a bit sheepish. "You were right. We *don't* know each other *that* well." He shrugged. "The only excuse I can offer is that I let things get a bit out of hand. You're worried about your sister and I'm worried about my son. And now someone is following us and God only knows the reason why. I guess we both needed some kind of release from the tension, some kind of reassurance, something tangible to..." He shrugged again.

Lisa didn't know quite what to say. She hadn't expected him to be embarrassed or to apologize, and she should have felt relieved. So why did she feel so... so disappointed? After all, she argued silently, it wasn't as if they were out to form a relationship of any kind. The only reason he had come along in the first place was in hopes that she could lead him to his son.

"Still friends?" he asked, a tentative smile on his lips.

Lisa immediately nodded, glad that he wasn't going to belabor the issue. "Still friends," she answered.

Gabe cleared his throat and glanced at his watch. "It's way past lunchtime." He reached down and shifted into first. "I think we need to find somewhere we can get a bite to eat and talk." *Somewhere very public and safe,* he added silently.

A QUARTER OF A MILE past the south traffic circle, the driver of the Lincoln pulled off onto the shoulder of the highway.

The man sitting in the passenger seat craned his neck, looking all around. "Okay, Parker, where the hell did they go?"

Judd Parker stared at the man sitting next to him. He didn't like Leo Jones. The son of a bitch was pushy and still had the stink of prison on him. "How should I know?" he shot back. "You were supposed to be watching, too."

Leo cursed, then glared at Judd. "Just shut up and drive. There's a fast-food joint about a half a mile down. They've got a pay phone, so pull in there."

"Maybe we ought to look around some more before you call him." Judd didn't want to think about the possible consequences if they lost their quarry. "Hell, I hope he don't blame me," he muttered.

"He's gonna blame both of us, stupid. And there ain't no reason to keep going around in circles. Just drive."

Both men remained silent until they pulled into the parking lot near the pay phone.

Leo opened his door. "Keep your eyes on that highway. If they're still around, they have to come this way sooner or later. I'll go make the call."

"Better you than me," Judd grumbled. Leo scowled, then stalked off toward the phone booth.

As Judd watched Leo press the numbers, he shuddered. Just thinking about how the boss was going to take the news was enough to give him the shakes.

The call was answered on the second ring, and Leo swallowed back the lump of fear lodged in his throat.

"Hey, boss, it's Leo."

"Did they hook up with Striker yet?"

Leo shifted from one foot to the other and swallowed again. "Ah, not exactly."

"Then why the hell are you calling me?"

Leo took a deep breath. "We lost them."

"You what?"

"They spotted us and—" Leo cringed at the string of curses that came through the receiver. Then there were several moments of silence, and sweat popped out on his forehead.

"I want Striker and I want what he owes me. I have to set an example here. If I let one get away, the rest will think they can do the same. I don't care what you have to do to find that bastard, but find him. And if you and that worthless Parker don't find him, neither one of you better show your face around here again."

There was a loud crash on the other end of the line. Leo winced and jerked the receiver away from his ear.

The bastard probably did it deliberately, he thought as he hung up the receiver.

"Well?" Judd asked when Leo leaned down, level with the open car window.

"What do you think?" Leo retorted sarcastically.

"He was pissed, huh?"

"Yeah, well, never mind. I've got me an idea. Just keep watching the road while I make another call."

ACROSS TOWN, Lisa followed Gabe to a row of double glass doors that led into a mall.

He paused and took a final look around the crowded parking lot. There was no sign of a black Lincoln Towncar, so he pushed one of the doors open and gestured for Lisa to enter first.

"Why a mall?" she asked, a bit breathless from trying to match his long strides.

Gabe glanced down at her. "Lots of people around. Easier to get lost in a crowd if we need to. Besides, there's probably a food court and I saw a movie theater across the street."

Lisa's mouth watered at the very thought of food, and she realized that she was hungry. "A movie theater?"

"Yeah, don't you like movies?"

"Well, yes." She paused. "But I think this is a pretty strange time to go to the movies."

Gabe chuckled. "You're right, but I'd be willing to bet you that Lincoln is sitting somewhere on Highway 71 near the interstate, just waiting, since that's the major road that leads south. If I were them, that's where I would wait.

"I figure if they have to sit there long enough, they might give up. And even if they don't, if we hang around here until later tonight, we might slip by them in the dark, so—"

Lisa grinned and finished his sentence. "So, what better way to pass the time than taking in a couple of movies."

Gabe nodded and kept walking in the direction of the food court. He could think of one particular way he'd rather spend his time. Just remembering how Lisa's lips had tasted and the way her bare, satiny skin had felt beneath his fingers was sheer torture, but he knew those kinds of thoughts could only lead to trouble. Gabe figured that under the circumstances, neither of them needed more trouble than they already had. Besides, he thought, if Lisa even suspected that deep down in his heart he considered Dixie guilty until proven innocent, he knew for certain she would leave him on the side of the road in a New York minute.

And every time he thought about the danger Danny might be in because of Lisa's precious sister, his stomach churned with fury. Danny was just a kid, a mixed-up kid at that. Gabe only hoped he would get the chance to tell his son how much he really cared about him, before it was too late. He would gladly agree to Danny's dropping out of school if he could just be assured that he was alive and well.

Once Gabe and Lisa had each selected and purchased food, they found a group of empty tables where they could eat and still keep an eye on the rest of the food court.

Lisa unwrapped her hamburger, lifted off the top bun and sprinkled it liberally with salt and pepper. "Who do you think those men are—FBI?"

Gabe shook his head and squeezed ketchup onto his French fries. "I can't see the FBI providing Lincolns, can you? Besides, those two weren't the same ones who questioned us in Shreveport."

"But who else would have any reason to follow us?" Ravenous, Lisa bit into her hamburger, and savoring the taste, she chewed slowly.

Gabe shrugged and took a drink of his soda. "I've thought about it a lot, and to tell the truth, I can't figure it out."

Gabe had thought about their situation, and nothing added up; yet, he couldn't totally ignore what they had found so far. For one thing, he still believed that there had been a struggle of some kind in Dixie's apartment. Another thing he couldn't get out of his mind was the way Striker's apartment had been ransacked. Either someone was looking for something or they were out to leave Striker a message he wouldn't soon forget. Gabe's instincts told him that somehow, both incidences were tied in to the men following him and Lisa.

Gabe sighed and glanced at Lisa. She was staring at her food and seemed lost in her own thoughts. She picked up the burger, eyed it, then placed it back on the tray. He saw her shudder and knew she was still thinking about the men who had followed them.

Six hours and two movies later, Lisa slid into the passenger seat of the Jeep, all the time searching the dim parking lot for any sign of a black Lincoln.

Gabe slammed the door, buckled his seat belt and started the Jeep. "If we take turns driving and don't make too many stops, we should be in Destin before daylight."

When they neared the on-ramp for the interstate, Lisa kept a sharp eye out for any vehicle that remotely resembled the Lincoln. "Do you see it anywhere?" she asked Gabe.

"Not yet," he replied. "I'm hoping they got tired of waiting."

"Me too," she murmured, straining her eyes and still searching the highway.

Several miles later, Gabe's low chuckle broke the silence between them. "If you don't stop jerking your head around like that, you're going to get whiplash. As far as I can tell, no one is following us now, so why don't you try to relax and catch some sleep? I'll wake you when we get to Baton Rouge and then you can drive for a while."

Lisa sighed. He was right, and she was tired. Besides, she thought, in the dark, with so many lights whizzing by, it was almost impossible to tell one car from another.

She twisted around and tried to get comfortable, then a thought occurred to her. "Are you going to stop in Ponchatoula?"

After a moment he finally answered, "No. By the time we go through, my aunt will be sleeping. I don't want to disturb her."

Lisa closed her eyes and contented herself with listening to the deep timbre of Gabe's voice.

"She helped me raise Danny after his mother died," he continued, "and this whole business has really upset her. She's not that young anymore and she needs her rest."

Lisa had wondered about Danny's mother, had wondered if Gabe was divorced or if she had died, but up until now, she hadn't felt comfortable asking him. "How old was Danny when your wife... when his mother died?"

When long seconds passed and Gabe didn't answer, Lisa decided that remembering his wife's death must have been too painful for him to talk about.

"Danny was just seven," he finally said. "Too young to really understand why his mother would never come home again."

The bleakness in Gabe's voice tore at Lisa's heart. Telling a seven-year-old child that his mother had died was beyond her imagination.

Gabe sighed. "I'm just thankful he didn't have to watch her suffer too long." He glanced over at Lisa. "She had breast cancer. One day she found the lump and six months later she was gone."

Lisa shivered. The threat of breast cancer was never far from any woman's mind. "That must have been hard on both of you."

"It was," he answered gruffly. "For the first year I didn't think I could go on without her. Then one day, Aunt Bessie sat me down and gave me a stern lecture about my responsibilities to Danny. She threatened to pack up and go back to Florida to live if I didn't shape up."

"It's never easy to let go," she murmured, her thoughts wandering back to the agonizing months following Barry's death.

"No, it's not," he agreed. "And at times, I still miss her."

Lisa felt a familiar heaviness fill her chest. There were still days when she missed Barry, too. "I know how you feel," she said softly. "Sometimes, when I wake up during the night and my mind isn't quite clear, I reach over and..." Her voice trailed away.

"I know," Gabe whispered, instantly regretting that he had caused her to recall her own painful memories. Her loss was a lot more recent than his own. He'd had years to cope with Brenda's death. Wanting to somehow console her, Gabe cleared his throat. "That feeling never completely goes away, but as time passes, the memories aren't quite so painful, especially if you can learn to focus on the good experiences that you shared."

He waited several minutes, expecting her to say more. When she didn't, he glanced over at her. Even in the dim light, he could tell by her even breathing that she had fallen asleep, and he wondered if she had heard him.

After checking the rearview mirror, he turned his gaze back to the highway.

Talking about Brenda after so many years seemed strange. Other than his aunt, he had never talked about his wife with another woman. But Lisa was different.

The more he learned about her, the more he realized just how much they had in common. But Gabe knew that there was more to it than that, more to the pull he felt each time he was near her. Beneath her tough exterior, she had a guileless naïveté and an honesty that were rare.

Gabe's stomach knotted. What a mindless jerk he'd been, coming on to her like a bull in heat earlier. He'd only had a few relationships since Brenda, but none that evoked the uncontrollable feelings he had experienced with Lisa, and without exception, he had always acted the perfect gentleman. To Gabe, being a gentleman was a source of pride.

Gabe cursed beneath his breath. It was just his luck that he'd finally found someone like Lisa, someone he could imagine spending his life with, only to know there wasn't a chance in hell of it ever happening.

CHAPTER EIGHT

LISA FORCED HER EYES OPEN. For a moment, she simply stared straight ahead, feeling slightly disoriented...and cold. As her mind began to clear, she shivered, rolled her head from one side to the other, trying to get the kinks out of her neck, then she glanced around.

They were parked in front of gasoline pumps at what looked like an all-night truck stop, but the station wasn't one she was familiar with. She held up her wrist to check the time, twisting her arm so that she could see the dial in the dim light. It was almost 4:00 a.m., and she began to realize that there was no way they could be in Baton Rouge. She had figured they would get into Baton Rouge a little before midnight. So just where in the devil were they? she wondered.

And where was Gabe?

She straightened and searched the parking area, her gaze coming to rest on the small café attached to the gas station. Maybe he'd gone inside to pay for the gas, she thought, peering at the entrance. There were several windows on the front of the building, but it was impossible to see inside.

When minutes passed and there was still no sign of him, she reached for her purse. She noted that the ignition keys were gone, so she figured he had to be around somewhere. She shoved open the passenger door. Feeling distinctly uneasy, she walked briskly toward the café.

She didn't like the idea that he'd left her alone, asleep and vulnerable in a strange place. Besides the fact that just anyone could have walked up and knocked her in the head or robbed her, there was always the possibility that the men who had been following them were still around, lurking in the darkness somewhere.

Lisa entered the small café, and squinted against the bright lights. The smell of bacon frying and coffee assaulted her senses. Country-western music blared from the jukebox and small groups of bleary-eyed truckers were seated throughout the room.

She stepped farther inside, her gaze drawn to a lone table located near a window. Gabe was sitting there, his hands wrapped around a cup of coffee. And he wasn't alone.

The woman leaning across the table was obviously a waitress. But unlike most waitresses that Lisa had seen, this particular woman's uniform was short, tight and fit her well-endowed body like she'd been melted and poured into it. The buttons on the front looked like they could pop off at any second. And it was just as obvious to Lisa by the woman's expression that she was giving it her best shot to serve Gabe more than just coffee.

To give him credit, Gabe looked a bit uncomfortable and kept shaking his head.

Lisa told herself that the spurt of anger she felt had nothing to do with jealousy or the waitress propositioning him—that was his problem. She assured herself that her anger stemmed from his thoughtlessness, from the fact that he'd left her asleep in the Jeep where anything could have happened to her.

At that moment Gabe looked her way, and if she hadn't been so furious, his stunned expression might have been comical.

While Lisa was listing all the reasons she had to be angry with him, Gabe was wondering what he'd done now to make her so mad.

The last hour of driving had been hell. More than once he'd caught himself falling asleep at the wheel, so he'd decided it was time to let Lisa drive for a while.

When he had first pulled into the truck stop, he had figured she would wake up, but she hadn't. Even after he had filled the gas tank and paid for the gas, he still didn't have the heart to wake her, so he'd decided to get a couple of cups of coffee to go first. He'd been careful to keep an eye on the Jeep when he'd gone inside the café. Once inside, he had changed his mind and decided to give her a few more minutes of sleep. He'd found a table near the window so he could keep an eye on her, and he'd ordered his coffee.

"Thanks a lot."

Sarcasm dripped from Lisa's words as she stood near the table, her hands on her hips.

The overly friendly waitress snapped her head around, her eyes wide with surprise. Lisa glared at her, jerked out an empty chair and sat. The waitress immediately took the hint and scrambled to her feet, looking first at Gabe then at Lisa.

Gabe was secretly relieved that Lisa had chosen that moment to make her entrance. He didn't like pushy women, and he was fast losing patience with the waitress and her not-so-subtle advances.

"I'd like a cup of coffee, please," Lisa directed her curt request to the waitress. Ignoring the woman's miffed look as she stalked off toward the counter, she turned back to Gabe. "Well?"

"Well, what?"

"Why didn't you wake me? I don't appreciate being left in the middle of nowhere, prey for any pervert, while you're off drinking coffee with some overendowed waitress."

Briefly, Gabe allowed his male ego to bask in the possibility that she might care enough about him to be jealous. And for a moment, he even allowed himself to fantasize that they could have a relationship. She would never admit it, not in a hundred years, but she *was* jealous, pure and simple, he decided. Why else would she have mentioned the waitress?

"Look, I didn't wake you because I thought you needed the sleep. And not once were you in any danger. I sat here to keep an eye on the Jeep." He stood.

"Enjoy your coffee." He threw down a couple of dollars. "I'll be in the Jeep when you're ready to leave."

Gabe knew he sounded cool and uncaring, but he couldn't afford for her to think otherwise and he couldn't explain without sounding like an egotistical jerk.

EARLY FRIDAY MORNING, hues of pale pink spread over the horizon, heralding the arrival of a new day. There wasn't much traffic, and ahead of Lisa, the highway stretched out and blended into the rising sun. It was a fantastic view, and Lisa's fingers tightened on Lover's steering wheel as she felt the familiar itch for her camera.

Next to sunsets, sunrises were her favorite time of day, a time when everything was fresh and new, when anything seemed possible. For years she had tried to capture the true essence of the spectacular event on film, but she was never satisfied with the results. She always felt that there was something missing, something that eluded the eye of her camera.

Up ahead, Lisa spotted a sign that indicated Destin was still twenty miles away. She yawned and blinked several times. Her eyes felt gritty and thoughts of a hot bath and cool, clean sheets floated in her head. She was tired of riding and tired of driving.

She rolled down her window and inhaled deeply, filling her lungs with the humid, salty air. The distant cry of gulls brought back a flood of bittersweet childhood memories of family vacations spent playing on the white Florida beaches and romping in the warm waves of the Gulf of Mexico.

For a fleeting moment she had the urge to share her thoughts with Gabe. Then she remembered the truck stop.

At the time she had thought she had a right to be angry, but now, in retrospect, she knew she had over-reacted. He had calmly explained his reason for letting her sleep, and although his explanation had been logical and reasonable, he had been polite and remote, almost as if he had instantly erected an invisible barrier that was plainly marked, no trespassing.

Lisa looked over at Gabe. Was he really asleep or had he simply closed his eyes to avoid conversation? After the way she had carried on, she wouldn't have blamed him if he would rather sleep than talk to her.

Gabe's broad chest rose and fell evenly, suggesting that he truly was asleep. Shifting her eyes between him and the highway, she allowed herself a moment of furtive observation. Barry had always had an innocent little-boy look about him when he slept, but there was nothing remotely innocent about the way Gabriel Jordan looked, awake or asleep, she thought.

With his dark, unkempt hair and his overnight growth of beard, Gabe appeared rough and rumpled. And in size alone, he was built entirely differently from Barry. For one thing, Gabe was much larger than Barry had been.

No, she thought, there was nothing innocent about Gabriel Jordan, and there was certainly nothing innocent about the way he kissed her, either.

Just thinking about the kiss they had shared, Lisa felt her face grow warm and her pulse accelerate, and she quickly turned her attention back to the road.

For the past three hours, she'd had nothing to do but drive and think, and trying to figure him out was making her crazy.

"How much farther?"

Lisa jumped at the unexpected sound of Gabe's voice. She flexed her fingers around the steering wheel. Telling herself to relax, she concentrated on breathing deeply before she answered. "About twenty miles," she finally said.

Gabe sat up and stretched, the action making Lisa even more aware of his size in the confines of the Jeep.

"What time was Striker's charter scheduled to leave?"

"Seven Saturday morning."

"Good," he said, smothering a yawn. "That should give us plenty of time to eat, rest up and find the marina. I'd like to keep an eye on that boat tonight, just in case he decides to show up early. But right now I'd give a week's pay for a good cup of coffee."

The first thing they did was find a motel. After Lisa and Gabe registered, they stowed their luggage inside their rooms, walked across the street to a pancake house and ordered breakfast.

Gabe was quiet during the meal, and Lisa could feel the tension between them, almost as if it were a tangible force she could reach out and touch. Each bite of food she ate grew more tasteless as each moment passed.

Finally unable to stand the prolonged silence another minute, Lisa dropped her fork on her plate and faced him. "I would like to apologize."

Gabe stared at her for several seconds before he finally shrugged. "No problem." He lowered his gaze, picked up his glass of orange juice and downed the remainder in one swallow.

Feeling even more uncomfortable than before, Lisa grimaced. "It's just that... well..." She paused, wondering how to explain. But how did she explain something she didn't understand? Since the first day she had met him, she'd been acting completely out of character. At times she didn't even recognize herself.

Gabe set down the glass. "Look. You're tired and I'm tired. We both need to get some rest." He reached for a packet of sugar, tore it open and stirred the contents into his coffee.

He'd easily dismissed her apology as if it were of no consequence, so there seemed to be nothing left to say. She shoved back her chair. "I am tired," she said briskly. Digging inside her purse, she pulled out her wallet. "This should cover my share." She shoved the money across the table, then stood. "I'm going back to the motel." Without waiting for his reply, she turned and marched out.

By the time she reached the motel, she noticed that Gabe still hadn't come out of the restaurant. For a moment, she looked longingly at the white beach that ran behind the motel and was tempted to take a stroll, in the hopes that the exercise would help clear her head and relieve some of her tension and stiff muscles from the ride.

Then out of the corner of her eye, she saw Gabe exit. She'd told him she was tired and wanted to rest. He might follow her if she went for a walk, and she wasn't sure she was up to another encounter just yet.

With one last wistful look at the beach, she turned and went to her room.

GABE WATCHED UNTIL LISA disappeared inside her room. Then he crossed the street. The brisk breeze off the Gulf was cool, and the beach was empty except for a couple of early-morning joggers. The soothing, rhythmic sound of the waves beckoned.

Slipping out of his shoes, he rolled up his pant legs. He should have talked to Lisa, told her what was on his mind.

Gabe kicked at a mound of sand. Hell, he couldn't even talk to his own son about how he felt, so why did he think he could make Lisa understand?

Walking closer to the edge of the beach, he stared out over the endless glimmering water. The best thing he could do was find Danny as soon as possible. Once he found Danny and got this business straightened out, Lisa could go her way and he could go his. The trick was keeping a lid on things until that happened. But for now, all he could do was hope that Striker would show up and that the bastard could give them some answers.

As TIRED AS SHE WAS, Lisa found it difficult to fall asleep. Finally, exhausted both in mind and body, she dozed off and on until midafternoon.

When she finally got up, she headed for the bathroom. While she showered, she mentally listed every possible thing that could have happened to make Gabe act so reserved, so distant.

The incident at the truck stop rated high on her list, but she had apologized.

Lisa turned off the shower and grabbed a towel. For long moments, she stood staring into space. From what he'd said, Gabe had been single a long time. Was it possible that he'd somehow sensed she was becoming too attracted to him? Did he imagine the poor widow was so starved for affection that she would jump at the first man who paid her a little attention?

Lisa closed her eyes and groaned. What else would he think after the way she had clung to him, the way she had kissed him and allowed him to touch her?

She quickly dried off and marched into the bedroom. As she jerked on her clothes, she tried to decide what she should do. *Nothing* was the only frustrating answer she could come up with, nothing except to make damn sure he didn't get the wrong idea again.

Besides, she thought, she had more important things to worry about than some egotistical male trying to protect his freedom, *if* that was his problem.

Still feeling a bit humiliated, Lisa was thumbing through the local telephone book when she heard a knock, followed by Gabe's voice.

"Lisa, are you up?"

Marking the number and address of Destin Gulf Charter, she laid the book down and opened the door.

He had changed into a pair of well worn jeans and a faded black sweatshirt. He had shaved and smelled shower clean, but he didn't look as if he'd slept any better than she had.

Stick to the reason we're here, she silently cautioned herself.

Motioning for him to come in, she walked over to the bed and picked up the telephone book. "I found the address of Destin Gulf Charter."

Gabe took the book and glanced at the page. "The desk clerk should be able to give us directions."

Twenty minutes later Lisa pulled the Jeep into a parking lot near the marina. Across the parking lot was a small white building with Destin Gulf Charter painted in large red letters on the side. Just behind the building was a long pier, but the slips where boats should have been docked were empty.

"Oh, no." Lisa turned to Gabe. "Do you think we missed him? What if he's already left?"

Gabe frowned. "There's only one way to find out." He shoved open the door and stepped out of the Jeep.

With one hand braced against the roof and the other hand on the door, he leaned down. "Do you want to come with me or wait here?"

"I'll wait here," she answered.

Several minutes passed before he finally returned. Once he was seated back inside the Jeep, he turned his head to face her. "Striker hasn't shown up yet," he said. "Destin Gulf Charter owns two boats, and they're both booked for fishing trips today. The receptionist said they weren't due back until around six."

Lisa glanced at her watch. "It's only four, so we've got a couple of hours."

"More than a couple, probably. But there's always the chance he might turn up early."

For several seconds Lisa stared at the empty pier, her thoughts on how to fill up the hours until the boats returned. "Since his charter is booked so early in the morning, doesn't it make sense that he would get here tonight?"

Gabe picked up on her reasoning immediately. "And if he gets here tonight, he needs a place to stay."

Lisa nodded and started the Jeep. She shoved the gearshift into first. "It's a long shot, but he might be staying at one of the hotels or motels. If we divided up the names in the telephone book, it shouldn't take too long to call each one." She shrugged. "We might get lucky."

Back at the motel, they decided that Gabe would take the first half of the alphabetized list and she would take the second, then Gabe left to make his calls from his room.

Two hours later Lisa had just hung up the phone on yet another dead end when she heard Gabe's knock.

She opened the door. "Any luck?"

He shook his head and stepped inside. "Nothing, how about you?"

Lisa walked back to the phone. "Nope, but I've still got a couple of possibilities left."

A few minutes later she sighed and hung up again. "Guess I was wrong."

Gabe had been staring out the window. He turned to face her. "Don't feel too bad. Like you said before, it was a long shot. He could be staying anywhere between here and Shreveport. Anyway, doing something was better than sitting around twiddling our thumbs."

Lisa sighed. "I guess so, but dammit, now we have to wait until tomorrow morning before we know if he's going to even show up. And if he doesn't, then what do we do?"

"Let's cross that bridge when we come to it. For now, I suggest we go find some dinner then head back to the marina."

Lisa grabbed her purse and stalked toward the door. "That's all we seem to do—eat, drive and wait," she grumbled.

Gabe chuckled. "Got to keep up our strength."

THE PARKING LOT across from the marina was dark, with only a couple of streetlights to lend small beacons of comfort. Except for the distant sound of crashing waves and an occasional car passing, for the most part, the marina was quiet and deserted.

Lisa checked her watch, then peered through the window. Gabe was nowhere in sight. Using the excuse that he needed to stretch his legs and that he would try to find a soft-drink machine, he'd left nearly an hour ago and hadn't returned yet.

Lisa shivered. The early-morning hours had cooled down considerably, and she wasn't sure if she was shivering from the cold, or from being worried about Gabe, or from uneasiness about being left alone.

Checking one more time to see if the doors were locked, she hunched lower in the seat. "There's absolutely nothing to worry about," she muttered. Saying the words out loud seemed to help. Besides, she thought, she still had Barry's pistol beneath the seat if she needed it.

Across the parking lot, she saw a large shadowy figure moving toward the Jeep. For a moment, she felt as if her heart had leaped into her throat. When the shadow finally took shape, she let out her pent-up breath. Where the hell had he been all this time?

Reaching over, she unlocked the passenger door and Gabe climbed inside. He handed her a canned drink.

"Sorry I took so long," he said. He popped the top on his own drink. "I almost ran into a security guard making his rounds and had to stay put until he left."

Lisa popped the top on her drink and took a long swallow. "Guess you would have a hard time explaining what you're doing lurking around at this time of night."

"I was not lurking," he grumbled. "But I am almost frozen stiff. Didn't expect it to turn so cold."

A few minutes later, a car pulled into the lot, and Lisa tensed, watching until the driver got out.

"Well?" Gabe whispered. "Is that Striker?"

Lisa shook her head. "No." When the man headed for one of the charter boats, Lisa sighed. "He must be one of the captains."

Within minutes another car pulled up. Again Lisa tensed.

"Bingo," she whispered the minute the driver stepped out of the car. "That's him." Her heart pounding, she reached for the door handle, but Gabe grabbed her arm.

"Not yet," he said. "We don't want to scare him off. Let him get on the boat first. Once he's inside, I'll go see what I can find out from him. If something happens, there's a pay phone across the road. Call the police."

Lisa glared at Gabe. "I did not come this far just to—"

"Keep your voice down," he cautioned. "Out here, sound carries."

Lisa gave a frustrated sigh. "Like I said—" she lowered her voice "—I did not come this far just to sit here and watch. I'm going, too. Besides, he knows me, and he'd be more willing to talk to me than a perfect stranger."

"Come on, Lisa, be reasonable. This is not some game we're playing. If he's the sleaze you say he is, things could get rough."

"I'm coming with you," she retorted, her voice a harsh whisper, "and there's nothing you can do about it."

Gabe just stared at her. "Aw, hell. I swear, you've got to be the most stubborn woman I've ever met." Silent seconds ticked by and she could hear Gabe's harsh breathing. "Damn," he muttered. "Okay, okay, we'll both go."

Their stealthy footsteps were almost silent on the wooden pier. Shoving the keys to the Jeep into her pocket, Lisa focused on the tiny light coming from the charter boat as she followed close behind Gabe. A sudden gust of wind kicked up and she shivered. As they drew closer they could hear the murmur of voices coming from inside.

There was a gap between the boat and the pier. Gabe took a firm grip on Lisa's upper arm and steadied her while she stepped from the pier onto the boat's deck. Once on board, he motioned toward a large porthole.

Since Lisa didn't recognize the gruff voice coming from inside the cabin, she figured it had to be the captain.

"Mr. Striker," he said. "I can't leave until my crew gets here. And besides, we agreed on payment up front."

Lisa plastered herself against the outside cabin wall. Gabe eased closer to the opening.

Kevin's laughter rang out, sounding harsh and ugly. "Look, you old bastard. I need to leave now—immediately. Do you understand?"

Gabe tilted his head closer to the porthole, then eased just far enough over to get a peek inside the cabin.

Striker was turned sideways but his attention was on the captain. Gabe could see the captain shaking his head.

"Not without payment first," the captain repeated.

Gabe tensed when he saw Striker reach in his pocket.

He pulled out a pistol and pointed it at the captain. "You wanna bet?" he said.

Gabe jerked back his head and leaned close to Lisa's ear. "He's got a gun," he whispered, just barely loud enough for her to hear. "Stay here, and run like hell if things go wrong."

Even in the dim light, he could see that Lisa's eyes were filled with both fear and panic, but Gabe didn't have time to reassure her. The important thing was to stop Striker.

Easing past Lisa, Gabe crept toward the cabin door. From his quick peek through the porthole, he knew that Striker's back would be facing him. If he could just get within tackling distance, he could probably jump Striker before he knew what hit him . . . and before he had a chance to pull the trigger. But everything hinged on how the captain would react.

Taking a deep breath, Gabe stepped soundlessly into the middle of the open doorway. He could feel the adrenaline rushing through his veins. The captain saw him but faked a sudden coughing fit to keep Striker's attention focused on him and away from the door.

Gabe took one last step forward, bent his knees and lunged. The second before impact, he slammed the heel of his hand against Striker's wrist, and the gun went flying. Striker let out a grunt of surprise. And both men hit the floor.

Striker bucked like a wild bull, but Gabe's size and bulk enabled him to pin him down long enough to get a stranglehold around his neck.

"Okay, that's enough!" the captain shouted.

Out of the corner of his eye, Gabe could see that the captain had the gun.

"Okay, buddy boy," Gabe said, tightening his arm against Striker's neck. "We can do this the easy way or the hard way. It's up to you." With one arm still around Striker's neck, Gabe balanced himself and stood, bringing Striker up with him. He shoved him in a nearby chair.

"Who the hell are you?" Striker glared up at Gabe. "Gabe?"

The sound of his name on Lisa's lips brought Gabe
up short, and for the moment he ignored Striker. She
was standing in the doorway, her face pale, her eyes
round and a bit glazed-looking.

"Are...are you all right?" she asked. Lisa tried her
best to appear calm, but each time she thought about
what *could* have happened, her legs threatened to
buckle.

Suddenly Gabe didn't feel too steady himself. Seeing Lisa so upset was unnerving. Then Striker suddenly groaned and let out a string of vile curses.
"Where the hell did she come from?" he muttered.

Gabe gritted his teeth, barely controlling the sudden rage that Striker's foul language sent surging
through him. "I'm fine," he quickly reassured Lisa,
then, lightning swift, he turned on Striker. He grabbed
him by his shirt and pulled him halfway out of the
chair. "Watch your mouth around the lady, you
slime."

"I'm calling the cops."

All three sets of eyes focused on the captain, who
still had a death grip on the gun.

Gabe released Striker, shoving him back into the
chair. Hands up in front of him, he turned to the captain. "We don't want any trouble, Captain, but I need
some answers from this piece of sleaze before you
make your call."

For a moment, the captain continued staring at
Gabe.

With his hands still in the air, Gabe tilted his head toward Lisa. "This lady's sister is missing and we think he might know where she is."

"Please, just a few moments." Lisa added her plea to Gabe's.

When the captain looked at Lisa, he seemed to soften a bit. "Well," he drawled, hesitating. "I guess a few more minutes won't hurt." He jerked his head to glare at Striker. "But just you remember, I've got the gun."

Gabe lowered his hands, narrowed his eyes and faced Striker. "Okay, buddy boy, I've got some questions and you'd damn well better have some answers."

CHAPTER NINE

KEVIN STRIKER GLARED at Gabe. "I don't have to tell you anything," he retorted, his tone full of cocky defiance.

Striker's arrogance sent a rush of fury straight to Gabe's head. Aware that Lisa was watching, he flexed his fingers and took a deep breath in an attempt to control his temper and to control the sudden urge to punch out Striker. Beating Striker unconscious wouldn't find Danny or Dixie, he reminded himself, and sometimes intimidation could work just as well.

Gabe narrowed his eyes. "Like I said before," he warned in a soft voice, "we can do this the easy way or the hard way. It's up to you. Now where is Dixie Miller?"

Striker slid his gaze to Lisa, then back to Gabe. "I don't know."

Gabe grabbed him by the shirt and hauled him off the chair. "Where is she?" He drew back a fist and Striker's eyes widened.

"I swear I don't know!"

So much for intimidation, Gabe thought. He tightened his hold, pulling Striker closer. "Where's the money you stole?"

"I don't know what you're talking a—"

Gabe punched him. Striker moaned and doubled over, holding his gut.

Gabe jerked him upright. "Once more," he said, drawing back his fist again. "Where's Dixie Miller and where is the money you stole?"

His face still contorted with pain, Striker tried to pull away. "Okay, okay," he cried. "Just don't hit me again."

Gabe shoved him back into the chair.

Striker hugged his middle, still gasping.

"I'm waiting," Gabe snapped.

Striker slowly raised his head. "I don't have the money— No! Wait." He threw up his hands to shield his face. "I'm telling the truth. I did steal it."

"How?" Gabe demanded.

"Ah, hell. I gave the stupid bank teller a song-and-dance story about Dixie being injured and unable to come in to open an account. The teller let me take the card with me for Dixie to sign. All I had to do was forge Dixie's signature, then bring the signed card back to the bank. The rest was easy since I'm an officer in the union, too. From then on I just made regular deposits to Dixie's account."

Striker bowed his head and stared at the floor. "Don't you see? I had to do it. There was no other way. They were going to kill me if I didn't pay them what I owed."

"Who was going to kill you?" Gabe demanded.

"I don't know his name, but he sent his goons after me. They said if I didn't pay, they'd kill me."

"Do you really expect me to believe something like that?"

"Hey, man, it's God's honest truth. I had a run of bad luck at the racetrack, and the bookie I used works for this hood."

Gabe continued to stare at Striker. "Okay," he said. "So you got in over your head and stole the union money to pay off your gambling debts, but—" he paused, his eyes narrowing to deadly slits "—that still doesn't answer my first question. Where is Dixie Miller?"

Striker shook his head. "I told you I don't know. Everything was working just like I planned until—" he shifted his gaze to Lisa "—until her sister screwed things up." His voice rose. "If it hadn't been for her and her boyfriend, I wouldn't have those bastards on my tail. They took the money. Took my car, too."

Lisa bristled. "That's a lie," she said, her icy voice full of contempt. "My sister would never steal from anyone."

"Oh, yeah?" Striker's voice was like a vicious snarl. "Well, I don't give a damn if you believe me or not, but if I ever catch up with her, I'll give her something worse than just a black eye."

Lisa gasped. "Black eye!" She marched across the room to where Striker was seated. Hands on her hips, she glared at him. "What did you do to my sister?" she demanded.

"Nothing more than she deserved," he shot back.

Gabe held up his hand. "Hold it right there. Both of you," he added, looking first at Lisa, then back at Striker. "And you—" He poked Striker on the chest with his forefinger. "You'd better explain."

Striker muttered a nasty expletive. "Hell, like I said, I had it all worked out. Dixie would get blamed for stealing the union money, and I was going to pay what I owed. Then everything started going wrong." Again, he turned and glared at Lisa. "I had Dixie and her boyfriend stashed in an old cabin for safekeeping, but they gave me the slip and took the money for themselves. Now those goons are after me, and if I don't get out of the country, they'll kill me."

Lisa turned to Gabe and grasped his arm with a grip of desperation. "Gabe, he's lying." Her face was pale; her expression was a mask of misery. "I know my sister, and she's not a thief. She wouldn't touch stolen money. Even if she did take it, she only did it to give it back. She just wouldn't..." As her agonized voice trailed off into a whisper, she released her hold and stared at the floor.

Gabe ached for her, knowing that she was trying to convince herself as much as she was trying to convince him.

Everything Kevin Striker said confirmed what Gabe had suspected all along. Dixie might not have stolen the money initially, but she did take it. Lisa wanted to believe her sister took the money to give it back, but Dixie was still missing and hadn't made any effort to contact the police. Whether Lisa wanted to admit it or not, her sister was involved up to her eyeballs. Gabe felt his gut tighten with anger. And somehow, someway, Dixie had dragged Danny along for the ride.

Suddenly a prickle of awareness danced across Gabe's neck. He jerked his head toward the door and froze. For long seconds, he was only conscious of his heart pounding in his chest.

Two men stood just outside. One was tall and one was of average height. Both looked vaguely familiar. And both held guns pointing straight at him and Lisa.

"Well, well, well," the taller of the two said with a sneer. "Look who we finally caught up with." He stepped farther into the cabin.

Lisa gasped and Kevin Striker cursed. Out of the corner of his eye, Gabe saw the captain's gun waver, but he was more concerned with keeping Lisa safe.

"Gabe?" Her voice quavered. With her gaze never leaving the guns, she blindly reached out for him.

Keeping a wary eye on the two men, Gabe pulled her close, placing himself between her and the interlopers. Her hands were cold and trembling. "Just stay calm," he murmured, trying to infuse his voice with more confidence and reassurance than he felt. "If my memory serves, these are the two jokers in the Lincoln."

A shudder rippled through Lisa and he tightened his grip. "But they can't be!" she exclaimed softly.

Gabe straightened to his full height. "Who are you?" He directed his question to the taller one. "Why are you following us and what do you want?"

The man ignored Gabe, his attention on the captain. "Drop it, old man," he snapped.

The captain steadied his gun, but his face was pale. "Looks like we have a standoff," he blustered. "Leave now and no one will get hurt."

The tall man chuckled as if he found the situation amusing. "There's two of us and only one of you. You're outnumbered." His voice hardened. "So drop it."

Hidden behind Gabe, Lisa couldn't see. Seconds ticked slowly by as she waited. Her insides quivered and her legs threatened to buckle. When she heard the clatter of a single gun as it hit the floor, she flinched, somehow knowing that the captain had given in first.

"Now, kick it over here."

The gun slid across the floor.

"What do you want?" Gabe snapped.

Striker let out a strangled sound. "He wants me. They're the ones I told you about."

The tall man laughed and waved his gun at Lisa and Gabe. "And thanks to your two friends here, we found you." He strolled over and slapped Striker on the back. "We've been looking for you, old buddy. When your *friends* showed up at your apartment, we decided they might know where to find you. Your apartment manager was kind enough to supply us with the name of your friends' motel."

The short man behind him laughed. "After some *friendly* persuasion," he added.

Lisa was still confused and still trying to assimilate how the men had managed to follow them despite their precautions. "We lost them in Alexandria," she whispered. She wasn't even conscious that she'd said the words out loud until the man walked around Gabe and smiled at her suggestively, his eyes raking her from head to toe.

"You just thought you lost us, sweetheart. You were looking for a Lincoln, so we switched cars." Suddenly he grabbed Lisa's arm and yanked her toward him.

Lisa screamed and fought him, but he was too fast and too strong. Within seconds he had his arm around her neck in a choke hold.

"Let her go," Gabe snarled. With his hands doubled into fists, he took a step but froze the instant he saw the man point his gun at Lisa's temple.

"Just stay where you are or your lady friend gets the first bullet," he told Gabe as he dragged her backward.

Gabe felt his knees grow weak. Lisa's eyes were wild with terror and her face was a white mask of fear. "If you hurt her," he warned, his voice a deadly growl, "I'll kill you."

The man ignored Gabe. "Parker! Get over here," he snapped. "Our friend, Striker here, needs some of that *friendly* persuasion."

The man called Parker hesitated, glaring at his partner. "I'd rather hold the woman," he said with a sneer, stepping farther into the room. Then he shrugged and gave a nasty chuckle that set Gabe's blood boiling. "Maybe later, after our old buddy Kevin tells us what we need to know, huh, sweetheart?" He winked and patted Lisa on the cheek.

Lisa tried to control the shudder of revulsion that rippled through her as she watched the short, loathsome man walk past. There was a roaring in her ears, and spots danced before her eyes as she struggled to breathe. She sought out Gabe, hoping that by concentrating on him, she could maintain some semblance of control instead of passing out.

Gabe held her gaze, but the look on his face—a look that told her that he'd die before he let Parker touch her—sent another rush of cold fear racing through her veins.

Parker stood in front of Striker and grinned nastily. "You can't say we didn't warn you, old buddy."

Striker turned a ghastly shade of gray. "I had the money," he cried.

"Sure you did," Parker drawled. "And you were going to bring it to us, right?" He laughed. "That's why you're down here on a charter boat. Now which knee should I shatter first?" he said, pointing his gun at Striker's left knee.

His eyes fairly popping with fear, Striker shrieked. "Wait! Her sister has the money. Just give me a little more time and I swear I'll get it. I just have to find her."

Lisa kept her eyes on Gabe as Striker continued to beg. She could tell by the determined look on his face, by the tense way he held himself, that he was just waiting for an opportune moment. She'd already seen him in action once, when he'd tackled Striker. With Parker's attention focused on Striker, Lisa knew that the only thing holding Gabe back was the gun pressed against her head. If she could somehow disarm the man holding her, then they would have a fighting chance.

Oh, God, she thought. Here she was trying to figure out how to fight a man with a loaded gun pointed at her head. Just the thought made her weak all over, and for a moment, she was afraid she was going to be sick.

Lisa took short shallow breaths and swallowed several times. She had to help Gabe. If she didn't at least try to help him, he could die. She couldn't let him risk his life because of her. Somehow, some way, she had to do something.

Gabe knew the exact moment Lisa made up her mind to act. Her face was still too pale, but her dark eyes grew even darker, and the look on her face was that same stubborn expression he'd learned to recognize, a look that he'd also learned to respect.

He wanted to shout, to tell her to just hang tight, but he couldn't without drawing unwanted attention to her. He tried to convey the message with his eyes, but her expression didn't waver. Either she wasn't getting his message or she was ignoring him. Since he suspected the latter, he did the only thing he could under the circumstances—he tensed in readiness. And he waited.

Lisa slid her gaze to the captain, but he was watching Gabe, almost as if he was waiting for a signal.

Her chance to help came unexpectedly. The man holding her got careless. He was so caught up in what his partner was doing to Kevin Striker that he loosened his hold around her neck and eased off the pressure of the gun.

Lisa knew it was now or never, and she offered up a quick prayer for courage. She just hoped that she could remember the self-defense tactics that Barry had taught her.

Her pulse raced. Adrenaline began pumping through her veins. Suddenly she opened her mouth, ducked her chin and sank her teeth into her captor's arm. At the same time, she brought her elbow back, aiming low for his groin.

The man howled with pain, dropped the gun and Lisa scrambled away from him.

The minute the gun hit the floor, Gabe shoved Parker into Striker. Then, lightning swift, he turned on the one who had held Lisa. He slammed his right fist into the man's gut, then followed up with another quick left blow to his chin.

The man went down, and Gabe grabbed Lisa's hand. "Let's get out of here!" he yelled, pulling her to the door.

Lisa didn't need further encouragement. Within seconds they were through the doorway. With Gabe fast on her heels, they jumped onto the dock and sprinted down the pier toward the parking lot.

"The keys!" he yelled. "Give me the keys!"

Still running, Lisa dug in her pocket. "Here." Like a runner in a relay race, she handed them to Gabe.

Within seconds he had the door open. He jumped into the driver's seat and turned on the ignition. The minute Lisa was inside, he shoved the gearshift into first and floored the accelerator.

Lisa quickly snapped on her seat belt. Only then did she venture a glance back at the boat, but since the cabin door was on the opposite side from the parking lot, she couldn't tell what was happening. "What about the captain?"

"He'll be okay. Those men wanted Striker and us, not him. The first phone booth we come to, I'll call the police . . . anonymously."

"Anonymously?"

Gabe shifted and turned a corner. "Even though Striker admitted he stole the money, he also said Dixie and Danny took the money from him. I don't intend to get bogged down with the police or the FBI until we locate Dixie and Danny and find out the truth. I'm sure Danny will try to contact me sooner or later."

Terrified and convinced that any minute she'd see either the thugs or Kevin Striker running down the pier to come after them, Lisa kept watching until they drove out of sight of the marina.

KEVIN STRIKER FLATTENED himself against the outside of the boat's cabin and waited, counting the seconds and also counting himself lucky. Leo Jones was out cold, and while the captain had been busy scuffling with Parker, he'd been able to make his escape. He knew from the sounds coming through the thin wall that the captain had overpowered Parker. He could hear the captain's booming voice radioing a message to the cops.

Kevin knew that any minute the place would be swarming with police. His instinct was to run like hell, but he didn't want to chance running into that big bastard Lisa had called Gabe, not yet, so he waited and watched until the Jeep drove out of sight. The minute it disappeared around the block, he scrambled off the boat onto the pier.

Stumbling and holding his stomach, he half ran, half limped the length of the pier. Any second he expected to either hear gunshots or sirens.

Once he reached solid ground, he ventured a quick glance over his shoulder. The boat sat quietly, and there wasn't a sign of life aboard. Still keeping a wary eye on the boat, he hurried to his rental car. Within minutes he turned left and headed west on Highway

98. In the distance, he heard the scream of police sirens.

Just as a precaution, he figured the first thing he had better do was ditch the rental car and get another one. The next thing he needed was a gun. Any pawnshop should do. Kevin grimaced. Now that his escape route had been cut off, he'd have to make alternative plans. With those goons behind bars, at least now he'd have a little more time, time to find Dixie Miller and get his money back.

Kevin leaned forward and fished out the extra billfold stuffed into his back pocket. Thanks to his own foresight and Dixie's boyfriend, he now had a good idea where to start looking.

Flipping open the billfold to the driver's license, he quickly glanced down and scanned the information. Daniel Gabriel Jordan III. Kevin frowned, again remembering that Lisa LeBlanc had called the man who was with her Gabe. Now that he thought about it, the man did resemble Dixie's boyfriend. Were they related? Probably were. Most likely father and son, he decided.

Kevin spied the birthdate on the license and raised his eyebrows. The age was right, but since when had Dixie begun robbing the cradle? Shrugging, he focused on the address. As he returned his full attention to the highway, a slow smile spread across his face. Yes sir, he thought, if he could get his hands on that money, getting out of the country would be a breeze.

GABE DROVE as if the demons of hell were after them, but for a change, Lisa was glad. His reckless driving gave her something to focus on. If she let herself think about everything that had just happened, she knew she would start screaming, and if she started screaming, she wasn't sure she could stop.

Once he was sure they were far enough away from the marina, he stopped just long enough to call the police.

Daylight was just breaking over the horizon. With each car that went by, she tensed, terrified that she would see the faces of the two thugs, or worse, Kevin Striker. It was only when Gabe pulled into the parking lot of a small motel that she realized they had left Destin behind and were now in another small town.

"I'll get us a couple of rooms," he told her.

Lisa watched him stroll toward the small office. The minute he disappeared inside, she scrambled to the driver's side. Reaching beneath the seat, she withdrew the holster that held Barry's old handgun. Unsnapping the catch, she pulled out the gun. Clutching it, she turned in the seat to stare at the highway that ran alongside the parking lot. With each minute that ticked by and with each car and truck that whizzed past, her grip tightened on the gun. She had often wondered if she would be able to fire the gun if the occasion ever arose. And even now she wasn't sure she could actually pull the trigger, but holding it made her feel better.

When Gabe returned, the first thing he saw was Lisa in the driver's seat, holding the gun. The next thing he noticed was her face. Unease crawled down his spine.

He approached her slowly. "Lisa, we're safe now," he said softly. She didn't so much as blink an eye. "We don't need a gun," he continued. *Easy does it,* he thought. "Why don't I put it back for now?" Cautiously he reached for the gun, but her grip remained firm. "Come on, sweetheart, let me have it." Patting her hand, he gently pried it loose from her fingers. "I promise they didn't follow us this time," he said, slipping the weapon back into the holster and sliding it beneath the seat.

For several seconds she still didn't move. Then she clenched her hands into tight fists, slid across the seat and stared straight ahead.

Gabe fumbled in his pocket, but it was empty. He needed a cigarette in the worst way, and he didn't even have a damn toothpick. Keeping a wary eye on Lisa, he got in behind the wheel and turned on the ignition. He wanted her to talk to him, but he suspected she was in shock. Gabe silently cursed as he pulled the Jeep around to the back of the motel. He knew next to nothing about how to deal with someone who had been traumatized.

The minute he parked the Jeep, he jumped out, went around to Lisa's side and opened her door.

"Come on, sweetheart, let's get you inside."

Lisa felt frozen to the seat, and she had to force her legs to move. As if in a dream, she was aware that

Gabe was there, trying to help her. His soothing, steady voice was a lifeline and it took everything within her to concentrate on what he was saying.

If she could just hold on until they were safe, she would be okay. She kept telling herself that they were safe, that there was no way the two men could find them. Gabe had promised they didn't follow this time.

He unlocked the motel room, pulled her inside and flipped on the light. He led her to the bed. "Sit here and wait. I'll be right back as soon as I get the luggage.

Lisa wasn't sure how much time passed before he returned. All she knew was that, for the moment, they were safe.

"It's not much," Gabe said, depositing the luggage on the floor and motioning at the room, "but we both need to get some rest since neither of us got any sleep last night." He closed the door, locked it, then walked over to another door located near the dresser. He was babbling, talking nonsense, but he didn't know what else to do. Maybe he should try to get her to a doctor, but he hoped that if he kept talking, she would snap out it.

"I was able to get connecting rooms," he continued. He walked over to a door in the middle of a wall and unlocked it. Through the doorway was another identical room. "I thought you might feel safer that way."

Something in her expression altered, almost as if something he'd said clicked. Lisa looked around, but he knew she wasn't seeing the room. Her eyes were still glazed and she was pale. She had a fragile look about her, almost as if any sudden move could cause her to shatter into tiny pieces.

He knew that she was holding onto her emotions by a thread, that she was holding at bay the reality of what they had just been through. And he also knew that all those pent-up feelings had to be dealt with. He only hoped she wouldn't freak out on him.

"We have to talk," he said softly. "Striker was our only lead and we have to decide what we're going to do next."

When she didn't respond but continued to stare at him, he tried another tack. "At least we know that Dixie and Danny are still alive," he offered. "And I still think they will contact us, sooner or later."

When Lisa heard the mention of her sister, the glazed look disappeared, and her eyes flashed with a sudden intensity so strong that he felt as if he were witnessing a volcano erupt.

"They're alive no thanks to Kevin Striker!" she shouted. "Lying bastard. I don't care what he said." She shook her fist. "My sister is not a thief."

Lisa jumped up from the bed and began to pace from one end of the small room to the other end. "Dixie would never be a part of stealing money from the union. She loves her job. And *if* she took that money from Striker—and not for one minute do I think she did—she only took it to give it back." Lisa suddenly halted near the only chair in the room. "Oh,

God," she whispered. "Why hasn't she called? Oh..."
She blindly reached out for the chair arm then collapsed into the chair.

Looking into her eyes was like reliving every minute of the horror they had just escaped from. Then she covered her face with both her hands and began to shake. Gabe rushed over to her and knelt down. He gently grabbed her shoulders. "Lisa, we're safe now," he murmured, knowing that her outburst was simply an emotional release and had more to do with the ordeal they had just been through than her sister's guilt or innocence. "They can't hurt you. We got away. By now they're probably in custody."

When she lifted her head, her eyes filled, and tears spilled over to trickle down her cheeks. Gabe couldn't help himself. He gathered her into his arms.

Up until now she'd been so brave, so gutsy and independently strong. Each time they had come up against an obstacle, she had bounced back and come out fighting. But witnessing her real vulnerability was more than he could take, and at that moment, he felt something deep inside him snap as he rocked her back and forth, murmuring reassurances.

Everyone had a breaking point, he realized. And just as Lisa had finally reached hers, he knew that he had reached his. He had no idea, not even a clue, how they would find Dixie and Danny now that their only lead was gone, but he could no longer deny or ignore what he felt for the woman in his arms

He had wanted to deny his feelings for her, had tried all along. Even on the boat, he had still turned a deaf ear to what his heart was telling him when he had been willing to die for her.

Gabe had always been a firm believer that love was something that took time to develop, took time to grow, not something that hit you in the gut and turned you inside out when you least expected it.

But you've never met anyone like Lisa LeBlanc, he silently acknowledged.

"Lisa, I…" His voice trailed away to a whisper, and as always, words failed him, so Gabe tried to show what he felt the only other way he knew how.

Loosening his hold on her just enough to find her lips, he kissed her with all the pent-up passion he had in him, the passion he could never find words eloquent enough to express.

Gabe was fully prepared to back off at the first sign she showed that this wasn't what she wanted too, but she didn't pull away. She clung to him, responding with a fervor that almost bordered on desperation.

For seconds all he could think about was the softness of her eager lips, the way her mouth tasted, warm and sweet with a touch of innocence, the little groans of pleasure she made, the way her small but perfect breasts felt pressed against his chest.

He could feel her heart thudding in rhythm with his own, and at that moment he knew with unfailing certainty that he wanted more than just a kiss, that just a kiss would never be enough between them.

But what about later? Right now, she's scared, vulnerable and needy. But later...

Gabe wanted to ignore the small voice of reason that kept intruding. But the voice kept nagging and wouldn't go away, and he knew he couldn't ignore it and still live with himself. He cared about Lisa, too much so to simply satisfy his own needs without considering the consequences.

Mustering every bit of control he could, he pulled away. "Lisa," he whispered against her lips. "I want you." He paused, giving her time to assimilate his meaning. "But I don't want to do this unless..." He seized her face between his hands, and knowing that he would see the truth in her eyes, he stared deeply. "I have to know... I mean, I—"

Her gaze never leaving his, Lisa placed her forefinger against his lips. The look in her eyes was a reflection of his own desire. She seemed to know and understand what he was asking, almost as if their minds were in perfect harmony.

"Yes," she whispered. "Right now, I need you too. My answer is yes."

CHAPTER TEN

As GABE effortlessly swept Lisa into his arms, she didn't dare question too closely the decision she had made. Nothing in her life made sense anymore. Everything that had happened during the past week had been like a nightmare, one that wouldn't end.

But through it all, through all the uncertainties and danger, she'd been able to rely on Gabe. His steady, unfailing strength and his genuine concern for her and her sister had been like a lifeline.

What she'd told him the day he'd first kissed her hadn't changed. She still didn't know him, not in the sense of time, but whether she'd known him for a day or for a year didn't seem to matter now. The only thing she was sure of at the moment was that she wanted him and she needed him. She needed a solid reality to hold on to, something that would blot out the horror of being chased and held at gun point. When Gabe reached the bed, he didn't release her immediately, but took her mouth in another searing kiss, a kiss that robbed her of every coherent thought and seemed to melt her bones.

When he finally pulled away, he eased them both down onto the bed. For a moment he hesitated, and a worried frown appeared on his face. Then he closed his eyes, and with a groan born of pure frustration, he shook his head.

"Gabe, what's wrong?"

After a moment he opened his eyes. "I'm afraid I've started something I can't finish, not the way I would like to, anyway."

Lisa swallowed hard. "I don't understand."

He turned his head to stare into space. "I didn't think. Dammit to hell, I just didn't think."

By this time, she was beginning to get alarmed. "Gabe?"

Shoving himself away, he stood and raked his hand through his hair. "I can't protect you," he said bluntly. "It's been a long time... I mean, I don't have any—I didn't plan for this..."

When it dawned on Lisa exactly what he was trying to say, she felt a sharp stab of disappointment. She should be glad that he cared enough to act so responsibly, she thought. So why wasn't she?

Then she smiled, a slow, knowing smile, as she raised up on her elbow and reached for his hand. "We don't have to go all the way." The moment she said the words out loud, she felt as if her face was suddenly on fire. She ducked her head and laughed. "Oh, God, how embarrassing. I sound like a teenager."

Gabe chuckled. "That's only fair since I feel like one."

His gruff confession did funny things to her insides, and slowly, she raised her head. What she saw on his face wiped away any doubts she might have had and gave her the confidence to reach out, take his hand and tug gently. He was a far cry from a teenager. He was a man, with a man's needs and a man's desires.

"There are other, almost as satisfying, ways," she said softly.

"I know." He allowed her to pull him down beside her. "But I'm not sure I can trust myself," he replied. "Each time I touch you, I can't seem to think straight."

"Stop worrying," she whispered, reaching for the buttons on his shirt. "*I* trust you, and between us, somehow we'll manage."

The look he gave her seared her to her very soul, and her fingers shook as she unbuttoned his shirt. When he shrugged out of the shirt, she couldn't take her eyes off him.

He was every bit as beautiful as she had imagined he would be. A liberal sprinkling of dark hair covered him, starting at the top of his broad, muscular chest and spreading downward, narrowing to a V over his hard, flat stomach. He was tanned and fit and all male. Her camera would love him, she thought absently, feeling the familiar itch she always got when she knew she was viewing a perfect shot.

"My turn," he whispered urgently.

Lisa let her fingers trail down his chest before she leaned away. Intending to rid herself of her sweatshirt, she reached for the bottom band, but he grabbed her hands and shook his head.

"Uh-uh." He turned her palms outward, drew them up to his lips and kissed each one. "I said it's my turn."

The feel of his lips against her palms was more erotic than she'd ever thought possible. She wasn't sure just what she'd expected, but it was clear that Gabe had his own ideas. He eased her down on her back and nuzzled her neck just below her ear, his hot breath making her shiver with need. With his hand, he started at her stomach and began a slow, sensuous journey, rubbing and gently massaging, and inching his fingers upward beneath her shirt.

By the time he'd almost reached her breasts, Lisa was breathing hard and her breasts ached for his touch. But instead of touching her there, he slid his hand beneath her back and unfastened her bra.

When he finally did touch her breasts, his fingers brushed lightly over the now-sensitive tips of her nipples, and the fire that had been building in her belly erupted into a raging inferno. When she cried out, Gabe covered her cry with his mouth, and at the same time, both his hands cupped her breasts, his thumbs teasing her nipples until they were hard.

He plunged his tongue into her mouth and explored it, tasting every hidden crevice. What he was doing to her was sheer torture, but it was beyond ecstasy, and as Lisa grabbed his bare back and kneaded his taut muscles, she didn't ever want him to stop his sensuous assault.

Suddenly Gabe enfolded her within his arms. In one fluid movement, he rolled over onto his back, and she found herself stretched out on top of him. Bracing her hands on his shoulders, she wiggled farther down. The pressure of him, swollen and hard, against her set off a yearning so strong that she began to tremble. It was only then that Gabe finally tugged her shirt over her head and threw it, along with her bra, aside.

Taking both her breasts in his hands, he sucked first on one, then the other. The feel of his rough tongue on her nipples and his hungry mouth pulling at her breasts sent her over the edge.

Lisa cried out and began to writhe, seeking to get even closer than their clothes would allow. After what seemed like an eternity, he finally let go of her breasts, grabbed her hips and pulled down hard, twisting and grinding, seeking to give her the release she was begging for.

With one last cry of passion, she felt her world shatter into a thousand pieces of undulating sensation, sending tremor after tremor of rapture surging through her core.

Afterward, for long seconds, she was too stunned to move. And all too soon the tremors eased and eventually died away. Feeling limp but thoroughly satiated, she finally collapsed against him.

Several minutes passed before she could think coherently. Gabe's hands were still clasped possessively around her hips. His breathing against her neck was shallow but harsh. And he was still rock hard against her thighs.

"Oh, Gabe," she whispered as she lifted her lower body and slid her hand down between them. "Let me—"

"No." He caught her hand, and in one easy motion, he shifted her onto the bed beside him. "Just be still for a few minutes."

"But I want to," she protested softly, stroking his whiskered cheek.

"I know." His voice was rough with strain. "But this time was for you. Next time, when I'm better prepared, will be my turn." He turned his head and lightly brushed a kiss against her forehead. Then with a groan, he pushed himself off the bed.

As Lisa watched him stiffly walk over to the window, she was well aware of the price he was paying for his unselfishness, and the thought was humbling.

As he stood there staring outside, filtered sunlight drenched him, and she was content to simply lie there and look at him.

He remained perfectly still, his back ramrod straight, then slowly, bit by bit, he seemed to relax. "You okay?" he asked, with his back still facing her.

Lisa knew exactly what he was asking. She also knew his question had nothing to do with their lovemaking and everything to do with their run-in with the two hoods.

"Better," she answered. "Much better," she emphasized, realizing that it was true. "I'm not exactly sure what happened. I do know that I've never been so scared in all my life, and I guess I just kind of freaked."

"You had every right to."

"I guess so, but—"

Gabe turned to look at her. "I know so. It's hard to face the truth sometimes, but to face it at gunpoint..." He shrugged. "For your sake, I didn't want to believe what Striker said about Dixie. But I suspected it all along. There was just too much evidence—"

"Whoa, wait a minute here." She pushed herself up to a sitting position. "Run that by me again. I'm not sure I'm following you."

Gabe shoved his fingers through his hair. He didn't want to hurt Lisa any more than she already had been, but it was time she admitted the truth. Admitting the truth now would be better in the long run than later. Now they could make plans. Farther down the road would be too late.

"Don't you think it's a little strange that Dixie hasn't contacted you or the police yet?"

"Are you suggesting that my sister stole the money from Striker deliberately and intends to keep it?"

"Not exactly."

When Gabe hesitated, Lisa felt a sudden chill she strongly suspected had nothing to do with being naked from the waist up. Spying her sweatshirt near the edge of the rumpled bed, she snatched it up and quickly slipped it over her head. But the chill didn't go away.

Maybe she was wrong, she thought, still hoping that her mind was playing tricks on her. Maybe she had simply misunderstood him. She wanted to be wrong. *Oh, God,* she thought, *please let me be wrong*.

Lisa drew in a deep breath and squared her shoulders. "What exactly *are* you suggesting, then?" she asked evenly.

Gabe cleared his throat. "At first I did think she was the thief. Even you have to admit there was a lot of circumstantial evidence against her. But now I don't believe she meant to get involved initially. I think—no, I know that Striker set her up to take the rap, but things didn't work out the way he'd planned. Dixie saw an opportunity and she took it, plain and simple. And I think that once Danny stops listening to his hormones and comes to his senses, he'll make her turn the money over to the authorities."

He paused, a thoughtful frown crinkling his brow. "If worse comes to worst, and we can find her before the cops do, we can persuade her to turn the money over. Then we can tell the police that the reason she hadn't turned it in before was that she was afraid that Striker or those goons would get to her first."

A bone deep shiver shook Lisa and she wrapped her arms tightly around her waist, hugging herself against the invasive cold. And still a part of her hoped, a part of her wanted to believe that Gabe couldn't possibly mean what he was saying.

"From the beginning you thought that my sister stole that money?" she whispered, her words both a question and a statement.

Gabe went very still as if just realizing that she was yet struggling with the fact that he could think that Dixie was guilty.

"All the evidence pointed to that possibility," he said gently.

"And now you think that Dixie stole the money from Striker on purpose, to keep it for herself." Her voice rose as she carefully slid off the bed to stand. "And—and you're insinuating that she's somehow lured a seventeen-year-old boy—your son—into helping her. In other words, no matter what I've told you and no matter how the *evidence* has changed, you think Dixie is guilty, one way or the other." She glared at him. "My God, what kind of monster do you think my sister is?"

"Lisa, I—" Gabe took a step toward her but the look she gave him dared him to come any closer.

"All this time I thought you wanted to help," she continued, "that all that *concern* you demonstrated was genuine. I can't believe what a fool I've been—"

"No!" In two giant steps, he closed the distance between them and grabbed her. "I do care about you, I—"

Lisa wrenched free and backed away from him. "You haven't heard a word I've said to you about my sister. All you cared about—I repeat, *all* you cared about was finding your son. The rest—" she motioned toward the bed "—the rest was a smoke screen, a slight diversion, a way to pass the time." Even as the hateful words spewed out, she wanted to stop them, but it was as if she no longer had control.

"You just played along, hoping I would lead you to your son!" she shouted. "What did you plan to do then?" When he started to answer, she threw up her hands. "No, wait! Let me guess. Since Danny is only seventeen, he's still a minor, and if you can prove that Dixie is guilty, then that lets your son off the hook. Well, let me say this one more time, one last time," she stated in a deadly, cold voice. *"My sister is no thief. Do you hear me?"*

"Lisa, please listen."

Lisa ignored the stricken look on Gabe's face. "No. I'm tired of listening to your lies," she snapped. "I want you out of this room ... now!"

Gabe opened his mouth, but she cut him off. "Don't—just don't say another word or I swear I'll leave you stranded."

Gabe told himself that her reaction was to be expected. She was just hurt at the moment. Her anger was directed at the truth, not him. After she'd had time to think things through, she'd calm down, then they could talk.

Taking a deep breath, he walked past her, picking up his shirt and duffel bag. At the door of the adjoining room, he hesitated, still hoping she would say something.

She continued to stare at him, her dark eyes full of contempt. Then she whirled around, her rigid back and stiff shoulders saying more than words could ever convey about how she felt.

With a small sigh of defeat, Gabe stepped through the doorway into the adjoining room and pulled the door shut behind him.

FOR LONG MOMENTS after she heard the door close, Lisa maintained her rigid stance and continued staring at the faded print on the wall. The silence in the shabby room was deafening, and a dull ache began to throb behind her gritty eyes.

Slowly, as if in a trance, she made her way to the bed. She took one look at the wrinkled coverlet and the dull ache grew sharper. It seemed impossible that only a few minutes had passed since she and Gabe had—

She winced. No, she wouldn't think about that.

Not now.

She just couldn't, not when she felt so confused, and . . . so damn empty.

Determined to put everything from her mind, she eased down on the bed and curled into a tight ball. She didn't want to think, not about being held at gunpoint by the two thugs, not about Kevin Striker or Dixie, Danny, or the stolen money and most of all, not about Gabe and his deceit.

Lisa moaned and squeezed her eyes shut. If she could just go to sleep, just sink into mindless oblivion for a while, then later she could sort things out. Later, after she'd rested, she would be stronger. Later she would deal with her ravaged emotions.

As GABE WAITED and listened on the other side of the door, he kept telling himself that eventually she would cool down. He hadn't imagined that there was something extraordinary between them, and it was incomprehensible to him that she could throw it all away without a second thought.

He sure as hell couldn't.

Surely, any minute, she would come through the door and want to talk. And if she didn't... Gabe didn't want to think about that possibility.

He dropped his duffel bag, pulled on his shirt and slowly buttoned it. "Lousy timing," he muttered.

She'd been through a lot in the past twenty-four hours. He should have been more thoughtful, more sensitive, and he should have waited until later to talk to her about Dixie.

If only she would give him the chance, he could help her. Together they could figure out some way to help her sister.

But first she'd have to open the damn door.

Several minutes passed, and when it became obvious that she wasn't going to, he turned, and with a sinking feeling in his stomach that he had blown the most important chance of his life, he walked to the bed.

A sudden rush of pure exhaustion swept over him
and Gabe sank down on the bed. He'd almost give his
right arm for a cigarette.

*"You never listen. You only hear what you want to
hear."*

The accusations in Danny's letter were like ghosts
haunting his mind.

Gabe groaned and sprawled on his back, bringing
his arm up across his eyes.

*"You haven't heard a word I said to you about my
sister."*

Gabe winced, and the sinking feeling in his gut
grew, like a deep gaping hole in his soul.

Could they be right? Both of them? All these
years . . . all this past week, had he only heard what he
wanted to hear? Had he been so pigheaded, so all-fired
self-assured and self-righteous that he had ignored the
opinions and ideas of the people who meant the most
to him?

IT WAS LATE AFTERNOON when Gabe finally dragged
himself up to sit on the edge of the bed. He'd tossed
and turned and dozed off and on, but he didn't feel
any more rested than he had before.

Typically for the time of year, the cool, pleasant
morning had turned into a hot sultry afternoon. The
small motel room was like a sauna, and Gabe realized
that he was covered with a fine sheen of sweat.

Pushing himself off the bed, he headed straight for
the window. Below it was a metal box that contained

the air-conditioning unit. Turning on the switch, he stood in front of it for several seconds, hoping the blast of cool air would help clear his foggy head, but all he could think about was Lisa.

Had she been able to sleep? Was she hungry? Was she still angry? Did she even care that he'd died a thousand deaths thinking about how she had coldly dismissed him and completely denied what they had shared?

Gabe grimaced and ventured a glance toward the closed connecting door. Now what? he wondered. Should he wait for her to make the first move or should he? Knowing how stubborn she could be and remembering how furious she was, he figured that hell might just freeze over before she'd admit she was wrong.

And what if she isn't wrong? What if you're the one who's wrong?

As much as he wanted to ignore that possibility, as much as he had tried all day to ignore it, he couldn't.

"Yeah, right," he muttered, finally acknowledging and accepting the fact that *he'd* have to be the one to apologize. *He'd* have to be the one to admit that he could have been wrong.

Then a sudden thought jolted him, sending a rush of panic through him. What if she didn't give him the chance? What if she'd taken off while he was sleeping?

Narrowing his eyes, he reached up and shoved the flimsy curtain aside. He squinted against the glare.

When he spotted Lover in the parking lot, he let out a heavy sigh. At least she hadn't left him stranded as she had threatened to do. That had to be a good sign, didn't it?

Gabe turned away from the window. First he'd take a shower, he decided. Then he'd phone his aunt, just in case Danny had called home.

The thought that he was procrastinating ran through his mind as he rummaged through his duffel bag and pulled out a clean pair of underwear, jeans and a shirt. Assuring himself that he wasn't, that he simply wanted time to think of exactly the right words to say to Lisa, he headed for the bathroom.

Twenty minutes later, Gabe ignored his growling stomach as he punched out his aunt's number. The phone only rang once before she answered.

"Aunt Bessie? It's Gabe."

"Oh, Gabriel, I'm so glad you finally called."

Gabe immediately detected tears and excitement in her voice. Suddenly afraid, he tensed. "What's wrong?"

"I've heard from Danny," she blurted out.

CHAPTER ELEVEN

BEFORE GABE HAD TIME to catch his breath, his aunt rushed on. "He's okay. Oh, Gabriel, thank God he's safe. But he wouldn't tell me where he was. I told him you'd been looking for him, and that I was sure you would check in sometime today, so he said he'd try again later tonight."

"Whoa, Aunt Bessie, slow down." Relief, like a warm spring rain, washed over him.

Safe. Danny was safe.

Gabe felt as if his whole upside-down world had just been righted. Over the past few days, he'd had his doubts about Danny's chances of survival, but up until now, he'd been afraid to give voice to them. He was just superstitious enough to believe that giving those doubts a voice might make them all too real, real enough to come true.

"Sweetheart, are you sure he didn't say where he was?"

"Oh, I'm positive about that. I asked him several times."

"Did he say anything else? Anything at all about—" Gabe hesitated. He wanted to ask about Dixie, but for the moment he'd forgotten that his aunt didn't know about her yet. For that matter she didn't know about Lisa, either, and Bessie would insist on being told every detail. Attempting an explanation right now would take up too much precious time.

"—anything at all," he finally finished lamely, glancing at his watch. It was four o'clock. If he and Lisa left immediately, he might just make it home in time for Danny's next call.

There was a pregnant pause on the line before his aunt finally answered. "No, I believe I remembered everything he told me, but let me check my notes. As soon as I hung up the phone, I wrote it all down so I wouldn't forget."

He could hear his aunt muttering, going over what she had written.

"No," she said brightly. "He didn't mention anything else."

Gabe couldn't help smiling. "You did good, Aunt Bessie. I'm sure you remembered everything just fine. If he calls again before I get there, make certain you tell him to keep calling until he talks to me."

"Oh, goodness," she replied. "Let me write that down so I can tell him word for word."

Before he hung up the phone, Gabe slowly repeated the message for his aunt again. For several moments afterward, he stood there with his eyes closed, his hand still resting on the receiver. Excitement invaded his entire being. He'd been given a second chance, a chance to set things right with his son.

Gabe turned and stared at the door to Lisa's room. Now if Lisa would just give him another chance....

Gabe sighed. He really didn't hold out much hope that she would, but at least now he had the perfect excuse to restore a semblance of peace between them, he thought.

Taking a deep breath, he walked to the connecting door and rapped sharply three times.

"Lisa," he called out. "Open up. I have to talk to you." Several seconds passed. He cocked his head toward the door and listened, but he didn't hear anything. Maybe she was sleeping.

"Lisa?"

He knocked again and called out louder. When there was still no answer, his pulse began to race. Was she simply ignoring him, or was she even in the room?

With a less than steady hand, he reached down and twisted the doorknob. He was surprised to discover that it wasn't locked.

Shoving the door open, he stepped inside and glanced around. The bed was rumpled and empty, Lisa's suitcase was open, and the faint sound of running water came from behind the closed bathroom door.

Gabe sighed. She was in the shower. Paranoid. He was just being paranoid, he thought as he stalked across the room. He pounded on the bathroom door. "Lisa? I have to talk to you, now!" he shouted.

Immediately, the shower stopped.

"What are you doing in my room?" Her voice was muffled, but even muffled, he could tell she was irate.

Gabe rubbed his neck. "Look, I just spoke to my aunt. Danny called her."

At first there was no response, then suddenly the door swung open. A rush of steamy heat hit him full force. The minute the steam dissipated and he saw Lisa, a different kind of heat hit him, a heat that came from inside his own body and spread rapidly to his groin.

Without makeup, the smattering of freckles across her nose and cheeks were more pronounced. Her wet hair was slicked back and still dripping. She was clutching the lapels of a flimsy cream-colored robe together, and it was obvious she hadn't bothered to dry off. The silky material clung to her, outlining her breasts, her dark nipples and the even darker place at the apex of her thighs.

"Are they okay? Did he say where they were?"

It took a monumental effort for Gabe to pull himself together, and for a moment, he wasn't sure he could talk. He swallowed hard and cleared his throat.

"Danny didn't mention Dixie at all." The minute he saw the spark of hope in her eyes die, he felt as if he'd just been punched. "But he's going to call again later tonight," he quickly added, hoping to wipe at least some of the disappointment from her face. "I figure if we can get on the road, we can be there by the time he phones, and you can ask him about Dixie then."

"She has to be with him. She has to be..." Her voice trailed away and her lower lip trembled. After a moment she cleared her throat and squared her shoulders. "Why wouldn't he just simply tell your aunt where he was?"

"I don't know, but I'm sure he has a good reason."

Lisa's head snapped up. "Unless—" she paused "—unless he was afraid to. He might think that Kevin Striker is still after them or...or they could have found out that the FBI is looking for them."

Lisa headed for her suitcase. "I wouldn't put it past those agents to bug our phones, and if your son is as smart as you say he is, then he's probably already figured that out."

She bent down to rummage through the clothes inside. The thin robe hugged her still damp hips, leaving nothing to the imagination. Again Gabe experienced a rush of heat.

Lisa abruptly straightened and turned to face him. Gabe knew by the look of sudden awareness on her face that there was no use pretending, no use trying to hide what he felt.

For an instant, he saw an answering flicker of desire in her eyes. Then it was gone.

"If you'll excuse me," she said curtly, "I'd like to get dressed. The sooner I do, the sooner we can get on the road."

Her words were cold and emotionless. A part of her might still desire him, he thought, but in her mind, he had betrayed her trust. And he'd always known from the beginning what the consequences would be for anyone who betrayed her.

The apology he had carefully rehearsed lodged in his throat, and he couldn't get the words past his tongue. She wouldn't believe him, anyway, he decided. Not now. Maybe not ever.

But could he really blame her? If the situation was reversed and she had accused Danny of being a thief, wouldn't he have reacted just as defensively, just as outraged?

Gabe felt as if a heavy weight had suddenly settled on his chest. "I'll take care of the motel bill and wait for you at the Jeep," he muttered. Maybe later he could try to talk to her. It was a long drive to Ponchatoula, plenty of time to apologize.

Feeling somewhat better, he turned away and walked back to his room, firmly closing the connecting door behind him.

Staring at the closed door, Lisa wondered how long it would take for the desire she still felt for him to go away.

Slipping off her robe, she slowly dressed in a pair of soft, faded jeans and a blue cotton-knit sweater. For the first time since she had buried Barry, she had allowed herself to trust a man. She had allowed herself to feel more than just friendship. She had thought that Gabe was an honorable man, someone worthy of her trust, someone she could depend on. How could she have been so wrong about him?

Lisa sighed and walked into the bathroom. She didn't have an answer, and time was running out.

She glanced at her hair dryer but decided that completely drying her hair would take too long. She picked up a towel and briskly towel-dried her hair.

Once Danny called home again, and they found out where he and Dixie were, they could finally get to the bottom of the whole ugly mess and get on with their lives. Gabriel Jordan would go back to his oil rigs in the Gulf of Mexico and she would return to Des Allemands and her studio.

Eyeing her reflection in the bathroom mirror, she combed out the tangles in her hair and pulled the still-damp tresses back, securing them with a wide barrette.

After a hasty application of makeup, she gathered her scattered toiletries into a canvas bag and marched back into the bedroom. Throwing the bag inside the suitcase, she closed it and yanked the zipper around the edges.

Why *hadn't* Danny mentioned that Dixie was with him when he had called? she wondered, still hovering over her suitcase. The thought had been nagging her since Gabe had first told her that his son had phoned.

What if Dixie wasn't with Danny? What if she *had* taken the money and run, as Gabe had suggested?

Lisa closed her eyes and dark anger bubbled inside, anger and shame directed at herself for even thinking such disloyal thoughts about her sister.

Her eyes suddenly snapped open. Gabe had done this to her, she fumed. She would never have suspected her sister of anything so underhanded if he hadn't planted the idea in her head in the first place.

Lisa took a firm hold of the suitcase handle and dragged it to the door. She would do well to remember just where *his* loyalties lay.

Opening the door, she pulled the suitcase to the other side, then yanked the door closed behind her. Setting her mouth in a grim line of determination, she headed for the Jeep.

From now on, she would make damn sure that Gabriel Jordan knew exactly where *her* loyalties lay.

GABE SAT in the passenger seat and stared straight ahead as the miles raced by. Dusk had faded into darkness, and the two hamburgers and large order of fries he'd gulped down earlier felt like a sour lump sitting in the pit of his stomach. Lisa hadn't spoken a word to him since they pulled away from the drive-up window of the fast-food restaurant in Pensacola.

He squinted in the dark at his watch. A couple of hours more and they should be in Ponchatoula, but each time he thought about apologizing to her, his stomach twisted into yet another knot.

He was both amazed and disgusted with himself. For years he had worked with some of the roughest men in the oil business, and never once had he hesitated to say what was on his mind. So why was speaking his mind to one tiny woman such a daunting prospect?

Because you love her, and there's a damn good chance you could screw up and lose her for good.

Gabe shifted uncomfortably in his seat and turned to stare at Lisa's shadowy profile. If he didn't speak up, it was certain that he would lose her. *Damned if you do and damned if you don't,* he thought.

"Lisa, I think we need to talk about what happened this morning. I want to apologize—"

"As far as I'm concerned, there's nothing left to say. We both made a mistake. Just chalk it up to the tension of the moment."

Gabe realized his error instantly. She'd completely misunderstood what he was trying to say. Her flip answer stunned him, but worse, her cool dismissal of their lovemaking was like an unexpected slap in the face.

He had been more than willing to admit that he *might* have made a mistake about her sister, but he'd be damned if he'd concede that their lovemaking was a mistake. Nothing in his whole life had felt so right.

"I think we're talking about two different things here. I'm apologizing for my high-handed attitude about your sister."

"So you've changed your mind *again?* Now you've decided that Dixie might be innocent, after all?" She laughed, but without humor. "I swear, you must think I was born yesterday. Give me a break."

"Dammit to hell," he roared. "I'm trying to tell you that I love you."

It was Lisa's turn to be stunned into silence, and it took every bit of concentration she could muster to keep from running Lover off the road. She gripped the steering wheel tightly.

"What kind of game do you think you're playing?" she asked through gritted teeth.

"No game," he retorted stiffly. "Just the truth this time."

"This time? Ha! That's a laugh. And what about next time? You wouldn't know the truth if it bit you on the butt."

The angry words seemed to just tumble out, and Lisa instantly regretted that she'd said them. And worse, she felt like a fool for resorting to such tactics. Even in the dark, she could sense Gabe's hostile glare.

In all her thirty-five years, she had never felt so out of control, and she'd never been more confused. Gabe seemed to know exactly which emotional buttons to push to keep her off balance.

"Look, I shouldn't have said that," she whispered. "And I'm sorry, but you don't love me. You know it and I know it, so let's stop playing games."

The silence seemed to drag on forever, then she heard him heave a weary sigh and shift in the seat.

"Just drive, Lisa. Just drive."

BY THE TIME they pulled into Gabe's driveway and he had curtly introduced her to his aunt, Lisa was sure she'd never felt so tense. A dull pain behind her eyes had steadily grown into a full-blown headache.

"Come in, Ms. LeBlanc. Come in." Gabe's aunt smiled, and she gestured for Lisa to enter the living room. Her eyes sparkled with bold curiosity.

"Please call me Lisa."

"Of course, and you call me, Aunt Bessie. Everyone does. I live next door, but since I knew Gabriel was coming home, I decided to wait up for him here."

Gabe followed Lisa inside. He bent down and hugged his aunt. "Has he called back yet?" he asked.

The sparkle in Bessie's eyes wavered. "Not yet, Gabriel, but Daniel said he would, and he's always been a truthful boy, so I'm sure he will." She reached up and patted Gabe on the cheek, then turned to Lisa. "Now, what can I get you? Some iced tea, coffee? Have you eaten supper yet?"

Lisa massaged the bridge of her nose. "Some tea would be nice," she said absently. "And if it's not too much trouble, I could use some aspirin."

Before Lisa realized what was happening, Bessie had her by the arm and was propelling her to the kitchen. "Of course it's not too much trouble. You just come right in here. I believe Gabriel keeps the aspirin on the shelf above the sink. We'll take care of that headache, then we can have a nice chat. You can tell me how you and Gabriel met."

The sweet old lady was about as subtle as a steamroller, but Lisa couldn't find it in her heart to mind Bessie's gentle, probing questions.

Half an hour later, Lisa was still sitting at the kitchen table across from Bessie. In front of her was a plate of freshly baked chocolate-chip cookies. Bessie had insisted that they were Gabriel and Daniel's favorite. Lisa eyed the plate, now half-empty, and debated whether to eat just one more. The waiting was beginning to get to her. Praying that the phone would ring, she picked up her glass of iced tea instead and took a sip.

"I must apologize for Gabriel's manners." Bessie shifted her eyes toward the kitchen door. "He's usually very congenial and hospitable."

Lisa almost choked. *Talk about looking through rose-colored glasses,* she thought. As far as she knew, *Gabriel* was still in the living room, and except to decline his aunt's offer of food, he hadn't uttered another word to either of them. The fact that he had left it up to Lisa to explain everything still irritated her each time she thought about it.

"It's just that he's been so worried about Daniel," Bessie continued, a frown of concern deepening the wrinkles in her brow. "That boy means the world to him . . . and me," she added. Her frown turned fierce. "When I get my hands on that boy, I intend to box his ears good and proper. He knows better than to run off without permission."

Lisa figured that Bessie was just upset and didn't realize what she had said. A picture of an almost-grown boy asking permission to run away formed in Lisa's mind, and she had to bite her lower lip to keep from laughing. Then she thought about Bessie's boxing his ears and took a hasty drink of tea to hide her smile. From what Gabe had told her about his son, she figured Bessie would have to get a stepladder just to reach Danny's ears.

The jarring ring of the telephone quickly sobered Lisa, and her heartbeat quickened.

"Lisa!" Gabe shouted from the living room. "Pick up the extension!"

Lisa shoved out of the chair and raced across the kitchen to the wall phone. She snatched up the receiver just in time to hear Danny's greeting.

"Dad, it's me."

To Lisa, Danny's voice sounded like a more youthful version of Gabe's, only not quite as cynical.

"I—" Danny paused. "Is someone else on the line?"

"It's okay, Danny. Dixie Miller's sister is on the extension. Is Dixie with you?"

"Yeah, she's here."

Lisa closed her eyes and offered up a silent prayer of thanks.

"But how did you know—"

Lisa interrupted Danny. "Is she okay?"

"Yes, ma'am, she's fine. A little shook up, but she's okay."

"Can I please talk to her?"

Gabe quickly spoke up. "In a minute, Lisa. First, Danny has some explaining to do." Taking her acquiescence for granted, he continued. "Where are you, Danny?" he snapped.

Lisa ground her teeth but bit back the sharp retort on the tip of her tongue. *Patience,* she told herself. At least she knew for certain that Dixie was with Danny and he had said she was okay.

"We're at a beach house in Gulf Shores," Danny answered. "Dixie said Lisa would know where."

The second Danny mentioned the beach house, Lisa knew exactly where they were. Before her parents' deaths, and for as far back as she could remember, her family had rented the same little house for the Fourth of July holidays each year.

"Danny, what about the money that was stolen?"

"We didn't take it, if that's what you're worried about."

"Dammit, boy, I didn't think you did. I just want to know how in the hell you got mixed up in this mess?"

"You're not going to believe me."

"Try me."

Danny's resigned sigh whispered through the phone line. "It's a long story. If the line is tapped—"

"If you didn't take the money then it doesn't matter if the phone is tapped," Gabe shot back.

"Yeah, I guess you're right, but—"

"Danny!"

"Okay, okay," he retorted, his voice tinged with rebellion. "Like I told you in my letter, I was tired of school. I wanted a job, so I applied for one with

Southern Phone about a month ago. Dixie was the one who I talked back and forth with each week. When an opening came, I hitchhiked up there for an interview." He let out a sound of disgust. "She took one look at me and knew I had lied about my age. At first she was pretty angry, but after she'd calmed down, she offered to give me a ride back to Ponchatoula, since she had planned to go see her sister for a couple of days, anyway.

"Her car broke down before we even got out of Shreveport. A friend of hers said he could fix it, but it took longer than he thought, so I ended up spending the night at her place. The next morning one of Dixie's old boyfriends showed up and started shoving her around. I—I tried to stop him, but..."

When Danny's voice broke, Lisa's heart went out to the seventeen-year-old who was trying so hard to be a man. A sudden picture of Dixie's apartment flashed through her mind—the end table on its side, the tiny animals scattered. It was clear that despite his size, the inexperienced boy hadn't been much of a match for Kevin Striker, and it was equally clear that Danny still blamed himself for not protecting Dixie.

Danny cleared his throat. "When I came to, we were tied up. He'd left us in a dumpy cabin out in the middle of nowhere. He came back a couple of times a day to bring us food and let us go to the bathroom, but the last time he was in a hurry and got careless. Before he showed up again I was able to work my ropes loose.

When he drove up I surprised him and was able to knock him out. Dixie and I escaped, using his car."

Danny heaved a sigh. "Anyway, it was later when we realized that the briefcase he'd left in the back seat was full of money. We were going to turn it in, but when Dixie called her friend Nicole, we found out that the Feds thought Dixie had stolen the money from the union. I guess we both kind of panicked...."

There was a long pause before Danny finally said more. "Dad? I didn't know what else to do, so I finally decided to call you."

Several seconds of silence ticked by before Gabe finally spoke. "Just stay put, son," he said, his voice strained with emotion. "We'll be there as soon as we can. And don't worry, we'll get this mess straightened out." He paused. "Let Lisa talk to Dixie for a minute—and, son?"

"Yeah, Dad?"

"I love you."

When Gabe heard Lisa's voice and her sister's answering sob, he slowly hung up the phone. Feeling more weary than he'd ever felt in his life, he sank down onto the sofa. Leaning forward, he propped his elbows on his knees and covered his face with his hands.

Lisa had been right from the beginning. Dixie was innocent. Completely innocent. And he... Gabe groaned. He was guilty of everything that his son and Lisa had accused him of.

CHAPTER TWELVE

As soon as Lisa heard her sister's voice, tears of joy sprang into her eyes.

"Dixie, oh, Dixie, I've been so worried about you. Are you okay?"

"Oh, Lisa," she sobbed. "I've been so...so scared. First Kevin—he...and Nicole said that— Oh, Lisa, the FBI is looking for me, and everyone at my office thinks I stole that money."

As Lisa listened to her sister's quiet sobs, tears rolled down her own cheeks. "Honey, don't," she pleaded. "I promise we'll get this all straightened out." Lisa paused, unsure exactly how to pose the foremost question on her mind. "Sweetie, did...did Kevin hurt you? Danny said that he shoved you around."

The answering silence was telling, and Lisa's imagination went wild. "Dixie, answer me. Did he hurt you?"

"N—no, not really. I mean, I'm okay now, thanks to Danny, but Lisa, please come and get me. And please hurry."

"Soon, sweetie, we'll be there soon. Just hang in there a little longer and remember that I love you."

"Me too," she answered.

"Now don't hang up. Put Danny back on. His aunt wants to speak to him."

Lisa motioned to Bessie, who had been waiting patiently for a chance to speak to Danny again.

Dixie is alive. She's safe. As Lisa handed the receiver to Bessie, the words chased around her mind until she felt dizzy with relief. She wanted to shout, to celebrate.

Lisa sighed with unbelievable relief. The truth would come out, and the whole ordeal would finally be over soon. Everything could finally get back to normal. They could get on with their lives.... Yes, she thought, life would go on ... but her life wouldn't include Gabe anymore.

Lisa frowned. It all sounded so simple. So if all of it was so simple, why did the prospect of getting back to *normal* suddenly seem so dull and unappealing? And why did the thought of never seeing Gabriel Jordan again cause her to feel so damn depressed?

"I'm trying to tell you that I love you." Lisa closed her eyes in an attempt to block out the words that had haunted her ever since Gabe had spoken them. *Impossible,* she thought. He had been playing mind games, she reminded herself.

But was it really impossible? she wondered as she slowly walked toward the living room. Had he been playing games? He had to have been, she thought. A man like Gabe didn't just blurt out that he loved a woman after only knowing her less than a week.

When she entered the living room, she wasn't sure what to expect. Gabe had been uncommunicative and sullen since she had flung his declaration of love back in his face.

He was sitting on the sofa, and when she stepped into the room, he lifted his head. For a second, she caught a glimpse of something in his eyes, a bleakness that bordered on pain. Then he stood and straightened to his full height. Reaching inside his front shirt pocket, he pulled out a toothpick, stuck it between his teeth, and in that instant, the look disappeared.

"How is your sister?" he asked, his voice even and much too polite.

"She's still a bit shaken from their ordeal," she said cautiously, "but she's young and strong. She'll be okay once we get this mess straightened out."

Gabe nodded his agreement. "It sounded like they've both been through the wringer." He paused. "Lisa, I want to . . . I . . ." He hesitated.

He's trying to apologize, she thought.

Gabe grimaced and shook his head. "Never mind," he finally said.

Lisa sighed. Never before could she remember being so confused about a man, and never before had she been so unsure about her own feelings. He owed her an apology, and even though they now knew that Dixie and Danny were safe, she still expected one.

"Are you up to traveling again?" Gabe's question broke into her thoughts. "If you aren't—I mean, if you're too tired, I can go after them by myself."

Lisa shook her head. "I've come this far. I intend to go all the way." The instant she said the words, she recalled the last time she had said them. Her face burned with embarrassment. One look at Gabe and she knew that he had remembered, too.

Biting her lip, Lisa quickly lowered her gaze and concentrated on her tennis shoes.

The silence that followed was so charged with tension that Lisa could barely breathe.

Finally Gabe spoke. "Where's Aunt Bessie?"

Lisa still couldn't bring herself to look at him. She waved toward the kitchen. "She wanted to speak to Danny."

"I'll just check on her," he said, "then we can leave."

As he walked out of the room, Lisa took a deep breath and closed her eyes. "I'm going crazy," she muttered, reaching up to rub her neck. Her throat ached and all she wanted to do was sit and cry. "Stark raving nuts," she whispered.

KEVIN STRIKER THOUGHT if something didn't happen soon, he was going to jump right out of his skin. He'd been sitting and waiting for what seemed like hours. Only once had he dared to leave, and then he'd been afraid to stay away for more than the ten or fifteen minutes it had taken him to drive to the gas station, use the john and grab something to eat and drink.

His stomach growled and he shifted then hunched farther down in the seat, his eyes straining in the darkness. The bag of potato chips and the package of cupcakes he'd picked up at the station were long gone.

The only bright spot of the whole evening had been when Dixie's sister and that big bastard with her had finally showed up.

Kevin grinned and gave himself a mental pat on the back for being so shrewd. He'd figured they would show up sooner or later, and he also figured, sooner or later, they would lead him straight to Dixie . . . and his money.

Kevin clenched and unclenched his fist. Every time he thought about Dixie, he was reminded of the one mistake he'd made—the only mistake he'd made— during the whole setup. Maybe if he hadn't been so damn squeamish about doing away with her, he wouldn't be sitting in some stuffy car, hungry and thirsty, in the middle of the night.

"Well, no more mistakes," he whispered. From now on, he intended to play to win, no matter who got in his way.

Suddenly the porch light at the house blinked on, and Kevin stiffened. The front door opened and sweat beaded his brow. Lisa, followed by Gabe, emerged and headed for the Jeep.

Rubbing his hand against his pant leg, Kevin glanced at the clock on the dashboard. There was only one reason that they would be going out at this time of night.

"Oh, yeah, baby. Come to Papa," he whispered, his hand on the ignition key.

THE DRIVE TO GULF SHORES, Alabama, was long, tiring...and silent. What little traffic there was on the interstate provided the only source of light for the dark night, since there was no moon or stars. The empty night seemed to taunt Lisa, as if it was a reflection of her life. Not since Barry had died had she felt so isolated, so alone. Not even the prospect of seeing her sister again could exorcise the feeling.

Halfway there, Gabe finally broke the silence. "If you'll pull over, I'll drive for a while."

Lisa didn't argue but immediately pulled onto the shoulder of the highway. The last thing she remembered before she gave in to exhaustion and slept was that Gabe had switched the radio to a country station.

THE SILENCE and cessation of movement woke her. Lisa blinked several times, trying to adjust to the bright lights. Out of the corner of her eye, she noticed that Gabe was just sitting there, as if waiting for her to wake up.

She could feel his gaze on her, and the notion was a little unsettling. She couldn't help wondering just how long he'd been watching her, and she remembered the last time she had fallen asleep at the truck stop. Feelings of tenderness and desire stirred inside her, feelings that she wasn't sure how to deal with. He'd remembered, and this time he hadn't left her alone in the Jeep.

As each moment passed she grew more uncomfortable. She glanced around, looking for a distraction. He had pulled Lover up beside the gasoline pumps in front of what looked like an all-night combination café and gas station.

She yawned and stretched. "Where are we?" she mumbled.

"Another mile or so and we'll be in Gulf Shores. The Jeep needed gas, and since you know the location of the beach house and I don't, I thought it would be best if you drove."

Before she could answer, Gabe shoved open his door and walked to the gas pumps.

Still fighting to keep her eyes open, Lisa groaned, fumbled around for her purse, then opened the door. She stepped outside and took a breath of the cool night air. It was going to take more than fresh air to wake her up, she decided. "I need coffee." She headed for the bright lights of the café. Belatedly remembering her manners, she hesitated and glanced over her shoulder. "Want some?" she called out.

Gabe nodded and chuckled. "Yeah, thanks. Are you sure you're awake?"

Lisa glared at him. "I'm awake," she muttered. She took another step but stopped and turned. "Gabe?"

He had just removed the gas nozzle from the pump. He looked up.

"Thanks."

"You're welcome."

Twenty minutes later Lisa steered the Jeep down a dark, narrow unpaved road. The beach house was located in an isolated area, away from the condos, hotels and commercial ventures that had sprung up during the past few years.

In the distance the sound of waves crashing against the narrow sandy beach that ran behind the beach house mingled with the distant rumble of thunder. A flash of light from behind gave her a start.

Just lightning, she thought, glancing in the rearview mirror. But without the moon and stars and without streetlights, there was no way to see anything but the pitch-black darkness that wrapped around them like a huge smothering blanket.

A tiny shiver ran down her spine, and she wondered if she would ever completely forget the harrowing episode of being followed and chased by the two hoods.

Gabe leaned forward and peered out the windshield into the darkness. "Sounds like rain."

The tone of his deep voice had a comforting, soothing effect, and she was almost able to shrug off the foreboding feeling that something wasn't quite right.

A few minutes later, Lisa rounded a curve in the road. Up ahead was a tiny beacon of light shining

through a front window of the beach house. She
pulled in beside the unfamiliar Toyota parked near the
front door. She eyed the vehicle suspiciously until
she remembered that Dixie and Danny had made their
getaway in Kevin Striker's car.

The minute she switched off Lover's engine, a
streak of lightning split the sky and a crack of thunder followed.

"Definitely rain," Gabe grumbled.

At that moment the heavens opened up and rain
poured. Lisa twisted around and groped behind the
seat, searching for her umbrella. Just as her fingers
found it, another streak of lightning lit the sky. Lisa
looked up and froze. Just for an instant she could have
sworn that she saw a man standing in the middle of the
road. "Did you see that?" she whispered.

Gabe turned in his seat. "See what?"

Lisa didn't answer immediately. Praying for another flash of lightning, she continued to stare at the
now-dark spot in the road. Then the lightning came
again, but the road was empty.

Lisa shuddered. "I thought I saw something, but
there's nothing there."

"I guess it's just that kind of night," Gabe offered
by way of reassurance. Gabe knew the notion was ridiculous—by now, Kevin Striker and the two hood-
lums were in custody—but several times during the
trip, he could have sworn that someone was following
them. He considered that the FBI could have a tail on
them, but even if they did, the thought was more

comforting than disturbing. If the FBI did show up, maybe they could finally get the whole mess straightened out right then and there.

Lisa gave a nervous laugh. "It is kind of creepy out here. I don't remember it being so...so isolated."

Deciding that he was simply paranoid after all they had been through, Gabe grunted a noncommittal reply. "If this rain ever slacks up a bit, take off for the house."

Lisa held out her umbrella. "I only have one, but I'm willing to share."

Gabe shook his head. "We'd both get soaked then."

"But—"

"Listen! The rain is letting up. Go!"

Lisa didn't argue. Grabbing the keys and her purse, she shoved open the door, popped the umbrella and took off for the house.

Gabe was already on the porch by the time she got there. He pounded on the door. "Danny, it's me. Open up!"

Several seconds passed before the door finally swung open.

"Oh, Lisa, I'm so glad to see you." Sobbing, Dixie pulled Lisa inside and threw herself into her sister's arms.

Gabe closed the door behind him. He wasn't sure what he had expected, but Dixie Miller was a far cry from the older, seductive woman he had pictured.

She and Lisa were the same size, and except for the age difference, at first glance, they favored each other almost enough to be twins, the most outstanding difference being their hair: Lisa's was a dark auburn and Dixie's was strawberry blond. And at the moment Dixie reminded him of a small lost child by the way she was clinging to Lisa.

Standing there and watching, Gabe felt even guiltier than before for the unflattering image he had painted of Lisa's sister.

He directed his gaze beyond the two women. In the middle of the small living room stood Danny, looking unkempt, haggard and more than a little apprehensive.

Gabe's heart turned over as his eyes devoured his son. There had been moments during the past week when he had thought he might never see Danny again. Now, as he looked at his only child, knowing what he'd been through, his heart swelled with sympathy and pride. He pushed past the two women, and in three strides he grabbed his son, hugging him close.

"Dad...I...umph!"

Gabe felt Danny flinch and he pulled away. There was pain etched in his son's eyes.

"Are you hurt?"

"Bruised ribs, I think."

Gabe reached out and gingerly lifted his son's faded T-shirt. "How did you get—" Anger, like a red-hot poker, jabbed him in the gut. Dark purple bruises radiated from Danny's left rib cage. "Looks more than just bruised to me," he said. "Did Striker do this?"

Danny tucked his head and shrugged. "How did you know his name was Striker?"

"Lisa—Ms. LeBlanc and I added two and two."

Danny lifted his head and frowned. "How did you get together with Dixie's sister?"

Gabe shook his head. "It's a long story, but for now, I want to get you to a doctor and see about those ribs."

"And I want Dixie's eye checked, too," Lisa called out.

Gabe turned and looked at Dixie. Her face was red and blotchy from crying, and faint purple splotches ringed her still slightly swollen right eye.

Another stab of anger shot through Gabe. "That bastard," he murmured. "If I ever get my hands on that little sleaze—"

The loud crash of the door banging against the living room wall stopped Gabe in midsentence. Lisa screamed and Dixie whimpered. Gabe snapped his head around and Danny cursed.

Standing in the middle of the doorway was Kevin Striker. A jagged slash of lightning lit up the sky behind Striker followed by a clap of thunder. He was dripping wet and his clothes were plastered to his skinny body, but it was the gun in his hand that commanded Gabe's attention.

Striker stepped inside, reached out and slammed the door behind him. He waved his gun toward Lisa and Dixie. "Back off," he snapped.

Lisa grabbed Dixie, and placing herself between Striker and her sister, she backed toward Gabe.

Even as adrenaline pumped through Gabe's veins, questions raced through his mind. How had Striker gotten away, and if Striker got away, did that mean the two hoods had, too? "What do you want?" Gabe demanded.

Striker waved the gun in Dixie's direction. "She knows what I want," he snarled. "She and her boyfriend have my money. I want it. Now!"

"You! You fo—followed us," Lisa accused. "It was you I saw."

At that moment, Gabe would have kicked himself if he had thought it would change things. He'd known, dammit. Deep down, he'd known all along that someone was following, but he'd chosen to ignore the feeling, chosen to ignore caution. "How did you find us?" he demanded.

A disdainful smile distorted Striker's lips, the kind of arrogant smile that had Gabe curling his fingers into fists and wishing he could have just one chance to wipe it off.

"I have my ways," he retorted.

"He took my wallet." Danny spoke up. "My ID has our address on it."

"Aren't you the bright young stud," Striker drawled.

Lisa felt a shiver ripple down her spine. Striker had been watching them, following them, just waiting for them to lead him to Dixie. And like two complete idiots, she and Gabe had done exactly that.

Why hadn't they called the police or the FBI to follow them to the beach house? she wondered. The answer was almost as unappealing as their present situation. She and Gabe had been too wrapped up in their personal feud to think further than their noses. Hindsight was a wonderful thing, she thought sarcastically.

"Danny," Gabe warned. "Let me handle this."

Striker snorted. "Yeah, *boy,* let your daddy handle things."

Gabe slid a quick glance at his son, willing him not to give in to Striker's taunts. By the way Danny's jaw was set and the daggers shooting from his eyes, Gabe figured he'd better distract Striker before Danny let his temper get the best of his intelligence.

Gabe took a step forward and Striker jerked the gun in his direction.

"I wouldn't, if I were you," he warned. "I have nothing to lose, and I sure as hell don't plan to spend the rest of my life behind bars in some stinking prison."

Gabe slowly raised his hands. "Okay, okay. There's no need to add murder to your list of crimes."

"All I want is the money. Either they give it to me or I start eliminating witnesses, one by one."

Gabe felt as if his heart were going to pump right out of his chest. "What guarantees do we have that you won't kill us all, anyway?"

Striker's lips pulled into a nasty smile. "You don't." He turned to Lisa and waved his gun. "Step out of the way."

Lisa drew herself up to her full height, narrowed her eyes and lifted her chin in defiance, reminding Gabe of a fierce lioness protecting her cub. "You go to hell," she spat out.

"No, Lisa, don't!" Dixie stepped out from behind her sister. "The money's still in your car, Kevin."

"Dixie!"

Dixie ignored her sister. "The keys are in my pocket. Just take it and leave us alone."

"Oh, God," Lisa groaned. "Don't you realize what you've done?"

"All he wants is the money," Dixie said, her voice choking.

"You shut up." Striker glared at Lisa, then turned his attention to Dixie. "Give me the keys," he demanded.

Dixie reached down and pulled a key ring from inside her pocket.

Striker wiggled his finger. "Now, nice and easy, bring them to me."

The sinking feeling in Gabe's gut grew as he watched Dixie hand Striker the keys.

"That's a good girl." Striker patted Dixie on the cheek. She flinched away and backed toward Lisa.

"You've got what you want. Now leave."

Striker leveled a nasty look at Gabe. "You shut up, too. I still owe you one for back at the boat. I don't plan to murder anyone unless I have to. I'm not stupid. But like I said, I owe you one."

"You in the house! This is the FBI. Come out with your hands up!"

Gabe recognized Johnny Monroe's voice instantly, and hope, like an eagle, soared in his veins.

Striker cursed and a red tinge of fury darkened his face. But for all his bravado, Gabe spotted fear in the man's beady eyes, fear and something else that caused his blood to run cold. Desperation. Desperate men were dangerous men.

Off to his side Gabe could hear Dixie and Lisa's sobs of relief, but Gabe knew they were a far cry from being rescued. He also knew that somehow he had to convince Striker to give himself up.

"If you give yourself up now, all you'll get is a prison term," Gabe said evenly.

"I told you to shut up." Striker raised the gun and pointed it at Gabe. "I'm not going to prison."

Suddenly lights flooded through the windows of the small room, and the agent's voice boomed out again. "We've got you surrounded. Give yourself up!"

Striker cursed. Keeping his gun pointed at Gabe, he sidled over to the door and flattened himself against the wall.

Gabe swallowed the lump of fear that seemed permanently lodged in his throat. His whole life was in this room. Danny. Lisa.

Just the thought of losing Danny made his knees weak, and he felt a trickle of cold sweat run down his back. And even if Lisa never returned his love, he wasn't sure he could go on living if something happened to her.

Still keeping a wary eye on Gabe, Striker eased the door open just a crack. "I've got a gun and people in here!" he yelled. "Anyone comes in and I start shooting!"

Gabe knew he had to do something. He took a deep breath. "I know a way out of this, Striker."

"Yeah, right," Striker snapped. "And I'm the Easter bunny."

"No, listen to me." Gabe paused for emphasis. "There is a way out, a way you can walk out of here and no one will get hurt."

"Well?"

"Use me as your hostage."

CHAPTER THIRTEEN

"No!" Lisa cried. But even as the words passed her lips, the look on Gabe's face told her that her protest was futile.

Gabe kept his full attention riveted on Striker and didn't so much as acknowledge that Lisa had spoken. "Taking me is the only way you're going to get out alive unless you give yourself up," he said.

Lisa knew by the way Striker stared at Gabe that he was actually considering the proposition.

"You said we still had a score to settle," Gabe reminded him. "What better way than taking me as your hostage? I'm you're best bet."

"Just shut up!" Striker yelled. "Shut up and let me think." Striker reminded Lisa of a cornered animal. His eyes shifted back and forth, and his grip on the gun was so tight that his knuckles were white. She could almost smell the fear emanating from him.

"Okay," he blurted out. "But don't think I won't kill you if you try any cute stuff."

In a sudden unexpected move, Striker stepped over, grabbed Dixie and shoved the gun in her side. Dixie cried out and turned pale.

"Just making sure you don't get any heroic ideas," Striker said with a sneer, his words directed at Gabe. "Now get something and tie those two up."

"L-i-s-a . . ."

The sound of Dixie's terrified voice tore at Lisa's heart. She glared at Striker.

Gabe latched on to her arm. "Don't even think it," he whispered harshly, his hand biting into her flesh. "Trust me. Please—"

Dixie suddenly yelped. Gabe and Lisa jerked their heads toward her. Striker had yanked her arm up behind her, and pain was etched all over Dixie's face.

"Stop that whispering or I'll break her goddamn arm."

Any thoughts that Lisa had of rescuing her sister flew out of her head. "Please," she pleaded. "Don't hurt her."

The satisfied look on Striker's face sickened Lisa, but her main concern was Dixie. "It's okay, hon," she told her, trying to inflect confidence and reassurance in her tone. "Just hang in there. Everything will be okay."

"Come on." Gabe nudged her toward Danny. "The sooner we get this over with, the sooner he'll let her go." Giving Lisa one last look that he hoped would comfort her, he glanced around the room for something he could use to tie them up with. Then he turned to Striker. "Any suggestions?"

Striker looked as if he was ready to explode. "How the hell should I know?"

"The blinds," Danny offered. "Use the cord from the window blinds, Dad."

Gabe eyed Striker, who nodded, then he walked over to the window. He reached up, and holding the blind with one hand, he gave a yank with the other hand, but the cord held fast. "I need to cut it," he said, looking over his shoulder at Striker.

"So?"

"I need scissors or a knife."

Striker cursed, but he released Dixie's arm long enough to dig into his pocket. Pulling out a pocket knife, he tossed it to Gabe. "Just remember who gets the first shot if you decide to try anything funny," he warned, making a show of jamming the gun farther into Dixie's side.

Dixie winced, but she bit her lip to keep from crying out again. Gabe leveled a cool look at Striker, but didn't bother to reply to his taunt.

His mind racing with possibilities, Gabe opened the knife and cut the cord into two pieces. He couldn't try anything now, but if he could somehow keep the knife, then he'd at least have a weapon for later. What he needed was a distraction, something that would occupy Striker long enough to forget about the knife.

Gabe turned toward Lisa and Danny, the knife in one hand, the cords dangling from his other hand. It was almost as if his son had read his mind.

"Oh, you're a real he-man, aren't you?" Danny yelled at Striker. "But only when it comes to women."

The moment Striker directed his attention to Danny, Gabe closed the knife and slipped it into his pocket.

"A real man wouldn't hide behind a woman's skirt," Danny taunted.

Gabe grabbed Danny's wrist. Turning so that Striker could only see the back of his head, he gave his son a wink. "That's enough, son."

"Oh, no you don't." Striker's words rang out.

With a sinking feeling in his gut, Gabe turned. *So much for the knife,* he thought.

"You—hero." Striker nodded at Danny. "Tie up your daddy's hands first."

All Gabe could do was stare at Striker. Had his plan backfired? Was Striker going to take Danny instead? *Oh God,* he thought. *Now what do I do?* His son needed a doctor, and Danny was just hotheaded enough to get himself into real trouble if Striker provoked him one too many times.

"The deal was you take me," Gabe retorted. *To hell with the knife,* he thought. He'd gladly do without the knife if Striker wouldn't take Danny. "Hiding behind a boy won't win you any Brownie points with the Feds."

Striker ignored him. "Just do it, boy, and tie his hands behind his back, not in front."

Gabe had no choice except to grudgingly submit his hands.

As soon as Danny had complied, Striker shoved Dixie toward him. "Now the women."

Gabe swallowed hard as he watched Danny tie Lisa to Dixie. He'd screwed up royally, and now Danny would have to pay for his mistake. He never should have suggested the hostage bit to begin with, he thought.

"Okay, boy wonder. On the floor with your hands at the back of your head. If you know what's good for you, you'll stay there until we're out of here."

Gabe almost sagged with relief, and he hoped what he felt didn't show on his face as he watched his son gingerly stretch out, belly down, on the floor. Any sign of weakness would be like waving a red flag to Striker. He winced, knowing that lying on the hard floor wasn't helping Danny's ribs. Then he reminded himself that it was a hell of a lot better for his son to endure some pain and discomfort than to be taken as Striker's hostage.

"Come on, hero." Striker waved the gun at Gabe, and Gabe walked toward him. Striker grabbed him by the shirtsleeve and pushed him in front of him. He opened the door just a crack.

The steady drizzle reflected in the glaring lights appeared surrealistic.

"Hey, you cops out there!" Striker yelled. "I'm coming out, and I've got me a hostage." He sneered. "A real hero. First, I want you to shut off those damn lights and back off. Second, if anyone makes a move or tries to follow us, I'll kill the hero."

Minutes seemed to drag by before a disembodied voice answered. Again, Gabe recognized it was Johnny

Monroe. "No one will stop you!" he shouted. "You have my word."

"The lights!" Striker shouted. Within seconds the lights were cut, plunging the front yard of the beach house back into darkness.

Using Gabe as a shield, Striker shoved the door open. Just before Striker pushed him outside, Gabe glanced back over his shoulder. His gaze first rested on his son. Danny looked worried, but he gave Gabe a thumbs-up sign.

Then Gabe looked at Lisa. Her dark eyes were wide and sparkled with the tears she was trying so hard to hold back. He wished he'd had more time to iron things out with her, to convince her that he really did love her. He could only pray that he would get another chance.

LISA MET GABE'S GAZE, and what she saw took her breath away. She would have to be a complete imbecile to miss the unspoken message he'd revealed in just that one piercing look—regret, desire and...love.

The sudden revelation hit her like a physical blow, but before she had time to completely absorb it all or to respond, Striker shoved him through the door, and they were both swallowed up by the night.

Lisa closed her eyes. He had really meant what he'd said. He did love her. Time and time again he had shown her how much, had always been there for her. Back at the boat he'd risked his life for her, and now he was doing it again. Just how much more proof did she need? she wondered. His death?

"Oh, God," she groaned, squeezing her eyes tightly against the tears burning behind her lids. No matter how hard she had tried to convince herself otherwise, he truly was an honorable man, a man she could trust, a man she could depend on...a man she could love. What a fool she'd been, she thought.

"Danny, hurry up. Something's wrong with Lisa."

The sound of her sister's voice followed by the touch of Danny's hand on her shoulder finally penetrated her misery.

"Lisa? Are you okay? Are the cords too tight?"

Lisa sniffed and took a deep breath. "No," she finally whispered. "I'll be fine once you get us loose." But she knew she was lying, knew she wouldn't be fine, and she wasn't sure she would ever be again if Gabe didn't survive. She'd missed her chance, been too blind to see and too deaf to hear. She'd done exactly what she had accused Gabe of doing. She hadn't been willing to believe in him. And now she might never get the chance.

Danny fumbled with the cords that bound them. "I'll have you loose in just a minute."

Still too numb to think past her own shortcomings, Lisa rubbed her wrist.

Suddenly the door burst open. All three froze at the sight of armed men swarming into the room. Then she recognized Johnny Monroe. "It's okay," she told Dixie and Danny. "Mr. Monroe is FBI."

"Which one is Monroe?" Danny demanded.

When the agent stepped forward, Danny narrowed his eyes and rounded on him. With his hands on his hips, his aggressive stance and his fierce, determined look, Danny looked so much like his father that Lisa had to bite her lip to keep from sobbing.

"Where's my dad?" he demanded.

Johnny Monroe shook his head. "Sorry, son, but they got away." His voice was matter-of-fact, neither sympathetic nor condescending. "We couldn't get a clear shot without putting your father in danger. But we've got a tail on them," Monroe continued, "and I've already called the local police to set up road-blocks."

The distressed look on Danny's face tore at Lisa's heart. Whatever differences Danny had with his father, it was clear that he loved him fiercely.

Danny shook his head slowly. "He shouldn't have done it," he said, not talking to anyone in particular. "He shouldn't have gone with that bastard."

"Believe me, we'll do everything possible to get your dad back safe and sound."

Danny simply turned away, walked to the door and stood, staring out into the darkness.

Monroe turned his attention to Lisa. "Are you and your sister all right?"

Lisa nodded. "I don't know how you knew where we were, but I'm glad you showed up."

For the first time that night, his stoic expression slipped. He seemed almost embarrassed.

"We should have been here sooner." He drew in a deep breath then sighed. "We had already tapped Mr. Jordan's phone, so when his son called we were able to pinpoint his location. Then we got word that the captain of Destin Gulf Charter had called the local police. After hearing what happened, we put out an APB on Striker. But we were too late. He'd already switched rental cars, so no one stopped him along the way. We had just driven up when we saw Striker go in." He paused and narrowed his eyes. "If only you had cooperated in the beginning, all of this might have been avoided."

Lisa bristled at the censure in his tone. "If we had gone along with you, you'd have thrown my sister in jail, and Kevin Striker would have been long gone by the time you figured out that he was the real thief."

As soon as the words were out, Lisa felt like digging a hole and crawling into it. She closed her eyes, appalled by the way she had just attacked Johnny Monroe. She truly *was* going crazy, she thought. One minute she was thanking him, and the next she was raging at him. Reaching up, she pinched the bridge of her nose. "I'm sorry," she whispered. "That was uncalled for."

Unable to say more, she whirled around and stalked off toward the corner of the room. Somehow she had to get a grip on herself. Gabe would be okay, she told herself. He was levelheaded and wouldn't take unnecessary chances. Kevin Striker would let him go. He just had to. Maybe if she kept repeating it over and over, she might finally believe it, she thought.

"Lisa?"

Lisa sighed and turned to face her sister. She took one look at Dixie's face and knew she had to get a grip on her emotions for her sister's sake. She couldn't help Gabe except by praying, but Dixie was here, and her sister needed her now.

Dixie ducked her head in a familiar gesture that Lisa recognized, one that had always signaled a confession was forthcoming. "I'm sorry...about everything, about our fight and about all of this. I shouldn't have said those things to you—you know, all that cutting-the-apron-strings business. And you were right about Kevin all along. I should have listened to you when I first started dating him, but..." Her voice trailed away to a whisper. "All I know to do is say I'm sorry."

"Oh, hon." Lisa gathered Dixie in her arms and held her tightly. Dixie was a grown woman and her sister, but their special relationship superseded that of mere sisters.

Lisa thought back to the last Saturday-morning phone conversation they'd had. Through circumstances neither had been able to control, she would always be the mother and Dixie the child, no matter what Dixie thought to the contrary.

"I should never have hung up on you. We should have talked it out. So you see, we all make mistakes—we're only human. The trick is to learn from those mistakes so you won't repeat them."

Lisa felt Dixie shudder. "Kevin Striker is one mistake I will *never* repeat," she said. "Oh, Lisa," she cried, "he never cared about me. He just used me. How can I go back to Southern Phone and face all of those people? I'm not sure I will ever be able to forgive myself for being so gullible. And poor Danny," she continued in a broken voice, "he tried so hard to protect me and got kicked in the ribs for his efforts and it's all my fault. And now his father is—"

"The important thing is that you and Danny are safe." Her heart ached for her sister. "Danny's dad will be okay. He just has to be," she said quietly. Her own eyes filled with tears. *Please let him be okay,* she prayed silently. *Please.*

GABE STARED AHEAD into the stormy night as the road markers whizzed by in a distorted blur. He felt as if every nerve in his body was on fire. The frantic slapping of the windshield wipers battled the driving rain. Streaks of lightning punctuated the rolls of thunder.

He looked down at the clock in the dash. An hour had passed, an hour that had felt like an eternity. He glanced at the speedometer and sucked in his breath. He had hoped that once they got in the car, he could somehow slow Striker down. Thoughts of throwing himself against Striker and other less than savory ideas had gone through his head. But with the blinding rain and at the speed Striker was going, he figured that neither one of them would live through an accident. Gabe decided his best bet was to continue to try to loosen the cord that bound his wrists. If he could get his hands loose and retrieve the knife, he might be able to force Striker to stop before the bastard could get to his gun. Anything else at this point was certain suicide.

Gabe wasn't familiar with the route Striker had taken, and except for an occasional expletive the man hadn't uttered a word since they had left the beach house.

Suddenly Striker cursed.

Gabe looked up. He stiffened and his heart began to pound. In the far distance he could just barely make out the flashing lights of two patrol cars parked bumper to bumper across the road.

Striker cursed again and stomped on the brakes, sending the car into a spin. With his hands tied, all Gabe could do was try to brace himself with his feet against the floorboard. Outside, the thunder roared and lightning cracked through the sky. Still spinning, the car slid sideways on the wet pavement, heading for the shoulder of the road. For a second, the headlights lit up a steep slope that led downward into a deep ditch. The car jolted, then slithered sideways again.

Gabe lost his footing and was slung forward. His head hit the dash. Even as a sharp pain and a kaleidoscope of sparks exploded behind his eyes, he was aware that the car had stopped. The sound of the rain pounding against metal surrounded him, fading in and out. With a tremendous effort, he tried to open his eyes, but his vision blurred and nausea rose up in his throat.

Don't pass out, he told himself. *You have to stay conscious.*

He glanced over at Striker. Gabe couldn't tell if he was alive or dead. Feeling a bit less nauseated, he struggled to straighten in the seat. Pain ripped through his head again, followed by a wave of sick dizziness. A huge black void opened, beckoning him with promises of rest and peace. He thought of how useless the knife in his pocket was. He thought of Lisa and Danny. Would he ever see them again? Then, with a moan of surrender and regret, he gave in to the blackness and closed his eyes.

THE JARRING RING of the telephone gave Lisa a start. She stiffened, her heart pounding in anticipation as she watched Johnny Monroe snatch up the receiver.

Within seconds, she sighed with disappointment and slumped back into the overstuffed chair she'd occupied off and on for the past three seemingly endless hours.

She could tell by the way the agent snapped out orders that the call was like all the rest they had received—another dead end.

A muffled groan from the sofa caught her attention. Danny, who was stretched out, shifted in an attempt to find a more comfortable position. His eyes were closed, and from the deep frown lines etched into his forehead, she could tell he was still in pain.

Stubborn, she thought. *Just like his father.* Monroe had offered to have a squad car drive him to the nearest hospital, and even though it was obvious he needed medical attention, Danny had flatly refused, insisting on waiting with her and Dixie in hopes they would hear some word about his father.

They were all waiting, she thought, looking around the room, her gaze coming to rest on her sister. Dixie was curled up in a chair near the sofa, her arms clasped around her knees, her head bent, hiding her face. From the few words she had spoken, Lisa knew her sister was eaten up with remorse. No matter how many times she had tried to reassure Dixie that she wasn't at fault, her sister firmly held on to the mantle of guilt.

Suddenly the air in the room seemed stale and the walls seemed to be closing in on her. For hours she had been sitting there, worrying and feeling so damn helpless. Every muscle and nerve in her body felt so tight that she knew she was almost near the screaming stage. She couldn't stand it another minute. She had to do something.

Desperate for a reprieve from the waiting, Lisa pushed herself out of the chair. "I need some fresh air," she whispered, hurrying toward the front door.

Outside, the few officers who had remained were gathered around a squad car, their hands wrapped around mugs of coffee and their faces reflecting the somber mood of the waiting game they were all playing.

She could feel their eyes on her as she headed straight for the narrow stretch of beach that bordered the gulf.

The sun was just beginning its daily journey, peeking over the eastern horizon, its rays bouncing off the gulf waters. A lone sea gull soared toward the shore, riding the cool early-morning breeze effortlessly.

Lisa stopped near the edge of the surf and watched, her bare feet sinking deeper into the gritty sand. For long moments, she breathed deeply, willing her aching muscles to relax. She tried to clear her mind and concentrate on the soothing sound of the waves and for a few minutes it seemed to work. But then the look on Gabe's face just before Striker had pushed him into the dark night flashed through her mind. Hot tears stung her eyes, and she wrapped her arms tightly around her chest. Inside, Dixie, Danny and Johnny Monroe waited. Outside, the other officers waited. All around, officers at roadblocks waited.

What good were the roadblocks? she railed silently. None of them had spotted Striker's car. None of the airports or bus stations had reported seeing him. It was almost as if he and Gabe had disappeared into thin air.

A heavy feeling of dread and foreboding threatened to overpower Lisa, the same feeling she had been fighting since she had seen Gabe walk through the door with Striker. Where were they? she wondered for the thousandth time. She had seen Gabe slip the knife into his pocket. Lisa shivered. Had he been able to use it? Was he safe? Or had Striker finally evened the score? Thoughts of Gabe lying somewhere, bleeding and hurt, nagged at her.

The lone gull cried out, signaling that he'd spotted his breakfast, then he dived toward the surf.

Lisa shivered again and turned to walk back to the beach house. In the real world, as in nature, only the strong survived. Gabe was stronger than Kevin Striker. And so was she. Gabe had asked her to trust him, and no matter how long she had to wait, she just couldn't give up hope. She had to keep believing that he was safe, that he would come back.

When Lisa entered the beach house, Danny was awake and had moved into the chair next to the phone. Johnny Monroe was nowhere in sight.

"Where's Mr. Monroe?" she asked.

Danny tilted his head toward the kitchen. "Making more coffee," he said with a grimace.

Suddenly the phone rang, the sound too loud in the quiet room. Danny jerked around and snatched up the receiver.

CHAPTER FOURTEEN

"YEAH, THIS IS Danny Jordan. Okay, I'll hold."

Lisa tensed and her heart fluttered. Dixie lifted her head and stared at Danny, her eyes eager and expectant. Johnny Monroe rushed out of the kitchen, a bag of coffee still in his hand. He stopped within a foot of Danny and stood there poised like a tiger ready to pounce.

"Dad?" Danny's eyes lit up and he grinned. "Oh, wow, we've been so worried about you— What?" Danny frowned. "Oh, sure. Okay."

For what seemed like an eternity, Danny just listened, the expression on his face sober and attentive. Lisa's stomach felt as if it were full of a million butterflies. Her thoughts rushed ahead. What would she say to Gabe when she talked to him? She couldn't just blurt out that she loved him, not in front of everyone. Besides, she thought, after everything that had happened, she wasn't sure he would believe her; he could misinterpret her change of heart as simply gratitude.

"Okay, Dad," Danny finally said. "We'll see you there. Yeah, me too," he added.

As she listened to Danny's last gruff response, a warm feeling welled up within Lisa. She was sure that

Gabe had just told his son that he loved him. Now if only he would say those words to her again, she thought wistfully.

Danny held out the phone to Johnny Monroe. "Dad says that one of your men wants to talk to you." The agent snatched up the phone.

Grinning from ear to ear, Danny turned to Dixie and Lisa, gave a war whoop and stood. "He's okay. A slight concussion, but he's okay."

"A concussion?" Lisa whispered.

Dixie chimed in. "Oh, no."

In the background, Johnny Monroe snapped out orders to someone over the phone, but it was several moments before Lisa could say anything further. Joy that Gabe was alive battled with disappointment that he hadn't asked to speak to her.

She swallowed the disappointment and concentrated on the fact that Gabe was alive. "Are you sure he's okay?" she blurted out.

"Yeah, are you sure?" Dixie asked.

Still talking on the phone, Johnny Monroe threw them an irritated look, then, covering his other ear with his hand, he turned his back on them.

"He said he was," Danny answered, glaring at Monroe's back. He signaled for Lisa and Dixie to join him on the sofa.

"About an hour after they left, Striker spotted a roadblock," Danny explained, his voice low. "Dad said Striker was speeding, and when he saw the road-block, he hit the brakes."

Lisa shuddered. With all of the rain, the pavement would have been as slick as glass.

"The car skidded and went down an embankment. Both of them were knocked unconscious, and since it was dark and raining cats and dogs, the cops at the roadblock never saw it happen. No one spotted the car until it got light."

Dixie laid her hand on Danny's arm. "I'm glad your dad is okay."

Danny was visibly emotional. "Thanks. He's been released from the hospital and one of the Feds is driving him home. He said for us to meet him there."

"What about Striker?" After all the terror he'd caused them, Lisa didn't really care if he was hurt or not, but she did want reassurance that he was in custody.

"He's still in the hospital but under guard. He'll live to go to prison."

"Good," Dixie said bluntly. "I hope they throw away the key."

Out of the corner of her eye, Lisa saw Johnny Monroe hang up the phone. She stood. "We would like to leave, if that's okay."

He nodded. "I think it's safe now. We'll need statements from all of you, but someone will be in touch about that later. Also we might need you to testify when Striker goes to trial."

Dixie stood. "Ah, Mr. Monroe, will you...will someone explain everything to my boss? You know— that I didn't steal the money."

For the first time since Lisa had met the agent, he almost smiled. "I'll take care of it personally," he said.

IT WAS MIDMORNING by the time Lisa entered the city limits of Ponchatoula. Dixie and Danny had slept most of the way, leaving Lisa with nothing but the oldies-but-goodies station on the radio to keep her company.

She had wanted to take Dixie and Danny to see a doctor, but they had both flat out refused. Dixie had said she didn't need a doctor to tell her she had a black eye. Danny had told her that he could wait until he got home and saw his father first.

The closer Lisa came to Gabe's house, the faster her heart seemed to beat. How was she going to tell Gabe that she loved him? In her mind she had rehearsed a hundred different ways, but none of them seemed adequate. And what if he had changed his mind, had had second thoughts? Then what was she going to do? Worse, what if he thought she was just saying she loved him out of gratitude?

By the time she pulled into the driveway, her hands were sweating from nerves and her fingers were stiff from the death grip she'd had on the steering wheel.

Gabe's aunt met them at the front door. "Oh, Daniel," she cried, grabbing him around the waist. "I'm so glad you're finally home where you belong. How could you have run off like that?"

Danny's cheeks turned red, and Lisa could tell what the hug cost him by the pained expression on his face. Still, to his credit, he didn't flinch away or complain as his great-aunt squeezed one last time before she released him.

"Oh, my." She turned to Dixie and Lisa, but frowned as she stared at Dixie's black eye. "What on earth happened to your eye?" Then, as if realizing what she had said, she waved her hand. "Please forgive my lack of manners. You must be Dixie," she said, giving Dixie a cheery smile. "I'm Gabriel's aunt. Come in, all of you." She gestured toward the door leading to the living room. "Gabe tried to wait up for you but he was exhausted. He just dozed off a few minutes before you drove up. I told him he should be in the hospital, but he wouldn't listen to me. I'm supposed to wake him—"

"No, don't..." Suddenly the prospect of facing Gabe was more than Lisa could handle. "I mean, there's no need to wake him right now," she hurried to add. "I'll just look in on him, if that's okay. We're all tired and could use some rest."

Lisa knew she was taking the coward's way out, procrastinating, but she justified her decision by telling herself that she needed to be rested and in full control when she talked to him.

Bessie gave her a knowing smile and nodded. "Go right on in there, hon. We'll be in the kitchen."

Lisa turned away but paused. "By the way," she said, facing Bessie again. "Danny—Daniel—needs to see a doctor. He's got some bruised ribs."

Bessie's lips tightened into a disapproving line and she glared at Danny. "Your father didn't mention you had been injured. Just how did that happen, and when were you going to tell me, young man? Now you just march yourself into the kitchen and call Dr. Ferguson. Tell him we'll be over within the hour, and on the way to his office, you can explain."

Looking sheepish and totally humiliated, Danny glanced at Dixie, turned an even darker shade of red, then stalked off toward the kitchen.

Dixie bit her lower lip, and Lisa could see amusement dancing in her eyes. Knowing Dixie, Lisa figured Danny was in for a razzing. Feeling sympathetic to his predicament, she knew that if Dixie teased him now, on top of everything else he'd endured, the poor kid would only be more miserable. Lisa felt the need to give her sister some kind of warning, but a stern look was all she had time for before Bessie hustled Dixie into the kitchen.

Lisa sighed. She had been so caught up in everything that had happened and her confusing feelings about Gabe that she had completely forgotten about all the phone calls Danny had made to Dixie, passing himself off as someone much older. Anyone with a pair of eyes could see that he had a crush on her sister.

And Dixie. Lisa shook her head. Before she had found out the truth, Dixie had actually encouraged him. *Poor Danny,* she thought. He had gotten himself into more than he had bargained for. And now he was having to suffer through the mortification of being taken to task by his aunt in front of Dixie.

Lisa tiptoed into the living room. She would have a talk with Dixie about Danny later, but right now, she had to see Gabe, had to see for herself that he was okay.

He was sprawled out on the sofa, the expression on his face drawn and weary, even in sleep. He had changed clothes, choosing the comfort of a jogging suit that had seen better days. Against the dark tan of his face and his dark hair, the white bandage wrapped around his head was a stark reminder of his injuries, injuries he had received when he had been willing to sacrifice himself for Danny, herself and even Dixie.

Lisa's throat suddenly felt tight, and she blinked several times, trying to stem the tide of tears that kept welling up in her eyes.

Since Barry had died, there had been a huge void deep inside her, an emptiness that she had thought no other man could ever fill. Looking at Gabe, she was startled to realize that the void no longer existed.

She knew that a part of her would always love Barry, would always cherish what they had shared, but Gabe had helped her realize that she had the capacity to love again—not in the same way, but in a different, equally fulfilling way. No matter what happened between them, she would always be grateful for the precious gift Gabe had given her, the gift of being a whole person again.

Leaning over him, she placed a gentle kiss on his cheek. His stubble felt rough and scratchy against her lips. He smelled shower clean, all male, and for a moment, she lingered, savoring the moment.

When she pulled away, he opened his eyes. "Lisa?" Her name was like a whispered sigh on his lips, and she froze. "Mm, thought I was dreaming," he said.

Lisa gave him an unsteady smile, but before she could respond his eyes fluttered closed again, and his chest began to rhythmically rise and fall, indicating he'd fallen back to sleep.

"I love you," she whispered with one last lingering look. Straightening, she turned and walked slowly toward the kitchen.

Dixie, Danny and Bessie were seated at the kitchen table. Dixie was happily munching on a chocolate-chip cookie and chatting with Bessie. Danny was sitting stiffly in his chair, his brooding eyes focused on the floor.

Time to leave, thought Lisa, once again feeling sorry for Danny. "Dixie, are you ready to go?" she asked.

Her sister glanced up and smiled. "Yep, whenever you are." She stood. "Thanks for the cookies, Aunt Bessie. See you around, Danny."

Then, in typical Dixie fashion, she flounced out of the room without a backward glance, completely

missing the wounded look on Danny's face as he
stared at the empty doorway.

"Danny?" He turned his head to look at Lisa. "I
never did really thank you for sticking by Dixie," she
said. "I know you got hurt trying to help her, and I
just want you to know I appreciate you being there for
her."

Danny lowered his gaze and a flush stole across his
cheeks. "I didn't really do anything."

Then, because she couldn't stand the hopeless expression she had seen on his face when Dixie had
walked out of the room, she added, "I'm sure we'll be
seeing each other again. Agent Monroe said there
would be a trial."

Danny nodded but he still didn't look up.

Lisa laid a hand on Bessie's shoulder. "Thanks for
everything. Tell Gabe..." *Tell him what?* she wondered. She finally shrugged self-consciously. "Just tell
him to take care of himself."

FOR THE FIRST FEW MILES, Dixie remained silent,
which worried Lisa. She'd never known her sister to be
at a loss for words.

"So. Do you have a thing for Danny's dad?"

Lisa glanced over at her sister, then returned her attention to the highway. She should have known that
the silence was too good to last. And, as usual, Dixie
had cut straight to the heart of the matter. "What if I
do?"

Dixie snickered. "You don't have to sound so defensive. Geez, the man is a hunk—ah, for an older guy, that is."

"And what about his son, the younger guy?"

"Oh, Danny's okay. He's a sweet kid, but he's *too* young for me. Besides, I've sworn off men."

"Oh, right. Sure."

"Well, I didn't say forever."

Lisa smiled. "No, you didn't, and don't judge every man by Kevin Striker. There are some good men around."

"Like Danny's dad?"

Her sister had a one-track mind, Lisa thought, but she nodded. "Gabe is one of a kind." She only hoped he would give her the chance to tell him how she felt. "But about Danny."

Dixie groaned. "I feel a Lisa lecture coming on."

"Well, you can't just ignore him. He's got puppy love written all over his face."

"Yeah, I know, but I figured that it would be better and much kinder to pretend I didn't notice. At least that way, his pride wouldn't be too badly damaged."

Lisa felt humbled by her sister's answer. And she was ashamed for not giving Dixie more credit. Dixie's solution reminded her of just how mature her sister had become. She reached over and squeezed Dixie's hand. "I'm sorry."

"Sorry? What for?"

"For still treating you like a kid instead of the grown woman you've become."

Dixie shrugged. "I think I've decided that being treated like a kid isn't so bad sometimes." She reached down and flipped on the radio, twisting the dial until a rock song filled the silence.

Lisa had no choice except to listen. She was too happy to have her sister back again. Soon she found herself *really* listening to the lyrics.

"...destiny calling. Forget about a traveling man. This is your destiny calling. It isn't a one-night stand."

Lisa felt sudden tears spring to her eyes as she listened more closely, the meaning of the words chipping away at her heart.

I feel your heartbeat pounding. I feel your breath in my eyes. I never knew your thoughts were so wild, or that smile was behind your sighs. This is your destiny calling. It rings of fate unveiling her plans. This is your destiny calling. It isn't a one-night...stand. On your knees and blow out all the stars for me, and never deny our love. When the morning comes I'll be in your arms. We'll let destiny's will be done. If we'd never been together before, anticipation couldn't be more exciting. So open up destiny's door. I'm here before you, ready, inviting. This is your destiny calling. Forget about a traveling man. This is your destiny calling. It isn't a one-night stand. As the strains of the song died away, Lisa swiped at the tears running down her cheeks. Gabe was her destiny, had been from the beginning. Was it too late to claim that destiny?

THE SLAM of the front screen door wakened Gabe with a start. He stared up at the ceiling, vaguely aware of a dull throbbing in his head. For a moment his mind seemed a jumble of confusion. Then slowly images began to sort themselves out. He'd been dreaming, and in his dream Lisa was bending over him, her dark eyes full of love and concern. He could still feel the brush of her lips against his cheek. She'd said she loved him. Had he been dreaming?

"Dad? Are you awake?"

The sound of Danny's voice chased away the remnants of the dream. Gabe tried to lift his head, but when he moved, the dull ache grew stronger. Gritting his teeth and fighting a wave of dizziness, he pushed himself up to a sitting position.

"Are you okay?"

Gabe fought against the urge to close his eyes and sink back down on the sofa.

"Maybe I'd better go call Doc Ferguson."

Gabe held up a hand. "No, just give me a minute."

"Sure, but you'd better get a grip fast. Aunt Bessie said she'd be back over just as soon as she warmed up some soup for supper. If she sees you looking all pale and sick, she'll call the doc again, for sure."

"Again?" Had he been so out of it that he didn't even remember seeing the doctor?

"Yeah, after Ms. LeBlanc finked on me, Aunt Bessie *made* me go see him. I told her it was nothing, but you know how she is when she sets her mind on something."

Gabe's memory kicked in and he almost groaned out loud. He'd been in such a fog that he'd forgotten about Danny's injuries. "What did he say? How are your ribs?"

"Nothing broken or cracked. Just bruised."

Suddenly Gabe remembered that Danny had mentioned Lisa. Maybe he hadn't been dreaming, after all. "Ah, Danny, where is Ms. LeBlanc...and Dixie?"

"They went home. Aunt Bessie was going to wake you but Ms. LeBlanc wouldn't let her. She—Ms. LeBlanc—was really worried about you, though.... Come to think of it, she was a lot worried about you." Danny paused, then gave his father a speculative look. "Have you and her got something going?"

"Would it upset you if we did?"

Danny shrugged. "She seems nice enough." Again, Danny paused, but Gabe could tell by the sheepish look on his face that he was trying to work up the courage to say something more.

"Ah, Dad...I'm sorry for causing you so much trouble. I didn't mean for you and Aunt Bessie to worry—that's why I sent the letter—but nothing turned out the way it was supposed to."

"It rarely does," Gabe said, his thoughts turning to Lisa. "But that's life," he added, more for himself than Danny. "Sometimes you just have to pick yourself up and try again."

"Ah, Dad . . . about school."

Gabe drew in a deep breath and let it out in a sigh of resignation. The throbbing in his head seemed more pronounced, and he wasn't sure he was up to discussing anything at the moment, especially something as important as Danny's whole future.

Then he looked at Danny, and his heart turned over. Danny had the same troubled look on his face that he'd had when he was ten years old. Self-conscious about his superior intellect, he had set out to purposely fail math just to prove he was like everyone else, prompting a visit from his teacher. Gabe winced, remembering how badly he'd handled the situation.

In the end Danny's teacher had been the one who had said all the right things and had persuaded Danny that he was special, and that special people had an obligation to use their gifts to the fullest. He had totally agreed with everything the teacher had said to Danny. He just hadn't been able to say it himself.

"You never listen. You only hear what you want to hear."

It was time he started listening and it was time *he* learned to say the right words, beginning now with his son.

Being with Lisa had taught him that lesson. She had once told him that sometimes people had to find their own way, that what parents wanted for their children wasn't always what was best for them.

"Danny, I want to understand," he said softly. "I know I haven't done such a hot job of it in the past, but if you'll give me another chance, I promise I'll try. I never realized you thought we were pushing you. Lord knows, I never meant to. All I wanted—all any parent ever wants—is what's best for their child. If what's best for you now is to drop out of school for a while and work, then I'll try to help you do that in whatever way I can."

For once Gabe figured he'd found the right words, if the look of relief on Danny's face was any measure to go by.

IN DES ALLEMANDS that evening, Lisa stacked dirty dishes in the sink. After days of eating in restaurants and fast food, a home-cooked grilled-cheese sandwich and tomato soup had tasted great.

Now if only Dixie would get out of the bathtub, she could have her turn, Lisa thought, fantasizing about a long, hot bath.

When she heard the loud knock at the front door, she groaned, wishing that whoever it was would just go away.

"Lisa?"

She instantly recognized Clarice's voice. "Oh, great," she muttered. "Just what I need right now." For a second, she was tempted to ignore her mother-in-law, but she figured ignoring her would only make matters worse.

With a sigh, she walked briskly to the front door, unlocked and opened it. "Clarice, what are you doing out this time of night?"

Clarice scowled. "As if you didn't know."

"Would you like to come in?"

"Of course I want to come in," she said, barreling her way past Lisa. "We've all been worried sick about you. The least you could have done was call."

Lisa prayed for patience. "I'm sorry I worried you, but I had to find my sister."

"And did you?"

Lisa nodded. "Yes, I did."

"Well, thank God for that, at least. Carla told me a man went with you." She glanced around the room. "I saw that his truck was still parked outside. Is he here?"

Lisa shook her head. "No, I guess he'll pick up his truck later."

Clarice frowned and looked confused. "Is he anyone we know?"

Lisa truly resented Clarice's inquisition, but didn't have the heart to say so. "No, no one you know. Look, it's a long story, it's late and I'm very tired. I promise, first thing tomorrow morning, I'll come over and tell you everything."

Clarice narrowed her eyes. "Carla says he's good-looking." She pinned Lisa with a shrewd look. "Well? Is he?"

Lisa did her best to keep a blank expression. "Yes, he is."

"Will you be seeing him again?"

"I hope so."

For long seconds Clarice continued to stare at Lisa. Finally she nodded. "Good. It's about time you stopped moping around and got on with your life. I don't how *Pépère* will feel about it. He still misses Barry, you know—"

Lisa nodded. "I know. We all do." She lifted her chin and took a deep breath for courage. "But life goes on, and so must we." *And sometimes destiny calls,* she silently added, knowing now where her destiny lay.

Clarice continued her scrutiny of Lisa, and suddenly she felt as if she were a bug being studied beneath a microscope.

"I'm glad to hear you say that, *ma chere.* You loved my Barry very much, but, as you say, life goes on. I think you have put yours on hold for much too long now." She shrugged. "I should have insisted you return to Shreveport after... after..." She shrugged again. "Maybe then you would have found someone else, but I was selfish. Having you here, I could pretend Barry was coming back, too."

"Oh, Clarice." Lisa wrapped her arms around the little Cajun woman. "Your son will always have a special place in my heart."

Clarice hugged her back, then pulled away. "I know, but I suspect your heart is big enough for another. Am I right?"

Lisa felt her cheeks grow warm and Clarice chuckled.

"Ah, well, it's time for me to go." Clarice opened the door. "And don't worry about *Pépère*. I'll talk to him for you. Coffee, in the morning?"

Lisa nodded.

A few minutes later, Lisa sat on the front porch swing and watched Clarice's headlights disappear into the darkness. For several moments, she savored the peace and quiet and the gentle swaying of the swing.

She had been wrong about Barry's mother. She had mistaken Clarice's genuine concern for interference in her life.

THE FOLLOWING MORNING found Lisa seated in a lawn chair on the tiny wooden dock that jutted into the small bayou behind her house. With her hands wrapped around a mug of hot coffee, she gazed out over the still waters and inhaled deeply the humid, earthy scents of the nearby swamp. On the opposite bank was a wooded area with live oaks draped with the Spanish moss so typical of south Louisiana. From a distance the moss had always reminded her of airy intricate lace.

The dock had long been her favorite place to sit. In the mornings as she watched the sun rise and the new day slowly come alive, she had always done her clearest thinking. In the evenings, the soft bayou sounds had always soothed and relaxed her.

Lisa sipped her coffee, the strong, warm brew warding off the early-morning chill. She wondered how Gabe was feeling, if he had been able to rest or if his concussion had kept him awake. She also wondered if Danny's bruised ribs were simply bruised or worse, cracked. Would Gabe call her today? Would he come to pick up his truck? Or should she call him?

Lisa sighed. Even if she called him, what would she say? Where would she begin?

She closed her eyes. No, she decided. She wouldn't call him. Sooner or later, he'd have to come get his truck. She could wait until then to tell him how she felt.

"Lisa?"

At the soft whisper of her name, Lisa froze. Her first thought was that she must have been dreaming, that her mind was so full of Gabe that she had conjured up his image.

"Lisa."

Her heart quivering beneath her breasts, she stood and turned around. She hadn't been dreaming. Walking toward her and looking larger than life in a pair of faded jeans and a New Orleans Saints' sweatshirt was Gabe.

"What are you doing here?"

Gabe tilted his head and gave her a puzzled look. "Do you want me to leave?"

"No, of course not, but how did you get here?"

"Danny dropped me off." He paused. "So...I can stay?"

"Shouldn't you still be in bed—I mean—" she gestured at the white bandage around his head "—aren't you supposed to rest?" It was then that she noticed his lips twitching with amusement.

"I probably should still be in bed, but—" he shrugged "—here I am."

Suddenly Lisa felt flustered and out of control. Somehow she had to get a grip on herself. She motioned toward the other lawn chair. "At least sit down, or would you rather go into the house?"

"Is your sister still here?"

Lisa frowned, puzzled at his question. "Yes. She's still asleep."

"Hmm, then let's stay out here. I could use a cup of that coffee, if it isn't too much trouble."

"No—no trouble. I'll just be a minute." Lisa was extremely conscious of Gabe's eyes on her as she hurried to the house. *Wonderful*, she thought. Here she was barefoot, wearing her oldest, most ragged housecoat. Her hair needed washing and she hadn't even taken time to brush her teeth yet.

Once inside, she rushed to her bedroom, slipped into a sweat suit and tennis shoes, pulled a comb through her hair and hurriedly brushed her teeth. She was almost to the kitchen door when she remembered that the whole point of coming inside was to get Gabe a cup of coffee.

Outside again, she handed Gabe the steaming mug. His eyes danced with amusement. "You shouldn't have changed on my account. I've seen you in a lot less."

Lisa flushed furiously. "Yes, well . . . it was chilly." She quickly seated herself in the lawn chair. She turned to face Gabe. "Ah, how's Danny? His ribs?"

A faraway look came into Gabe's eyes, a look that Lisa wasn't sure how to interpret, but strangely reminded her of someone who had just been given an unexpected gift.

"Danny is fine," he said softly. "Just bruises." He reached inside his pocket and pulled out a folded piece of paper. "I want you to read this."

Puzzled, Lisa took the paper. "What is it?" She unfolded it and glanced at the first few lines. "This is the letter Danny wrote you, the one you told me about. Why—"

Gabe held up a hand. "Please, just read it."

Lisa frowned, then shrugged. For some reason, it seemed important to Gabe. She began to read. When she'd finished, she refolded it and handed it back to him. "I don't understand."

Gabe wasn't sure he understood, either. After they had released him from the hospital, he had spent a lot of time thinking about his past on the way home. Being faced with the possibility of losing both Danny and Lisa had hit him in a way that nothing had since the death of his wife.

He just knew that he had to start explaining some-where, and the letter seemed like a good place to be-gin. "Danny accused me of never listening, of hearing only what I want to hear. He was wrong. I did listen, but when it came to talking, to explaining how *I* felt, I could never find the right words. It was almost as if I had blocked off my emotions.

"When Brenda died, I guess a part of me died with her. Looking back, I realize now that I was angry at her for leaving me. You see, I had planned to grow old with her, to raise Danny with her and to have other children together..." His voice trailed away and he stared out over the bayou, as memories of the past clouded his eyes.

Lisa thought her heart would break. She could well understand how he had felt. She wanted to wrap her arms around him and comfort him, something she suspected he had never allowed anyone to do for him. She had felt the same anger when Barry had died, but by the grace of God and Barry's loving family—es-pecially Clarice—she'd worked her way through it. To her way of thinking, the difference between the way they had handled their grief was as simple as the dif-ference between a man and a woman. Why was it, she wondered, that men had such a hard time expressing their feelings?

Fast on the heels of that thought, Lisa suddenly be-gan to realize just exactly what Gabe was trying to do. She knew that he was a man whose feelings, like the sweetest of waters, ran deep. He was an honorable man, a man who had been willing to risk his life to save her. And if she had needed any more proof that he loved her, he was giving it to her now. Love meant trust, and Gabe was trusting her enough to bare his soul to her.

He finally cleared his throat and took a sip of coffee. "You know," he said, "instead of dealing with all that anger, I ignored it. As the years passed, it seemed easier and easier...until now. Danny's letter made me *have* to deal with it. I had no control over Brenda's death, but if I lose Danny, I'll have no one to blame but myself." He cleared his throat again and turned to her. "I guess that doesn't make much sense, but what I'm trying to say is, by the same token, if I lose you, I'll have no one to blame but myself, either."

He rushed on before she had a chance to respond. "Danny and I talked, and for once I really listened and heard what he was trying to say. I think we made a good start, and I'm hoping that some way you and I can do the same. Whether you believe it or not, I want you to know that I meant it when I told you I love you. If you'll just give me the chance, I'd like to try to convince you."

Lisa's heart began beating so hard that she was sure Gabe could hear it. "I don't need convincing," she whispered. "I've been agonizing over what to say to you, and *I* would like some time to convince *you* that I feel the same."

"Are you saying what I think you're saying?"

She nodded. "I love you, too." Before she realized he'd even moved, she found herself caught up in his arms.

"You've got it, lady," he whispered. "All the time you want, but—" He suddenly pulled away and stared at her, a worried look on his face. "Not *too* much time, huh? I mean, we're not talking about months and months here, are we?"

Lisa smiled and laughed, then shook her head. She felt so full of happiness that she was afraid she would burst. "No, not months and months," she reassured him. "In fact, probably just one month would do it, don't you think?"

The look of relief on his face was comical. "Whew. For a minute there, you had me worried."

She reached up and caressed his jaw, loving the freedom of touching him. "Can we kiss and make up now?"

Gabe's blue eyes darkened and seemed to smolder with desire as they focused on her lips. He pulled her close, letting her feel just how much he wanted her. "My thoughts exactly," he said hoarsely just before he covered her lips with his in a kiss that stole her breath, her soul and her heart.

EPILOGUE

One month later

LISA PACED the length of her bedroom, did an about-face and resumed her pacing. She stopped by the window, pushed the curtain aside, looked outside and frowned.

The day was perfect, with the sun shining and the temperature an unseasonably comfortable seventy-five degrees for the middle of the May afternoon. Two huge white awnings had been erected between the back of the house and the bayou. Beneath one were rows and rows of chairs set up church-style, with an aisle down the middle. Within the hour, those chairs would be filled with smiling, laughing people—friends, business associates and relatives that Clarice and Bessie had insisted on inviting.

Beneath the other awning, white coated caterers hustled about preparing the wedding cake table, the bar and the food table. Off to the side a small band gathered and began warming up their instruments. And everywhere she looked there were overflowing baskets of spring flowers.

What had started out to be a quiet simple wedding had turned into a major event. Lisa glanced at her watch, shook her head and turned away. They should have eloped, she thought, but she hadn't stood a chance against Bessie, Clarice and Dixie. All three had taken over the minute they had learned that Gabe had proposed and she had accepted.

Just premarital jitters, she thought. Surely it was only logical that she would be nervous.

She wandered over to the dresser and stared at her reflection. Fingering the strand of pearls around her neck, her wedding gift from Gabe, she smiled. The pearls were perfectly matched and felt warm against her skin.

Gabe had taken some long-overdue vacation time, and after only two weeks of their supposed courtship, he had declared that they had had enough time to get to know each other. She had wholeheartedly agreed, especially when she considered that getting married seemed to be the only solution to ever getting any rest again.

She turned away and frowned. She just hoped that Bessie, Clarice and Dixie knew what they were doing. It had only taken them two additional weeks to throw together a wedding that should have taken months to prepare.

"Lisa?"

At the sound of her name, she turned to face her sister.

"You're not dressed yet," Dixie accused. "For Pete's sake, everyone will be here soon. And stop chewing your fingernails. You'll ruin the manicure."

Lisa glared at her sister but dutifully tucked her hands behind her back. "Are Gabe and Danny here yet?"

Dixie hesitated. "Well...no, not yet, but I'm sure they will be any minute—"

"Then what's the hurry? There can't be a wedding without the groom and the best man, and besides, all I have to do is slip the dress on."

Lisa glanced at the dress hanging from the door frame. She felt even more nervous about the wedding dress than she did about the wedding. Maybe she had been silly—at her age—to buy such a dress, especially since this was her second marriage. Still, the dress wasn't exactly white, more of an ivory color—the silk confection had cost her the earth—but it *was* the traditional wedding dress style complete with a headpiece and a short veil. And from the moment she'd seen it, all she could think about was Gabe unbuttoning each of the tiny pearl buttons that ran down the back. Even now, she could feel her stomach tighten in anticipation.

Dixie walked toward her, a puzzled look on her face. "Lisa, what's wrong?"

Lisa gestured toward the window. "It's too much—all of it. We should have had just a small quiet ceremony."

"Well, you should have told Gabe."

"Wha—what do you mean?"

"According to Aunt Bessie, he's the one who wanted all the stops pulled out, the whole works and no expense spared. It seems that when he was married the first time, neither he nor his wife could afford much at all, just a hasty, justice-of-the-peace thing. When he learned that you and Barry had had the same type of ceremony, he told Aunt Bessie that since this would be the last wedding for both of you, he wanted it done right."

Lisa's heart lurched and tears sprang to her eyes. How had he known that secretly she had always regretted not having the kind of wedding that young girls dream of? When she and Barry had married, she had pushed aside those dreams for reality. She had consoled herself that a large splashy wedding didn't make a person any more married than standing before a justice of the peace. And somewhere along the way, she had forgotten how to dream.

She reached up and touched the silk dress. Who would have ever guessed that a big gruff man like Gabe could be such a romantic?

A warm glow started in the depths of her soul and spread throughout her being. One good turn deserved another, and there was one last thing she needed to do, one last gesture she had put off for much too long. She turned to Dixie and smiled. "Do you remember Barry's first cousin, Joel?"

Dixie nodded. "He's the one with all that wavy hair and blue eyes."

"I want you to find him and give him a message for me, but first—" she motioned toward the wedding dress "—all of those buttons are going to take forever to fasten. Will you help me with the dress?"

While Dixie was busy concentrating on fastening the pearl buttons, Gabe was standing in Lisa's driveway, glaring in his truck side mirror at the crooked bow tie around his neck. Danny and Bessie hovered just behind him.

"Daniel, help your father with that tie."

Danny rolled his eyes. "I'd be glad to if he would turn around and hold still."

With a frown of impatience, Gabe turned and faced his son. Within minutes Danny had executed a perfect bow.

"Oh, my," Bessie gushed, staring first at Gabe and then at Danny. "You two have to be the most handsome men in the world." She pulled out a handkerchief from her purse, dabbed at her eyes and sniffed. Then, straightening, she glanced at her watch. "Goodness, look at the time." She took both men by the arm. "We really must move along. Have you got the ring, Daniel?"

Danny patted his breast pocket. "Got it."

"And Gabriel, please try and remember to do everything the way we rehearsed it, especially the part about kissing the bride. Kiss her *after* the ceremony, not before and in the middle."

Gabe nodded and pretended to scowl at his aunt. "It's much more fun the other way."

Danny snickered and Bessie giggled.

Fifteen minutes later Gabe, Danny and Dixie stood before the minister. Suddenly the small band broke into the strains of the traditional wedding march.

Gabe turned, and the moment Lisa appeared, his eyes widened and his heart began to race. She was being escorted by the old gentleman everyone called *Pépère* who, despite his age, stood tall and walked with a steadiness that belied his years.

Lisa was a vision of beauty, and Gabe had the sudden urge to grab her and hold her close, just to make sure she was real. But what really got to him was the look in her dark eyes. They hypnotized him and seemed to glow with a serene inner light, reflecting all the love he felt inside.

To hell with tradition, he thought, and the moment she reached his side, he leaned over and kissed her with all the passion and love that he felt for her.

A collective gasp came from the guests, and somewhere off to the side, he could hear his aunt whispering, "Not now, Gabriel. Not now." Only when the minister cleared his throat for the third time and the guests began to laugh did he finally, reluctantly, release her.

The traditional ceremony didn't take long, and as they took their vows, no one in the crowd doubted their sincerity or the obvious love they shared.

As if in a dream, Lisa said, "I do," and instantly found herself caught up in Gabe's arms again, his warm hungry lips covering hers. When he finally released her, she felt dizzy with happiness.

The band struck up a rowdy, fast-paced Cajun tune, and the guests crowded close, all extending their congratulations.

Two hours later the wedding party was still going strong, with no sign of the guests leaving anytime soon. Lisa and Gabe had just left amid a shower of rice.

Carrying plates ladened with jambalaya, garlic French bread and cups of punch, Danny and Dixie wandered toward the dock near the bayou.

"Did you taste the seafood gumbo?"

Dixie smacked her lips. "Boy, did I, but the crawfish was the best I've ever had." She sat in a lawn chair and made an attempt to balance her plate on her knees, hold her punch and eat. "So, how's the job working out?"

Danny grimaced. "Pretty grimy." He plopped down on the wooden dock beside her, set his punch on the ground, and while he pushed the jambalaya around on the plate with his fork, he noticed that there was still some tell-tale dirt beneath his fingernails. "I never realized that road construction was such hot dirty work."

"Do you miss school at all?"

Danny looked up at her. "What I miss is the challenge of the classes—you know, the academic part. Already I've been trying to figure out how to approach Dad about going back next semester."

Dixie laughed. "And I thought only women had a monopoly on changing their minds."

Danny quickly ducked his head and began to eat.

"Hey, I was only kidding. I'm sure your dad only wants what will make you happy."

Feeling more embarrassed by the moment, Danny decided it was time to change the subject. "Did you get a subpoena?"

Dixie had just taken a bite of food, so she simply nodded.

"Me too, and I can't wait to put that character behind bars."

Dixie swallowed and took a quick sip of punch. "I think it's great the way things have worked out. Lisa and your dad, I got a promotion, you have a job, and last but not least, Kevin Striker goes to jail."

THIRTY MILES EAST, Gabe and Lisa entered the bridal suite of the Ponchartrain Hotel in New Orleans. Lisa had wanted to change clothes before they left the wedding party in Des Allemands, but Gabe had spirited her away without giving her a choice. Her face was still burning from all of the smiles and knowing looks they had received on their way through the hotel lobby, and when she remembered her earlier fantasies about Gabe unfastening all the tiny pearl buttons on her gown, she felt her face grow even warmer.

Gabe generously tipped the bellman, then firmly closed the door.

"Oh, Gabe, look. There's champagne and roses and— My goodness, look at all of this food."

But Gabe wasn't looking at the food as he reached up and pulled his bow tie loose. He had eyes only for Lisa. "Did I ever tell you that the perfume you wear drives me crazy?"

Lisa frowned. "I don't wear perfumes or colognes. They make me sneeze."

Gabe shook his head. "Oh, boy, then I'm in big trouble." He shook his head again. "Well, did I tell you how beautiful you look today?"

Lisa smiled, loving the way he was devouring her with his eyes. "Only about every five minutes."

Gabe shrugged out of his tuxedo jacket and tossed it on a nearby chair. "And did I tell you how much I love you?"

Again she smiled, and with her gaze never wavering from his, she slowly walked toward him. "I lost count of the times." She reached out, pulled his hands down to his sides, then slowly began to unbutton his shirt. "By the way, did I mention that I love you, too?"

Gabe swallowed hard. With the release of each button, she kissed the bare skin the shirt had covered. "I can't remember," he lied, his voice raspy and a little gruff. "Maybe you'd better tell me again." And she did, several times before she finally freed him of the shirt and cummerbund.

Lisa ran her hands up and down his rock-hard chest, luxuriating in the feel of the dark, rough hair that began at his neck and tapered into a V beneath his trousers.

Gabe groaned. "Is it my turn yet?"

Lisa leaned forward and kissed each of his nipples, then pivoted, presenting her back to him. "I've been dreaming about this since I first saw this dress."

"Just the buttons alone must have cost you a mint."

While he alternately nibbled at her neck and unfastened the buttons, shivers of anticipation rioted through her. When he had worked his way down to her midback, she heard his swift intake of breath. "You're not wearing anything underneath this—no bra." She felt him fumble with a few more buttons, then he slipped his hands beneath the back of the dress, slid them around to the front and cupped her breasts. It was a tight fit, but not as tight as the feeling deep in her belly.

Lisa groaned as his fingers rubbed against her nipples until they were so hard that they ached. "Oh, Gabe, you're driving me crazy."

He nibbled at her ear. "That's what you get for buying this dress with all of those damn buttons."

All too soon, as far as Lisa was concerned, Gabe withdrew his hands and finished unfastening the buttons. She stepped out of the gown, then turned and faced him, wearing nothing but a strand of pearls, a scrap of silk panties, a lacy garter belt, sheer stockings and satin pumps.

Gabe couldn't take his eyes off her, and desire, like a bolt of lightning, electrified him. He kicked out of his shoes and jerked off his socks, but when he reached for the fastener at the waistband of his pants, Lisa playfully swatted at his hands. "My turn again," she whispered, sinking to her knees in front of him, and taking her time releasing the fastener, lowering the zipper and sliding his pants down over his hips.

Gabe closed his eyes and tried to concentrate on anything but what she was doing to him. Much more and he was sure he would explode.

"Lisa," he groaned and reached down. With a firm grip beneath her arms, he pulled her up for a hard, thorough kiss, then nudged her toward the bed. "One good torture deserves another, don't you think?"

"Oh, definitely," she whispered, a sensual smile of anticipation pulling at her lips. She kicked off her shoes and lowered herself onto the bed, then leaned back on her elbows.

Gabe kneeled down in front of her and ran his hands up her leg, enjoying the silky texture of the stocking against her warm skin. He released the garter and slowly peeled away the stocking, then he turned his attention to the other leg.

Slow, sweetly agonizing minutes passed as he took his time loving Lisa. She had never dreamed that a man his size could be so gentle and yet so strong. And she had never dreamed that his large body covering hers could make her feel so loved, protected and cherished.

When he finally entered her, whispering how much he loved her, she was more than ready for him. Then the tremors began and they both lost control. Lisa held on, eager to take the journey that would forever meld their souls as one.

Later, both of them satiated and glowing, Lisa snuggled close to him, his arm wrapped around her, holding her firmly to his side.

"I have a surprise for you," she whispered.

Gabe turned his head until they were nose to nose. His eyes twinkled. "I can't imagine anything better than what just happened."

"I sold Lover," she blurted out.

Gabe went very still, but his heart began to race.

"It's time—past time," she rushed on. "I don't *need* it anymore... not like before. Clarice's nephew, Joel, has been after me for months to sell it to him. We finalized the deal right before the wedding."

Gabe sighed. "Oh, sweetheart, come here." He pulled her on top of him and held her close. He knew what it had cost Lisa to part with the Jeep, the last link with her late husband, and he could think of no words adequate enough to express the way he felt, except, "I love you, Lisa."

And those were all the words that Lisa needed.

Relive the romance...
Harlequin and Silhouette
are proud to present

by Request™

A program of collections of three complete novels by the most requested
authors with the most requested themes. Be sure to look for one volume each
month with three complete novels by top name authors.

In January: **WESTERN LOVING**   Susan Fox
                                          JoAnn Ross
                                          Barbara Kaye

Loving a cowboy is easy—taming him isn't!

In February: **LOVER, COME BACK!**   Diana Palmer
                                          Lisa Jackson
                                          Patricia Gardner Evans

It was over so long ago—yet now they're calling, "Lover, Come Back!"

In March: **TEMPERATURE RISING**   JoAnn Ross
                                          Tess Gerritsen
                                          Jacqueline Diamond

Falling in love—just what the doctor ordered!

Available at your favorite retail outlet.

REQ-G3

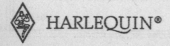

HARLEQUIN®   Silhouette

My Valentine 1994

Celebrate the most romantic day of the year with
MY VALENTINE 1994
a collection of original stories, written by
four of Harlequin's most popular authors...

MARGOT DALTON
MURIEL JENSEN
MARISA CARROLL
KAREN YOUNG

Available in February, wherever
Harlequin Books are sold.

HARLEQUIN ®

VAL94

MEN MADE IN AMERICA

Fifty red-blooded, white-hot, true-blue hunks
from every State in the Union!

Look for MEN MADE IN AMERICA! Written by some
of our most poplar authors, these stories feature fifty of
the strongest, sexiest men, each from a different state in
the union!

Two titles available every other month at your favorite
retail outlet.

In March, look for:

TANGLED LIES by Anne Stuart (Hawaii)
ROGUE'S VALLEY by Kathleen Creighton (Idaho)

In May, look for:

LOVE BY PROXY by Diana Palmer (Illinois)
POSSIBLES by Lass Small (Indiana)

You won't be able to resist MEN MADE IN AMERICA!

Where do you find hot Texas nights, smooth Texas charm and dangerously sexy cowboys?

Crystal Creek reverberates with the exciting rhythm of Texas. Each story features the rugged individuals who live and love in the Lone Star State.

"...Crystal Creek wonderfully evokes the hot days and steamy nights of a small Texas community."   —*Romantic Times*

"...a series that should hook any romance reader. Outstanding."
   —*Rendezvous*

"Altogether, it couldn't be better."

   —*Rendezvous*

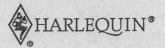

Harlequin proudly presents four stories about *convenient* but not *conventional* reasons for marriage:

- ◆ To save your godchildren from a "wicked stepmother"
- ◆ To help out your eccentric aunt—and her sexy business partner
- ◆ To bring an old man happiness by making him a grandfather
- ◆ To escape from a ghostly existence and become a real woman

Marriage By Design—four brand-new stories by four of Harlequin's most popular authors:

CATHY GILLEN THACKER
JASMINE CRESSWELL
GLENDA SANDERS
MARGARET CHITTENDEN

Don't miss this exciting collection of stories about marriages of convenience. Available in April, wherever Harlequin books are sold.

MBD94

HARLEQUIN®

Don't miss these Harlequin favorites by some of our most distinguished authors!
And now, you can receive a discount by ordering two or more titles!

HT#25409	THE NIGHT IN SHINING ARMOR by JoAnn Ross	$2.99	☐
HT#25471	LOVESTORM by JoAnn Ross	$2.99	☐
HP#11463	THE WEDDING by Emma Darcy	$2.89	☐
HP#11592	THE LAST GRAND PASSION by Emma Darcy	$2.99	☐
HR#03188	DOUBLY DELICIOUS by Emma Goldrick	$2.89	☐
HR#03248	SAFE IN MY HEART by Leigh Michaels	$2.89	☐
HS#70464	CHILDREN OF THE HEART by Sally Garrett	$3.25	☐
HS#70524	STRING OF MIRACLES by Sally Garrett	$3.39	☐
HS#70500	THE SILENCE OF MIDNIGHT by Karen Young	$3.39	☐
HI#22178	SCHOOL FOR SPIES by Vickie York	$2.79	☐
HI#22212	DANGEROUS VINTAGE by Laura Pender	$2.89	☐
HI#22219	TORCH JOB by Patricia Rosemoor	$2.89	☐
HAR#16459	MACKENZIE'S BABY by Anne McAllister	$3.39	☐
HAR#16466	A COWBOY FOR CHRISTMAS by Anne McAllister	$3.39	☐
HAR#16462	THE PIRATE AND HIS LADY by Margaret St. George	$3.39	☐
HAR#16477	THE LAST REAL MAN by Rebecca Flanders	$3.39	☐
HH#28704	A CORNER OF HEAVEN by Theresa Michaels	$3.99	☐
HH#28707	LIGHT ON THE MOUNTAIN by Maura Seger	$3.99	☐

Harlequin Promotional Titles

#83247	YESTERDAY COMES TOMORROW by Rebecca Flanders	$4.99	☐
#83257	MY VALENTINE 1993	$4.99	☐

(short-story collection featuring Anne Stuart, Judith Arnold,
Anne McAllister, Linda Randall Wisdom)
(limited quantities available on certain titles)

	AMOUNT	$
DEDUCT:	**10% DISCOUNT FOR 2+ BOOKS**	$
ADD:	**POSTAGE & HANDLING**	$
	($1.00 for one book, 50¢ for each additional)	
	APPLICABLE TAXES*	$ _____
	TOTAL PAYABLE	$ _____
	(check or money order—please do not send cash)	

To order, complete this form and send it, along with a check or money order for the total above, payable to Harlequin Books, to: **In the U.S.:** 3010 Walden Avenue, P.O. Box 9047, Buffalo, NY 14269-9047; **In Canada:** P.O. Box 613, Fort Erie, Ontario, L2A 5X3.

Name: _____

Address: _____ City: _____

State/Prov.: _____ Zip/Postal Code: _____

*New York residents remit applicable sales taxes.
Canadian residents remit applicable GST and provincial taxes.

HBACK-JM